The Hare

12-13

The Hare

•

CÉSAR AIRA

Translated by Nick Caistor

A NEW DIRECTIONS PAPERBOOK ORIGINAL

First published in Spanish as *La Liebre* by Emecé, Buenos Aires; published in conjunction
with Agency Michael Gaeb/Berlin

Manufactured in the United States of America
New Directions Books are printed on acid-free paper.
First published as a New Directions Paperbook Original (NDP1257) in 2013
Design by Erik Rieselbach

Library of Congress Cataloging-in-Publication Data
Aira, César, 1949–
[Liebre. English]
The hare / César Aira ; Translated by Nick Caistor.
pages cm
ISBN 978-0-8112-2090-3 (alk. paper)
I. Title.
PQ7798.1.I7L513 2013
863'.64—dc23

2013003580

10 9 8 7 6 5 4 3 2 1

New Directions Books are published for James Laughlin
by New Directions Publishing Corporation
80 Eighth Avenue, New York, NY 10011

Contents

THE HARE

1: *The Restorer of the Laws*

BATHED IN SWEAT, EYES ROLLING, THE RESTORER OF THE Laws leapt from his bed and stood swaying for a moment on the cold tiles, flapping his arms like a duck. He was barefoot and in his nightshirt. Two pristine white sheets, twisted and knotted by his contortions during the nightmare, were the only covering on the brass bed with leather thongs, itself the only piece of furniture in the small bedroom where he took his siestas. He picked up one of the sheets and mopped his soaking face and neck. His heart was still pounding from the memory of the horror, but the mists of his befuddled sleep were gradually lifting. He took one step, and then another, pressing his feet flat on the floor to enjoy its comforting coolness. He went over to the window and pushed back the curtain with his fingertip. The courtyard was deserted: palm trees, the sun beating down, silence. He walked back over to the cot but did not lie down again; after a moment's thought, he sat on the floor with his legs out in front of him, his back straight. The chill of the tiles on his bare buttocks gave him a brief shock of pleasure. He lifted his knees to begin his abdominal exercises. He put his hands behind his head to make them harder work. At first he struggled a little, but soon the movement became automatic,

3

rapid, gravity-defying, so that he had time to think. He did a hundred at a stretch, automatically counting them off in tens, while his mind raced. He reconstructed the nightmare in all its details, as though this were a self-imposed punishment. The sense of well-being produced by his physical exertions helped dissipate the terror of his memories. Or more exactly, rather than dissipating it, the gymnastics made it manageable, like another number he was counting off. He was not unaware of the general meaning of those phantoms which visited him at siesta time. They were the one, the two, the three, the four, the five, the six, the seven, the eight, the nine, the ten. How mistaken those illiterate scribblers were if they thought it was the shadow of his crimes that was being cast into his sleeping consciousness. That would be counting backward: ten, nine, eight, seven, six, five, four, three, two, one. The fact was, it was the complete opposite; and if his enemies made this kind of mistake, it was precisely because by definition opposition was the point from which everything was seen backward: what obsessed him were the crimes he had not committed, a feeling of remorse at not having reached the end of his count. One, two, three, four, five, six, seven, eight, nine, ten. He had been too soft, too conventional. They said he was a monster, but what he regretted was the fact that somewhere along the way he had missed the opportunity of truly becoming one. He was sorry he could not be his own opposition, so that he could build up a picture of himself from both sides, like a neatly executed piece of embroidery. One, two, three, four ... it was his imagination that had failed him, and without imagination there could never be true cruelty. Five, six, seven, eight ... his dreams were the reverse image of the cryptic accusations published against him in those Liberal rags, first *El Crap*, then *Muera Rosas* (what imbecilic names!). The world turned upside down. Nothing but literature. The key to his dreams was barely more than regret at life passing by. What he lacked was true inventive genius, poetic agility. Nine ... he recognized the fact and was sorry for it, in this somewhat brutally frank exchange he was having with himself. But where, where, where on earth could he discover the talent necessary to change the wild reversals of the Montevideo hacks into reality, into life, into something authentically Argentine? Ten. A hundred.

While the other man was writing out a page, Rosas downed half a liter of gin with cold water. A small glass per line, which seemed to him by no means excessive. It enthralled him to watch someone write. He considered it one of the few spectacles with an intrinsic worth, which demanded nothing of the spectator. Nothing, that is, beyond a little patience, which was a quality he possessed in abundance: so much indeed that he sometimes thought he had little room for anything else. He felt that the time taken for his oral intentions to be transformed into a properly constructed and well-written page of writing was brief in the extreme. That was why he was so insistent on its neatness. It might seem that nothing was happening, but he saw nothing less than a transferral between two people; in the study's shadowy atmosphere, he could make out the faint outline of a phantom. Gestures always created a perspective, especially if they were the gestures of writing. The movement of arm, hand, eye, and pen was an intention blown up like a bladder filled with phantoms. Those phantoms were one person becoming another. He perceived all this through a shimmering haze, as if all the objects around him were coated in a sublime sheen. This was the effect of the drink in the stifling afternoon heat, but it was also part and parcel of the scene itself. He told people he had discovered that gin was the best defense against the heat; what he did not say was that in fact the heat did not trouble him. In truth, creating a pressing need for the illusion of cold when it was hot, or vice versa, could be a marvelously effective way of giving utterances reality; that must be why the human race, in its prototype of the English, spoke so meaningfully of the weather all the time. It was a world within a world, but instead of being theater this was serious, for real. Perhaps that was the meaning behind the drinks he poured himself: cold water for altering the temperature, gin for the sheen without which there could be no inclusions, or they could not be seen. It all came down to the transferral from one state to another, from one body to another, one possibility to another. Which was why, in the end, it was he and not somebody else who was the Restorer of the Laws, and was precisely that and nothing else. He was that because ... Why? No, the reason had slipped from his mind at the same lightning speed it had entered. He shrugged; mentally of course. The moment of understanding had flashed by before he could seize it. He stood as stiff as a mummy for an indefinite length of time, his mind empty. His only movement was to lift the glass to his lips. All at once, the secretary handed him the sheet of paper, a model of neatness. The other hand held out a pen, for him to sign with.

•

Once the day's work—so slight as to be almost nonexistent—was over and done with, Rosas went to sit in the arbor and wait for Manuela to serve him his maté drink. He liked to spend this intimate, family time of day relaxed in thought. Paradoxically, to do this he left his mind a complete blank. Impossible as it might seem for someone with such a high opinion of his own brain, he achieved this with no difficulty. There were quite a few birds singing, and three or four dogs mingled with the children at play. Behind him, a semicircle of lemon trees purified the air; opposite him, a big osier willow whose branches sprouted directly from the ground seemed like a wild ikebana put there for his entertainment. The beaten earth under the bower had been rapidly sprinkled in his honor. Sometimes, his mind fixed on nothing, he could almost believe he was the only man on earth, the only truly living human being. There was not a breath of wind, but the heat was by no means intolerable. Ugly and pallid, Manuelita came and went from the kitchen, carefully carrying his drink. Her beloved papa only drank half a dozen matés in one of these sittings, so it was not worth setting up a stove outside. She stood waiting while he sucked up the liquid with a shocking noise. Rosas found his favorite daughter neither attractive nor intelligent; on the contrary, he thought her an idiot. An idiot and a snob: that was Manuelita. The worst thing about her was her irredeemable lack of naturalness. A puppet made of offal. "She's one of my worst habits," he would confide to his friends. He was bewitched by this girl, but had no idea why. There was a fundamental misunderstanding between them—that much he could see, but not an inch further. She was convinced her papa adored her. He wondered how on earth he had managed to sire her. Fortunately, there was always some doubt as to paternity. Maternity on the other hand is always beyond question. Whenever he looked at Manuelita, Rosas felt himself to be a woman, a mother. For several years now he had been toying with the idea of marrying her off to one of his fools, Eusebio. It was his secret plan, the scandalous delight of the impossible. But the real scandal lay in the fact that, as is well known, the impossible is the first thing to become reality. So that when one day he saw that the scribblers were attributing this very idea to him in their rags, his consternation knew no bounds. Naturally he had never breathed a word about it. Yet they not only wrote about the plan, but as usual accompanied their conjectures with drawings full of scrolls of words. Of course, as with all opposition, these brutes had only a limited number of clues to work from, they had to make and unmake their jigsaws from just a few pieces, which meant that it was not really so remarkable that they should come to the conclusion: Daughter-Fool. But even so, it was astonishing, as Rosas saw it: is it possible to penetrate someone else's incongruity? One's own or anyone else's, it made no difference, as he saw it. Even the most outrageous fantasy created at both its extremes, that of excess and of lack, the incongruity on which daily life was based. Although it was possible of course that the Unitarians had latched onto his idea by the kind of allegory they were so fond of, the Restorer was "hunting" the fatherland using an idiot full of wind as his shotgun. At this point Rosas, who was never very good at orthography, got into a muddle; but that did not matter at all, since what was allegorical to them was real to him, which meant that the misunderstanding became cosmic, universal, a law of gravity. In fact, the idea had occurred to him one day when Eusebio had been close to death from being tortured too much with the bellows. It would have been perfect to have married them in articulo mortis, because that would have avoided all practical consequences while retaining the symbolic value of the marriage. Manuelita already had a widow's face. "My widow," Rosas would sometimes mutter in his daydreams, although none of those who heard him ever understood whether he was talking about Manuelita, the Heroine of the Nation, women in general, Eusebio, the fatherland, or himself.

His two final audiences that afternoon had been granted to an elderly black woman and to an Englishman. The black woman had come about a trifling matter, a crass personal tragedy, but Rosas made it a rule always to receive his beloved darkies and play Solomon for them—an attitude they welcomed with a gratitude bordering on adulation. Rosas had a theory that before long, Argentina would be a country of blacks. He might even see that day arrive, if he lived long enough. He therefore took pains to keep them in the foreground politically, as privileged subjects of the Law and Justice. This cost him little, while at the same time he could see the inevitability of misery and stupidity which made this black nation a fiction. Today's black woman came accompanied by her two eldest daughters. She was a dreadful specimen, who although she must have been only forty years old, looked a worn-out sixty. She launched into her story with heartrending sobs and cries. The interview took place on the main porch of the house, which at that time of day afforded some shade. Foremost among the sadistic onlookers secretly rejoicing in the scene was Manuelita, all dressed up in scarlet ribbons and bows, feigning compassion. She was a hopeless actress, poor thing. Her complete lack of naturalness! The Restorer listened stony-faced, his gin glazing everything over as he sat in his sandalwood chair. Whichever way he looked at the problem, there was no answer: after thirty years of married life, the plaintiff's husband had gone off with another woman. There was no solution. According to the black woman's tearful account, once the man in question had committed incest with his elder and younger daughters, he felt there was nothing more to be gained from the marriage as far as sexual gratification was concerned. Anyone could understand that. From this point on, the abandoned wife's argument degenerated into one long moan of complaint. The Man in the Marble Mask felt that when complaining reached such a pure, ecstatic state as this, it gave him a good opportunity to think. The reasoning did not move forward at all, and seemed as though it never would. What did she want him to do? Have the man castrated? That would be easy, all too easy. But she herself must have realized this would get her nowhere. Manuelita was shedding crocodile tears, the two daughters were busy studying her afternoon robe so they could copy it, while the black woman herself never took her eyes off the Solomon from Palermo, who meanwhile was lost in a reverie about how the female body deteriorates. This train of thought (which could be summed up by the question: what does a woman have to offer, once she has lost the obvious?) led him off down unexpected paths, until all at once an idea, as bright as the sun, came to him as to how the woman might keep her husband. An infallible, impeccable method that was simple to apply and yet was guaranteed success. It was odd she had not thought of it herself, but then if she had, it would have occurred to all women, including her rival, which meant it would no longer be effective. And it had occurred to him, precisely to the one person who by definition would never need to keep a man in his bed. Strangest of all was the fact that he could not tell the person involved of the solution he had found, but had to sit there silent and motionless. Not because he was afraid of seeming ridiculous (he was far beyond that) but because there was a kind of logical imperative of silence which came into play just when saying something might have been useful. He stared at the black woman, she stared back at him ... there was a momentary impasse, but once he had arranged a concession for her offal stall at the slaughterhouse, she calmed down completely. That was more than enough for her to leave contented. And her husband? He decided that was a lost cause. They had reached no conclusion about the matter. Or had they? He wondered whether the woman had been able to read his thoughts.

As for the Englishman, he appeared at the most agreeable moment of the afternoon. He was accompanied by his nation's Consul, who was like one of the family. Rosas also received them on the porch, which had by now been cleared of all prying eyes and contained two extra seats. The newcomer looked to be aged around thirty-five, and was dark-skinned, with jet black hair. He did not look English, but Rosas had noticed that some Englishmen could be like that, almost Indian-looking. Rosas himself looked more like the other kind of Englishman, fair-haired and ruddy-cheeked. At first he thought his guest was ugly, although he was fortunate enough to be small, like an oriental. But when he spoke, in a more than passable Spanish, he became almost attractive, in a serious, reserved kind of way. They exchanged small talk. Clarke, as the Englishman was called, was a brother-in-law of Darwin, who had sent the Restorer greetings. There followed more empty remarks about the weather, journeys, this and that. What Rosas sought to convey above all was the atmosphere of the place, the time of day, the domesticity of the scene, which he was sure made a strong political impact. By now, the homely circle was complete, and went spinning on above and beyond Manuela's absurdities. Manuelita divided the whole of humanity into "cousins" and "gentlemen"; she could see no further than that. The Englishman spoke of his intention of traveling into the interior of Argentina once his preparations were completed. This information verged on the unnecessary, so they did not waste much time discussing it. Both of them considered they knew as much as they could about the other. The previous day, Rosas's police had determined that Clarke was in fact the person he claimed to be, that the schooner he had landed in had sailed from Valparaiso, and that beneath the cloak of a naturalist and geographer in the service of the British empire there was nothing worthy of note. Of course, it would have been much more interesting if there had been, which meant there probably was. The police had their limits. Rosas deplored the fact that good manners prevented one from asking people straight out what they were really up to. A different sort of courtesy was needed, he thought.

"My friend," he said, as if rousing himself, "allow me to show you some tricks I can perform on horseback, then you can tell me if horsemanship is as advanced in Great Britain."

The Englishman nodded and settled back to watch. He was immediately startled to see Eusebio's head appear in front of him. Eusebio was a dwarf little more than a yard high, almost half of which was accounted for by his huge head. He had come in response to a whistle the Restorer must have given at some point during his conversation or one of the pauses, but which the others had been unaware of. Eusebio must have been extraordinarily vigilant toward anything that concerned him, which is what made him a monster. Nor was there any need to repeat the name of the horse that the Restorer ordered him to bring: Repetido.

There followed a spectacle that the Restorer of the Laws rarely neglected to offer his European visitors. Repetido was a piebald of indeterminate race, neither Arab nor American; slender, with large hooves like a caricature cat, stiff-backed and with a small, featureless head. The two Englishmen turned their chairs to face the wide glacis that served as a track; the courtiers broke off their conversations to look on adoringly. Manuelita arranged her scarlet bows, the trace of an inane smile still on her face. She was convinced that exhibitions of this sort were customary in high society. The supreme horseman, First Centaur of the Confederation, galloped around in circles to warm up his mount, but did not need do this for long: Repetido pranced and bucked, then sped along like a tame streak of lightning. Rosas had narrow, tight buttocks, which made it seem as though he were never firmly seated on the horse. This made it all the more natural for him to lift his feet backward until his ankles were crossed over its rump. He kept the same position and increased his speed, then the next time he passed by lifted his feet high into the air, at the same time plunging his head between his hands, which he kept flat on the saddle, so that it looked as if he were falling from a tall building. The first round of applause rang out. The third time he rode past, his feet were level with the horse's ears; at the fourth, his body was completely horizontal. After that, he swung right underneath his mount's belly, rode standing up, stood on one foot, knelt down, knelt facing backward holding the reins with his feet, then with his teeth as he touched the soles of his boots with the palms of his hands. At first, Rosas carried out each of these feats with a virtuoso deliberateness on the darting Repetido, then gradually speeded up while his mount continued at full gallop, and concluded his display with a series of spectacular pirouettes that drew thunderous applause from the onlookers. There were two kinds of exercise in his performance: the easy ones that looked spectacular, and the difficult ones that did not. Rosas could impress with either, at no great cost to himself, depending on how knowledgeable his public was. But since Rosas had no way of knowing this beforehand, and since there was usually a mixed audience anyway, he had adopted a routine which included both kinds of tricks, performing the easy ones the hard way, and vice versa.

On their way back to Buenos Aires, the two guests let their horses set their own pace. They took the low road, enjoying the evening air as the English often do, saying little to each other; the silence of the empty fields allowed them to speak without raising their voices even though their mounts went different ways around the ruts in the track. They watched as a startled chaja bird scrambled away from them in panic, falling all over itself as it did so. Both of them simultaneously thought of the Restorer. Plump pigeons bent the branches of some terebinth trees almost down to the ground. No doubt they were settling for the night. To their left, the dun-colored river was as still as a lake; only where the water lapped against the edge of the green-tinged shoreline was there any sign of movement, and then only if one peered closely. Thoroughly familiar with this landscape, the Consul ceased to pay it any attention, and concentrated instead on political matters. This meant he was neglecting his guest, but that did not worry him unduly. He was one of the old school of diplomats who considered it no part of a consul's duties to act as a guide for his fellow countrymen. He kept his courtesies to a strict minimum, and on this occasion felt he had more than done his duty with the visit to the country's main attraction, the Dictator. Besides which, there were two further considerations: first, if it were true that Clarke intended to travel into the interior, he could obviously look after himself in Buenos Aires; and second, politics gave him a lot to think about: so much indeed that twenty-four hours a day were not enough. So the Consul became completely engrossed in his own thoughts. Clarke meanwhile let his horse pick its own way. Rather than staring at the land, he was looking up at the sky, which was a wash of purple, with broad streaks of blue and pink. It was still stiflingly hot, and the atmosphere was oppressively humid. The silence was crisscrossed by the whirring of insects.... When the Consul raised his eyes again he was intrigued by what Clarke was doing. He had let go of the reins and his hands were busy doing something at the level of his stomach. From behind, the Consul had no idea what this might be. He pushed his horse on, twisting to one side so that he could find out without seeming indiscreet. Clarke was concentrating so hard he did not even notice. He was holding a small metal box open in his left hand, and doing something inside it with his other hand. The Consul recognized the apparatus as a chromatograph. It was made up of rows of tiny metal rings, into which Clarke was inserting needles with a dexterity that spoke of long practice. The Consul moved no closer. More than a waste of time, the operation seemed to him sinister: it was like sticking pins into the soft colors of the sunset.

A few days later, with all his preparations for the journey to the interior completed, the naturalist made another trip out in this same direction, but this time he rode considerably further, to a village north of Buenos Aires where a well-known painter lived in seclusion. On this occasion, Clarke traveled alone. He set out in the early morning, enjoyed a solitary picnic mid-route at around eleven, took a siesta under a weeping willow on the riverbank, then continued unhurriedly on his way, at little more than a snail's pace. Below a certain threshold of speed, he found it hard to direct the horse: he was unsure whether they were advancing or not. He wanted to find the painter awake, but knew that whatever allowances he made, he always underestimated the length of siesta that people slept in these tropical climes. There was no well-defined track, and nobody seemed to be about. Just

once he met a cart driven by a black man dressed in a green liv-
ery as brilliant as a parrot's plumage. A child of about four or
five ran in front, shooing off the pigeons that settled in the path
the cart was inching its way along. The draught animals were a
spectacle in their own right: twin white oxen, which had been
so badly castrated that with the passage of time (they looked to
be hundreds of years old), they had taken on the appearance of
Japanese bulls, with swollen dewlaps and so many folds of white
skin dangling from their backs that they appeared to be covered
in sheets of marble, like Bernini statues in Rome. The two men
greeted each other with great courtesy as they passed. At the
time, it seemed to Clarke that the black man was wearing a pair
of eyeglasses, but afterward he was not sure he had seen correctly. A little further on, where the riverbank became steeper,
he saw a group of creatures which from a distance he took to be
crabs, but which turned out to be hedgehogs lying uncurled in
the sunshine. A curious thing happened. The hedgehogs, which
are the most timid creatures imaginable, saw him at the very moment he caught sight of them, but instead of reacting as a group,
they did so one by one, and though this was a very rapid process, Clarke was able to see how each of them took flight. Not
that it could really be called a flight: hedgehogs move extremely
slowly, but if frightened, they do contrive to disappear somehow
or other. As Clarke watched, each of them rolled up into a ball,
and this meant they all began to roll down the riverbank and into
the water. One after the other, until there was not a single animal
left, before the Englishman had so much as dared to blink.

Prilidiano's siesta was shorter than usual that afternoon, but it was not without its disturbing phantoms, which was normal, far too normal. It was pure habit, as with children. And this man, so important for Argentine history in his century, had a great deal of the child about him. He was plump, impetuous, imprudent, fearful, a slave to his passions, the plaything of the wildest fantasies. Every day he conjured up this theater of horror within the confines of his villa at the top end of San Isidro village: but only while the sun shone, because he always slept a dreamless sleep for all the hours when it was below the horizon. He was unmarried, with no close family, and no servants since he had placed himself in the hands of Facunda Lopez, who had started out as his cook, but by now had also taken over the duties of maid, housekeeper, gardener, and even groom. Facunda was a well-rounded woman of around forty years, who had no need to learn any erotic tricks to keep her master in the palm of her hand, because he was already there, and always would be. Whenever she talked to herself—and sometimes when she was speaking out loud too, as she was no model of discretion—she called the painter "Repetido," because he always made love in exactly the same way, without any variation, and never missed a day, with his childlike insatiability. She went to him, without fail, when his siesta was coming to an end; she watched him pretending to be asleep for a moment, then flung herself on him.

For several months now, Prilidiano had been painting a picture for his own pleasure. It was the first time he had done this, without the painting being commissioned. Just for himself, not to be sold. This had unnerved him somewhat: at first he had doubts as to what kind of art might emerge from this gratuitous act. Painting with his usual excruciating meticulousness, he watched as the image slowly took shape, and it was just like any other. Perhaps it was art after all. He worked even more slowly than usual, because he was painting in his spare time. His original idea had been to paint Facunda sleeping her siesta naked. Naturally, the painting was and always would be his secret. But precisely in order not to let slip even a fraction of that secret, which was far more valuable than the canvas itself, he wanted to paint Facunda a second time, in the same bed, alongside the first figure. Muddleheaded as he was, he did not realize that this meant he would be portraying two women rather than the same one twice. By the time he caught on, it was too late. This totally confused him. He was a genius, but things like this were always happening to him. At least he had learned his lesson. And since he truly was the Repetido, he went on learning it siesta after siesta.

Although not unknown, visits to the villa were rare. When the Englishman turned up in mid-afternoon, the two inhabitants of the house were still sleepy. Facunda came out to hold his horse. She asked him who he was and what he wanted. After he had told her, Clarke began to feel it was impertinent of her to insist so much on whether he really wished to see the painter. Of course he did. Did he wish to see him, or to have his portrait painted? If the latter were the case, he would need to learn to be patient. He had chosen the slowest artist in the world. Annoyed at this unwanted and trivial advice, Clarke strode into the living room without waiting for the woman to invite him in, and sat down. Within a minute, the artist appeared. Clarke thought it must be his son, but it was the man himself. He was not in the

least as Clarke had imagined him: a plump, dark-skinned youngster, turning bald although no one would have taken him to be
more than twenty-five, and with the asymmetrical, slanted eyes
of a lunatic. He had no manners, but the Englishman had enough
for them both. Clarke explained he had been given the address
by an aunt of the house owner, and then launched into discreet
praise of the painter's work. This was the first time that Prilidiano had heard anything of the sort. He agreed with everything he
was told, with a charming ingenuousness. Facunda, who had apparently disappeared for good, suddenly reappeared in the room
with a bottle of chilled claret and two glasses. In the twinkling
of an eye, the two men downed half the bottle. As he warmed
to his visitor, the painter confessed he was thinking of traveling
to Europe to become a little less ignorant. Clarke spoke strongly
against the idea. Prilidiano had all he needed for his development
in Argentina. The artistic scene in Europe was exhausted; before
much longer all the old world painters would start emigrating to
the new. What about technique? the painter asked. He already
had more than enough. And the old masters? When it came down
to it, the Englishman said, they were not worth the effort. They
continued in this vein for some time. Prilidiano was sorry he did
not have any of his paintings in the house to show his enthusiastic
admirer. He did have one, that of the two Facundas, but that was
not finished and besides, it was not something to show to others. What he could offer were a few works hanging on the walls
of the living room. Clarke stood up politely. They turned out to
be pictures woven in wool and esparto grass by Manuelita Rosas, who had given them to the painter. Clarke stared at them

without the slightest idea of what to say. They were abominable, wretched. Over the previous few days he had seen perhaps half a dozen portraits by Prilidiano in Buenos Aires salons. He thought them better than Reynolds and Gainsborough put together, the sign of true genius, not so much for the incredible psychological insight into their sitters they demonstrated, though that in itself was sublime, but for the way they created a surface. In that, they were beyond compare. Prilidiano achieved a visual clarity that was pure visibility, a way of taking the surface to the surface of the picture and making the two come together, of creating painting at the precise point where the viewer was—unbeknown to himself—wishing it might be realized. The painter's triumph went far beyond the teasing interplay of ingenuity and knowledge. Manuelita's ridiculously labored woolen offerings were the exact opposite. Could it be out of sarcasm that the genius had them hung in his living room, and was showing them off in this way? Clarke found it impossible to decide.

Once they had exhausted their discussion about painting, they sat down again and turned to the visitor's plans. Clarke was a naturalist, and his intention was to travel into the hinterland to study several animals, and one in particular, which a number of scientific institutions in Europe were interested in.

"Well," Prilidiano said lightheartedly, "if you take a good embalmer along with you, I suppose you'll be able to get some fine specimens."

No, that was not the Englishman's intention at all. He said that the last thing he wanted to do was to embalm anything. He was not aiming to collect things, quite the opposite. He briefly outlined the new theory according to which some animals were descended from others, which meant there was no point in preserving them in any one fixed form. Nor was there any point taking them off somewhere else because according to another, complementary theory, in ancient times all the continents had been joined together as one ... the painter's mind was filled with confusion. His guest might just as well have been talking Greek. He preferred to change topics, especially as something had occurred to him.

"So, you're going out ... into the desert?"

"Yes."

"But isn't that where the Indians are?"

"Well, yes."

"But my friend, as soon as they set eyes on you, they'll kill you!"

"I hope I'll have the chance to take proper precautions."

Prilidiano did not insist, because his gadfly mind had already gone into reverse. However absurd the idea about some animals being descended from others might be, it had given him a notion as to how he might resolve the dilemma of his painting of Facunda taking her siesta. Which at the very least was proof that some ideas can descend from others. But he did not stop there (he always promised himself he would pick up the threads of his thoughts later on). It was no great matter that the Indians kill a traveler; that was a risk to be run like so many others. The question needed to be posed on a more general level. How could one be happy traveling? Wasn't it a contradiction in terms? For years, he had been postponing his study trip to Europe because he could not imagine a life other than the one he was living, down to its minutest details. On the one hand he placed too much importance on happiness; on the other, he did not consider it so important that he should go in search of it. Painting and love were everywhere or they were nowhere. In a flash of inspiration of his childish, impish brain, Prilidiano got to the bottom of Darwinism and turned it completely upside down. Every change meant turning full circle. Eternity itself was a process of change, it was the present, the proof of happiness, and each and every one of these words was interchangeable.

"I'd really like to go with you," he said, gloriously inconsistent, "but I can't. I have so much to do!"

Before his expedition into the desert, Clarke paid a second and final visit to Palermo to say farewell to the Restorer and to thank him for providing him with a guide or "tracker," a gaucho by the name of Gauna or Guana. He called on Rosas one Saturday afternoon at the epiphanic hour. After they had paid Manuelita the customary compliments, they shut themselves in Rosas's office to talk. As usual, the Restorer looked relaxed and unkempt, his face bright red from all the wine he had drunk during a gargantuan barbecue he had eaten with the provincial governors. He smelled of grilled meat and wine. He had kept abreast of all the Englishman's movements. That was the advantage of having a secret police, although it was no secret to anybody that he had one: he got to know everything about everybody else. But by the same token, they all knew everything about him, because in order to have a police force, he had to live a public life. Consequently, the two of them wasted no time on practical matters. Instead, they talked about languages. Clarke's Spanish was particularly good for a foreigner, something which he modestly put down to an innate talent. Rosas considered himself blessed with the same talent, to a remarkable degree. He had never put this to the test, nor did he need to do so, because his certainty required no proof. With such a gift, he was saying, he would like to try not such simple languages as English or French, but something really difficult like the babble of the black people. He might at any time decide to study and then write a grammar of the Argentine Bantu language. The Englishman nodded his assent.

"And please don't think," Rosas went on, "that I would be driven to this out of boredom, as I have no lack of things to keep me busy. And I do not mean simply political matters. If only you knew how many domestic problems I have to deal with! Take this fellow, for example ..." A little boy, one of his countless illegitimate children, had sneaked into the study, and was watching them from the depths of an armchair. "He has got it into his head to start squinting recently, and I'm worried he might get caught in a draught and stay stuck like that forever. I know that physiologically my fears are groundless, but I can't help it, I can't shake them off. He, however, could shake off his wretched habit, but he persists in it because he knows how much it upsets me." The boy, a silent and pleasant-looking child, focused on them both perfectly well; perhaps he had no idea even of how to squint. "Although I must admit that when I was his age, I spent my whole time cross-eyed. But I'm not the kind of parent who is happy simply to say: 'I was seven too once.'"

In response, Clarke merely nodded. He considered Rosas a

genius; if not for languages, then for his "small talk." This latest digression, for example, had been a ruse to find out just how much Clarke knew about Indian societies. But Clarke was not that stupid. Of course he knew what squinting meant to the Indians. Moreover, he was one of the few Europeans of his day who could have explained it in one of the native American languages. He had no intention however of telling the Restorer this, not even to fill a gap in the conversation.

"Well," Rosas said, "are you hoping to discover a secret?"

Clarke replied that this was perhaps not the best way to describe his endeavor. The Legibrerian Hare he had been speaking of, which was the principal, if not the only, object of his expedition, was no secret. If it had been, how could he possibly expect to discover it with the limited means he had at his disposal, alone and lost in the vastness of the desert? Yet at the same time, it had to be one, for it to be worth all this trouble. Correctly phrased, the question would have to be: "What is so hidden that it is necessary to travel the globe to find it, but at the same time is so visible that it can be found simply by going to look for it? By definition, such a thing must be anywhere and everywhere, wherever one may be, in this very office...."

"But it's not here," Rosas replied, pretending to look under the table.

"That's because the definition implies a circumlocution, because every definition can be considered a nominal one, and ..."

Rosas had followed him as closely as he was able, but even so his mind had wandered almost from the beginning, once he had grasped the main idea. He had sniffed Manuelita in there somewhere. Whatever else the famous Hare might or might not be, his daughter was it as well. And by his own hand. He had made this foolish girl the most completely visible element of his politics, but without providing any explanation, which was what made things visible. Darwin had been pointing in the same direction, but he had been so timid it was almost pitiful; he had found it necessary to base it on what Rosas had least need of: belief. As ever, an Argentine had got there first. He felt so pleased, so full of himself that he immediately took several decisions he had been hesitating over: first, to commission a full-length portrait of Manuelita from Pueyrredon's son; second, to lend the Englishman Repetido for his journey; and third, to accede to the request he had received the previous day from the mother of Carlos Alzaga Prior, an aspiring young watercolor artist, and recommend that Clarke take him along. Everything fitted in, everything was part of the system ... he sat motionless for a moment, lost in the contemplation of his own grandeur.

2: The Legibrerian Hare

TO CARRY ON SPEAKING, CAFULCURÁ TOOK THE CIGAR from his mouth with the slowest of gestures, wreathed the whole while in a cloud of smoke that gave off a medicinal odor. He muttered the words with his eyes half-closed, as he sat bare-chested on the leather mats strewn on the floor of the tent.

"Wouldn't you say," he said, "that travelers to the desert always come to impose some kind of law?"

Clarke spread his arms cautiously, palms outstretched: stated in such general terms, the proposition was irrefutable. The Indian chief's way of speaking, which Clarke was listening to after an incident-free journey since setting out from Buenos Aires two weeks earlier, had a certain effeminate quality to it, at least on first acquaintance (but this was an impression which, like so many others, vanished with greater familiarity); an uncertainty, something imprecise which itself was not easy to define precisely. Which made it all the more difficult to find oneself in agreement with him on any point in particular.

"One law," Cafulcurá went on, "is made by a legislator; the other is the kind which already exists in nature, and which we only call 'law' by extension."

"Or vice versa," the stranger ventured to suggest, since he knew that the Mapuche word for "law" could also mean many other things, among which were "venture," "suggest," "stranger," "know," "word," and "Mapuche."

The chieftain nodded modestly, as if he himself had spoken. He breathed in the smoke once more, rolled his head vaguely, then continued his speech in the same slow drawl he had been using for two or three hours now:

"What the traveler does not know is that when this law is made and/or discovered, it creates a magic circle around itself, from which escape is no easy matter."

A lengthy silence.

"I beg you not to read anything threatening, or even prophetic, into my words, Mr. Clarke. Simply take them as a description, or a 'law' if you like. This circle around a law is a world in miniature within our world, which itself is a miniature. We create the world to fit in with our personal system, so that man can become world. In other words, so that the miniature can become miniature. But miniatures have their own laws, you know. It is not only space which can become minute: it also happens to the corresponding time, which becomes extremely fast. That is why life is short."

Cafulcurá fell into a thoughtful silence. The clouds from the herbs he was smoking wafted thicker and thinner. Layers of the perfumed haze rose high into the roof of the tent, which apart from the two of them was occupied only by three sleeping women, three dogs, and an extraordinarily large hen. Clarke sat silent as well. For the first time in his life he was aware of a direct continuum between the topic of conversation and the words used to express it. As they interacted, their values were exchanged: the vertiginous speed Cafulcurá had referred to became instead the immense slowness of real time. This inversion only served to strengthen the continuum. At this hour of the afternoon, Clarke also felt somewhat drowsy, which meant he had to make an effort to concentrate. He was drinking cold tea. The Indian chief was drinking water, or something resembling it. It was relatively cool in the tent, despite the torrid heat outside.

"I was just thinking," Cafulcurá said all of a sudden, "of what you were telling me. Your brother-in-law is a genius, there's no doubt of that. When I met him, I thought he was simply a likeable young man; but after what you've said, I'll have to change my judgment. Nothing unusual in that. But I should say: he's a genius in his own field. I myself have sought to convey similar ideas, but—and look what a strange case of transformation this is—I always did it by means of poetry. In matters like these, it's important to win people's belief. But in this particular case, it so happens that we Mapuche have no need to believe in anything, because we've always known that changes of this kind occur. It is sufficient for a breeze to blow a thousand leagues away for one species to be transformed into another. You may ask me how. We explain it, or at least I explain it ..."

He paused for a while to consider how he did explain it.

"... it's simply a matter of seeing everything that is visible, without exception. And then if, as is obvious, everything is connected to everything else, how could the homogeneous and the heterogeneous not also be linked?"

In the Huilliche tongue, these last two nouns had several meanings. Clarke could not immediately decide how they were being used on this occasion, and asked for an explanation. He knew what he was letting himself in for, because the Indians could be especially labyrinthine in these delicate issues of semantics: their idea of the continuum prevented them from giving clear and precise definitions. On this occasion, however, his sacrifice was not unrewarded, because Cafulcurá's digression, starting from the sense of "right" and "left" that the two words also had, ended thus:

"We have a word for 'government' which signifies, in addition to a whole range of other things, a 'path,' but not just an ordinary path—the path that certain animals take when they leap in a zigzag fashion, if you follow me; although at the same time we ignore their deviations to the right and left, which due to a secondary effect of the trajectory end up of course not being deviations at all, but a particular kind of straight line."

"Oh, yes?" said Clarke, who after first thinking with a start that the topic of the reason for his journey was finally being broached, soon found himself drifting off again. He was staring at the chieftain's hair as the old man looked down at the ground, showing him the top of his head. It was the blackest hair Clarke had ever seen, glistening with bright blue tints. Not a single white strand. At his age, this was remarkable. He must dye it, the Englishman thought; the knowledge these Indians had of chemistry was more than sufficient for that; they knew so much in fact that it was odd that in this case the color they had achieved looked so artificial, so metallic. As he looked more closely though, he became convinced it was natural after all. There were many astounding things about this man, and this could well be yet another one.

"Every single change ..." Cafulcurá went on, drawling even more exaggeratedly as he returned to the theme of Darwinism, "even a change in the weather ..."

At that moment, the noise clearly audible for some minutes outside the tent became even louder; there was the sound of galloping horses (though this was nothing unusual, as the Indians rode on horseback even when they were only visiting their neighbor's tent), then Gauna came in, apologizing.

Cafulcurá looked at him, a lost expression on his face.

"What's happening?" Clarke asked him. His guide had turned out to be someone shrouded in mystery. As a guide, he left a lot to be desired. While Clarke waited for a definite excuse to regret having brought him, he had grown used to the idea of being constantly surprised by the gaucho.

"Everybody's gone to see a hare that took off," Gauna said.

"You don't say!" Clarke looked across at the chieftain, who shrugged his shoulders in one of his typical gestures.

"Go and see if you like," Cafulcurá said.

The Englishman did not need to be asked twice. He was stiff, bored and felt nauseous from the cold tea and the smell of herbs. Ever since their arrival forty-eight hours earlier, they had been moved around constantly. Although this was always done with the utmost politeness, it was beginning to get him down. The Indian elders apparently needed to hold private conversations

about fifty times a day, which meant the strangers were asked
to leave, and then moved from the new place allotted them half
an hour later: always with humble apologies, but with that half-
sarcastic fatalism that the Indians were so practiced in. They had
assured Clarke that this was not normal, far from it. It was just
that he had arrived at a bad moment. Now at least he had the sat-
isfying opportunity to leave out of choice. Moreover, the reason
in this case was intriguing. Taking an obvious precaution, he had
been careful not to say a word about the hare, but he was afraid
that, as so often happens in these matters, he had let it slip anyway, so that all the many interesting allusions to the animal he
had heard were a kind of joke at his expense.

He left the tent heaving a sigh of relief. The light outside was
devastating. Everything in Salinas Grandes was the harshest
white. He had no need to ask Gauna in which direction the event
was taking place, because several Indians were heading toward
it at that very moment. He leapt on to Repetido. He could see
where all the Indians were gathered, about two thousand yards
away. The tents of the Mapuches' imperial capital were arranged
in loose semicircles that did not obscure the view on any side.

"Can a hare really fly?" Gauna asked him.

"Only if it's thrown in the air," he replied crossly. Gauna had
an irritating way of asking questions, with a hint of malice in his
voice. He must be half Indian, though his yellow, wrinkled face
made him look more Chinese.

Their ponies covered the distance in no time. When they arrived, there were more children than adults present, and the latter were busy playing a game of hockey with a ball of rags. Clarke

was taken aback. He caught sight of Mallén, one of Cafulcurá's favorite shamans, sitting quietly on his horse away from the main group, staring down at his fingertips. He rode over to him, followed by Gauna.

"What's all this about a hare?" Clarke asked him without preamble.

"I know as much as you do. I've just got here."

Typical reply.

"I heard that a hare had taken off," Clarke insisted.

"If that's true," replied Mallén, "it must have done so before I arrived."

A small group of children close by them were staring up into the sky. Without saying another word to the shaman, Clarke went over to them and asked the same question. It seemed to him that the children were more polite, more rational—presumably because according to Indian standards, they were less so. They told him that yes, a little white hare (they used the same word for "white" as for "twin") had taken off into the air, and they believed they had spotted it high in the sky. However, after the verb "taken off" they had used an extra word, the Mapuche enclitic (*i'n*), which served to emphasize the past tense. It could mean "a minute ago," "a thousand years ago," or "before."

This made the whole thing extremely suspect, but Clarke still threw his head back and looked up. For a while, the children tried to give him indications, using the stars as points of reference, since with their keen eyesight they could see them even during the day. Clarke soon gave up. In fact, he could not decide from what they said whether they were talking about a real animal,

or a star of the same name. He went back over to Mallén, where
Gauna was waiting for him too. Meanwhile, almost everyone had
joined in the game of hockey: there must have been a hundred
Indians playing, having a whale of a time. The horses galloped
in every direction, frequently crashing into each other, to loud
cheers from the spectators. In one of these collisions, an Indian
was knocked to the ground, and broke his neck. After that, the
game quickly petered out. As they were riding back to the camp,
Clarke spoke his thoughts out loud:

"I wonder if that tale about the hare was something real,
something that really happened, or whether it was some kind of
ceremony or ritual?"

Mallén nodded, showing interest, but no desire to express his
own opinion on the matter; to him the difference seemed to be
negligible, a mere intellectual quibble. In order to say something,
he commented:

"Not here, but further south in regions where we once lived,
the winds are so strong that no one would be surprised to see a
small animal, a hare for example, flying over their head."

They were joined by a single rider also on his way back to the
camp. Mallén greeted him with a sudden burst of enthusiasm,
then turned to introduce him.

"Do you two know each other? Alvarito Reymacurá. Mister
Clarke from England."

"Yes, we met yesterday," said the Indian. He was one of Cafulcurá's countless children, and a personage of some importance in
the court. The son of a giant, he was himself rather small, but he
was attractive and had the reputation of being obsessed with sex.

Mallén made some comment about the spectacle they had vainly hoped to witness. Alvarito responded with a brief cackle, although he gave no hint of a smile, which was something the Indians never did.

"How can one see what's already been, my dear Mallén?"

He must immediately have felt that his comment was out of place, and corrected himself harshly:

"But who cares about that kind of nonsense?"

"Well," Mallén said with a deep sigh, "if I'm not mistaken, I think our distinguished visitors were quite interested."

Alvarito corrected himself a second time, turning ninety degrees on the horse's back as though in a swivel chair, until he was facing directly toward Clarke (though he was staring at the ground). He said:

"Of course, of course! For anyone who has not seen it, it's of undoubted interest. Even if they never get to see it."

"It's disappointing, isn't it?" said the Englishman.

"No, no, not in the least!"

Mallén was silent. Then he said he had things he must attend to, and tapped his mount on the neck, urging it off in another direction.

"Goodbye," Alvarito called out to him.

"Be seeing you."

"I wonder, Mister Clarke, if you would care to come and have a cup of tea at my tent, although I'm afraid it must be in a dreadful mess."

"I'd love to."

"And Mister ..."

"Gauna, at your service."

So Gauna came along too. Alvarito's tent was nearby, in the first line of the village. As they dismounted, several small greyhounds came to rub themselves against the Indian's legs. The Indians always left their horses without tying them up, and Clarke decided to do the same.

They went in. All the tents were exactly the same, inside and out. A group of about ten Indians were playing cards in the center of this one.

"I'm sorry to disturb you, friends, but these gentlemen and I would like to talk on our own for a while."

"Don't mention it, Alvarito!" one of the men said, picking up the cards without mixing them. "We'll go over to Felix Barrigón's."

And so they left. Soon afterward, two women came in with some rolls of leather, which they spread out on the ground for mats. The three men sat down and the host called for some tea. Once they were settled, Alvarito Reymacurá crossed his eyes in a squint that seemed almost superhuman, and stared down at the ground. This was a sign of great courtesy that few in the village had offered Clarke until now; this made him feel better. They began to talk.

Summing up the various replies Reymacurá gave to the Englishman's hesitant questions, and stripping them of their many contradictions, vague points, and digressions, what he conveyed was more or less the following:

"As the perspicacious traveler has quite rightly noted from the attitude of the wise shaman, the question about the reality of the hare which caused all the fuss today was irrelevant. It was something which, literally, was of no interest to anyone. To explain why, as indeed to explain any other lack of interest, one must return to general principles, which might seem to bear no relation to the original question. To put it simply, it could be said that for centuries the central political problem for the savages has been that of the discontinuity of territory." He did not propose to go into details, partly because it was too complicated, and partly because it spoke for itself. What other problem could the wide open spaces of the pampas have, if indeed they had any, apart from that of discontinuity? As a result of many years pondering this problem, the Indians had constructed a whole logic of continuities, and this had to be borne in mind when even the most trifling event took place. The Mapuches were constantly creating continuities, and so adept were they at this that they no longer even needed to employ visible or virtual connections, but simply used the continuity itself to perform that function. "Take for example what happened today," Alvarito said. "The hare runs, but by definition it must run across territory. If for example it is running on the continent, it cannot be running on the island. But then if it takes off and lands on the other side of the channel separating the continent from the island, then it is doing so, isn't it? It is like that sad story," he added, heightening still further the rather stilted mannerisms of his way of talking, "of the Indian who was leading his three-year-old son by the hand in some celebration where there were crowds of people. At one point his attention wandered and he let go of the boy for an instant: when he looked again, he had vanished. The only thing left on the ground close to the despairing father's feet was the paper windmill the little boy had been carrying. A kidnapping? Fate? He never saw him again.

"None of this," he explained, "involved any complicated reasoning. On the contrary, they were all children's stories, they could be followed with a minimum of attention. The hare has big ears, which allow it to hear what is normally inaudible, even what is very far off. But the hare is also the emblem of speed. It is so fast that it makes one think of that other world in miniature in which time is all squashed together. And in the process, we move unconsciously from the 'real' hare to its opposite pole...."

"But there has to be some element of reality," Clarke butted in.

"Always, always!" the Indian responded emphatically. "You should know that better than any of us, if, as I have heard, you are a naturalist."

Clarke nodded.

"We Indians are very ignorant, very stupid; we cannot grasp either the very tiny or the very large, and we don't know much about what's in between. At best, we only occasionally pay attention to what we are told, then we have the effrontery to forget it.... The hare may be a character in a tale, and that tale may fly over disconnected territories, and always reach the other side of the earth.... As you know, my father has based his government on fables; there is no need for me to tell you any, because you might misinterpret them; he even sets himself up as the hero of a fabulous tale for his subjects...."

At that moment two elderly shamans came into the tent, bowing and whispering into Alvarito's ear. Such was his interest in what they were telling him that he immediately uncrossed his eyes.

"Show him in," he finally said to them, and to his two guests: "I must beg you to wait outside for me while I deal with a most

important and pressing matter which has arisen. It will only take
a minute, then I'll be all yours ... to continue with our most interesting talk."

Without ceasing for a moment to offer his apologies, he led
them to the tent's back entrance, where he gave instructions for
them to be attended to. Several women were sitting in the shade
of awnings; they at once laid out mats for them and offered them
tea. As they then immediately returned to their entertaining conversation, Clarke and Gauna were left with nothing else to do
than to stare out into the distance. From time to time, groups
of horsemen sped by, without any obvious destination. The salt
flats gave off a blinding dry white glare. One of the groups of
riders had the effect of silencing the women, who all stared after
them. The two men did not notice anything special about the
riders, but from the comments that followed they learned that it
had been Juana Pitiley, Cafulcurá's favorite wife, who was setting
off for Carhué to undergo a water treatment for her old bones.
Alvarito's wives were young (as he was also, since he could be
no more than thirty), they had viper's tongues, and there on the
back porch of the tent they had an enchanting, ungroomed look:
they looked far prettier when they were not smeared with their
ceremonial grease.

After about an hour an Indian came out of the tent and said
that Reymacurá begged them to excuse him, as his timetable had
become terribly complicated, but he would come and see them
that evening if he could find a free moment, etc., etc. Resignedly,
Clarke walked round to the front of the spacious dwelling with
Gauna, and the pair of them mounted and rode off.

They set off along the avenue containing the chieftains' tents, until Clarke shook off the torpor that all the tea and the waiting had induced in him and asked himself in a sudden panic where they might be heading. He had no desire whatsoever to get into conversation with Cafulcurá again, or with anyone else for that matter. His head began to ache at the mere thought of it. He looked round him. Gauna was lost in his own thoughts, with a black look on his face, though there was nothing unusual about that. Clarke asked him what had happened to the young watercolorist, whom he had not seen since that morning.

"I think he went to bathe in the creek," the gaucho replied.

"We could also go and cool off a bit, don't you think?"

Gauna shrugged. He raised his arm and pointed to the far side of the encampment. "It's over there."

They sped off at a gallop. Repetido was marvelously docile. Because of the way the tents were lined up, and because Clarke felt he had no right as a guest to cut between them as the Indians did, they had to travel in a circle until they reached the perimeter of the capital, then turned sharply to the left. The plain dipped gently in front of them, and although the slope was almost imperceptible, they felt as though they were constantly pitching forward. Their mounts were happy. The clear air showed signs that the afternoon was drawing to a close. The sun was no longer as blinding as it had been throughout the day. From dawn to dusk, it gave the sensation that tiny prismatic crystals were floating above Salinas Grandes, reducing everything to a white sheen.

The river ran narrow and cool through beds of osiers. A large number of bathers had spent the day in its streams and on its banks. About two hundred horses were standing loose near an open, treeless beach which seemed to be the official bathing place. Indians were sleeping, sunbathing, or playing cards, while children scampered noisily in and out of the water. The two new arrivals dismounted and walked for a while. As they went upstream, they came upon groups of youngsters who were enjoying themselves in more secluded recesses. One of them was Carlos Alzaga Prior, who approached them, his hair dripping. They sat together on a grassy high bank overlooking a calm backwater.

"Have you been having a good time?" Clarke asked Prior, treating him familiarly because he was so young.

"First class. What about you two?"

There was a silence. Gauna was still wrapped in his own thoughts. Finally, Clarke said: "Not so good. These Indians are always talking to themselves."

The youth burst out laughing, but they did not feel like joining in. The Englishman had come to think he had acted hastily when he had agreed to take Prior along. In fact, it had been very irresponsible of the young man's parents to give him permission to undertake the journey to the perilous desert as though it were a trip round the family estate. Parents like that, Clarke surmised, were the sort who would most readily accuse him of being responsible if anything happened to their son, in a classic defense mechanism of laying the blame elsewhere. As for his artistic apprenticeship, that had obviously been an excuse, because Clarke had not even seen him pick up a brush. Prior gave them a detailed account of his prowess at swimming, diving, and so on. His chatter eventually wearied Clarke, who suggested he return to his friends. Prior did so at once, a broad smile on his face.

"What a child," Gauna muttered when he was out of earshot.

"Señor Gauna, you were fifteen once," Clarke chided him.

"But he's been smoking something. Didn't you see how dilated his pupils were?"

"The truth is, I didn't notice."

They sat in silence for a while. They gazed idly at people swimming by them in the river. Birds were singing in the trees. In front of them, the sun dipped toward the horizon.

"Tell me frankly, Señor Gauna, is something bothering you?"

"Lots of things."

"Such as what?"

"For example, the fact that the Indians are such great liars."

This interested Clarke. Not because he needed confirmation that they were caught up in a web of lies, but because it might be useful for him to know what reasons his tracker had for saying so.

"Take that story of the 'hare' which 'took off,'" Gauna said, a sarcastic emphasis in his voice. "Did you believe that?"

"There wasn't much to believe, that's for sure."

"But it's as if they were making fun of us!"

Hearing this remark, the Englishman's curiosity took on a defensive edge. There was no doubt Gauna was treating him as stupid, because it was to him that almost all the comments had been addressed. He asked Gauna for an explanation. Gauna had one ready, and Clarke could not deny it was both ingenious and surprising.

"They say: the hare 'took off.' In Mapuche, that verb can also mean 'was stolen,' 'was made to vanish.' We have no reason to know of these double meanings, so we understand it in its first sense, and they go on with the joke at our expense; even when you ask them if what happened is real or an interpretation, they can permit themselves to lie with the truth, as they always do. And between you and me, I reckon that 'hare' is the name they give to some valuable object. I don't know whether you've noticed their habit of giving very valuable objects names. OK, so there's a robbery. When we reach the spot where they've caught the thief, or an accomplice, who knows, they put on this horse ballet for us, stare up at the sky, play the fool, like that idiot Mallén. Meanwhile under our very noses, they are dealing with the culprit...."

"You mean that poor man who fell from his horse? But that was an accident!"

"Yes, an 'accident' ... And on top of it all, that hypocrite Reymacurá starts to give you a metaphysics lesson! But he couldn't help letting a few of the most obvious sarcasms escape, like that story about the father who lost his son. Can you tell me what on earth a tale like that had to do with anything?"

"I took it as another example, and a very appropriate one. He was saying that a stolen child reappears as an adult somewhere else, and so establishes a continuity between different places and times."

Gauna did not even bother to contradict him. Clarke had in fact taken this example (though he did not say this to Gauna) as a delicate touch by their Indian friend, because Clarke himself had been a foundling adopted and raised by a well-to-do middle-class family in Kent. It was hardly surprising that the Indians knew this, thanks to Rosas's secret police, who were bound to have discovered it.

"And another thing," Gauna went on. "An hour later, Caful-curá's wife sets out on a journey. Some coincidence, don't you think?"

"But that fellow has thirty wives or more! There must always be one setting off on a journey somewhere."

"But precisely that one, Juana Pitiley, the only one who is rich and powerful?"

He had really gone too far with his suspicions. The Englishman thought it better to change tack, and offered a kind of abstract summing up of their discussion.

"Words in Mapuche seem to have pretty unstable meanings."

"No more so than in other languages."

"I can assure you that's not true of English."

"I don't know English, but if I look at Spanish, it's just as ambiguous. For example, you can give your own name to anything you like: that tree, for instance—look at those low branches, don't they look like a chair? If I came to have my siesta here every day, I'd end up calling that tree 'chair.' ..."

"Good God!"

Gauna closed his mouth. After a while, he opened it again:

"And anyway, you can't deny there's a contradiction in the very fact of their speeches. We all know that savages show 'an invincible repugnance toward speaking, except when it is absolutely necessary.' Yet you yourself said a while ago that your head was spinning from all the chitchat you had to put up with. So that these people's game consists in finding 'absolute necessity' where we see nothing but smoke rings."

"And that seems suspicious to you too?"

"Yes, sir! Very suspicious!"

"Tell me something, Gauna, you don't talk like a gaucho. Did you go to school as a boy?"

At that, Gauna lapsed back into being a gaucho again, mute and introspective. He gazed down at the tracks the busy ants were making on the ground. Tearing off a blade of grass, he chewed on it, then finally seemed to make up his mind:

"Of course I went to school. I ..."

That was as far as he got, because the reappearance of Carlos Alzaga Prior made him fall more silent than ever. The boy came to tell them he was going back to the tents with his new-found friends.

"But who are they?" Clarke wanted to know.

Carlos offered to show him, beaming like an idiot all the while. He led Clarke up a nearby bank and pointed out a group of young men and women. Most of the women had bulging stomachs in various stages of pregnancy.

"Come on, I'll introduce you!"

"No, thanks."

A lot of people were diving into the water.

"Did you have a swim?" Carlos asked him.

"The truth is, I'd love a dip."

Carlos encouraged him to have one. The sun was still high enough for him to dry off afterward. They agreed to meet at dinner time. Clarke undressed and dived into the water, which turned out to be freezing. He was quite a good swimmer, and the exercise relaxed him; what with being on horseback and having to squat for all the conversations, he was very stiff. By the time he got out, Gauna had gone. He threw himself down on the grass and dozed. The sky had turned pink, the birdsong became more evocative, haunting. He saw some huge wild cattle lumber down for their evening drink. Through the leaves of the trees, in his drowsy state, he watched as the sky became a dark blue, and the tree trunks slowly turned black.

When he returned to the beach, there were only a few Indians left. They all greeted him with elaborate courtesy. His horse stood waiting. He set off at a walk in the dusk.

At night, everything was fire. In the universal classification, the Mapuches were a fire culture. They lit them on any excuse, and enjoyed them immensely. At every step, near and far, fires, torches, bonfires shone out, creating marvelous reflections on the bodies of the Indians, whose nightly pleasure was to daub themselves in grease from head to foot. Neither Cafulcurá, nor Alvarito, nor any of the main chieftains appeared, busy as they seemed to be with their political conversations. Gauna and Clarke ate grilled meat with some tight-lipped ministers: Carlos Alzaga Prior came by for a minute to say he would be spending the night with friends. Gauna, who had not managed to take a siesta, retired early. Clarke sat for a while outside the tent, smoking a pipe, watching the fires and the Indians passing by. He was about to go and lie down when Mallén appeared.

"How are you, Mister Clarke, have you eaten?"

"Scrumptiously."

"I'm glad. I'm sorry we haven't been able to look after you properly, but something urgent cropped up ... you know how it is."

"Oh, yes? Something urgent? A war? I suppose you couldn't tell me anyway?"

"No, no. Nothing that serious, trifles really, the same as usual."

"But you yourself told me yesterday that it wasn't usual for you to be so busy."

"That's true, but you will admit that sometimes, the usual can pile up."

"True enough."

"By the way, tomorrow there is a gap in the protocol, and Cafulcurá asked me to convey his invitation to you. For my part, I should also like to offer you a rather fuller apology for our lack of courtesy."

"I'm all ears."

Mallén had not sat down. The two men were standing talking next to the entrance to the tent, and the shaman darted a glance inside. He seemed unwilling to speak there, as if afraid Gauna might be listening. This was a groundless fear, as they could both clearly hear the gaucho's snores.

"Let's walk a little, if you're not tired."

They set off in the direction of the nearest bonfire.

"I trust your tent is comfortable."

"Fine, thank you. Are you expecting Namuncurá soon?"

"Not at all. He could be away weeks if he feels like it."

Clarke had been surprised at being lodged in the tent of the chieftain's son and heir, who was away on a trip. Especially since all the man's wives were still in occupation.

When they had walked some distance, Mallén began to stammer, in the typically ceremonious manner which meant he was about to say something he had previously thought over.

"In the first place, I'd like to say how sorry I am that your visit has coincided with these ... shall we say, special circumstances.

All this surveillance, all these security measures ... they must have been a burden to you."

Although Clarke had been unaware of anything of the sort, he thought it wiser to keep quiet.

"But how were you to know that Cafulcurá is to celebrate his seventieth birthday soon, and that he is cautious enough to take some old-standing prophecies seriously? Cautious isn't the word! ... Well, with him, one never knows. I also wanted to talk to you about that. I don't think I'd be wrong in saying that certain of our chieftain's characteristics must have seemed to you, at the very least, surprising. I don't intend to make excuses for him, but some of them do have their explanation. I've known him for countless years now, and I think I understand him better than anyone. So I beg you to take what I am going to say as a corrective to your impressions, but one that in no way implies any disrespect for your perspicacity. Bear in mind that this incoherent old man, high on grass, who gave you all the rigmarole about the continuum, has for the past fifty years borne on his shoulders all the responsibility of governing an empire made up of a million souls scattered throughout the south of the continent, and has done, and will continue to do, a pretty good job. From his youth onward, Cafulcurá has worshipped simplicity and spontaneity. But one can't help thinking, and as soon as one does, all simplicity goes to the devil. And also, to be truly spontaneous, one would have to say 'spontani*e*ty,' wouldn't one?"

The joke was different in Huilliche of course, which was the language they were speaking in. But it survives the translation.

"Which explains," Mallén went on, "his consumption of hallucinogenic grasses, although I must admit it's gone a bit far of late. He uses them to create images, which interact with words to create hieroglyphs, and consequently new meanings. Given the prismatic nature of our language, there is no better way of bringing out meaning, in other words, of governing. And also, given that his own personal standing is based on his position as a man-myth, how could he think in any other fashion? He's looking for speed, speed at any cost, and so he turns to the imaginary, which is pure speed, oscillating acceleration, as against the fixed rhythm of language."

By now, they had reached the opposite crescent of tents, and so the shaman invited him to turn back. In the distance, the sound of feasting and quarreling could be heard; fires gleamed all round in the darkness.

"There's no moon tonight," Mallén said.

As they came up to Namuncurá's tent once more, Mallén finally explained what the chieftain's invitation consisted of.

"Tomorrow at noon there'll be a hare hunt nearby in your honor, if you're free. Good: I can assure you that this time you won't be disappointed as you were today, although I can't bring myself to believe that any hare will fly. We don't want you to get a bad impression of us. Up to now, we've given you too many words and not enough action, haven't we? But without words, there can be no experience. Although without experience, there can be no words—or anything else, for that matter."

3: The Hunt

DURING THE HUNT THE NEXT DAY, CLARKE DID NOT SEE
a single hare, and could have sworn that no one else did either.
He was not sure, but had nobody to ask, or even to exchange
opinions with; Gauna, who had begun talking to some idle old
men in the hope of drawing them out, declared he had no intention of going; and the young watercolorist did not even bother
to put in an appearance all morning. Around midday, a band of
tall, haughty Indians came to tell Clarke they were waiting for
him. This was a select group of about a hundred adults, all of
them extremely well mounted. The athletic figure of Cafulcurá
towered stony-faced above another group, who must have been
his personal bodyguard. He did not greet Clarke even from a distance. In fact nobody greeted him, but then he did not know anyone in the party. They set off toward the east, at a brisk trot, but
without too much haste. It was a sunny day like the previous one;
as they rode, a searching breeze refreshed their bodies. Clarke
was riding along with the men who had come to fetch him; like
all the other Indians, they were smeared with a foul-smelling
grease. Repetido was the only horse with a saddle. The Indians' mounts, all of them light-colored ponies with extravagant

markings, did not seem to be any better or swifter than his. They gradually increased their speed. As he had no idea where they were going, Clarke could not calculate how long it might take them to get there. The land was flat as a billiard table; the grass muffled the sound of their hooves. Lapwings traced wide circles of alarm in the sky. Clarke was riding in the midst of the group, so that the explosive flight of any partridges would not cause him such a shock. He had learned this precaution from Gauna, who gave a start and lifted his hand to his heart whenever a bird's whirring escape caught him off guard. But the gaucho thought too much, unlike Clarke, who was the most outgoing of men. Apart from the warriors around Cafulcurá, who carried long lances, the rest of the Indians were unarmed, out for pleasure.

They must have gone three or four leagues, drinking in the cool air, rising and falling in extended cadences on the backs of their horses, when they suddenly came to a halt in a spot that was the same as all the others—because they were all the same—but was broader, more spacious still (the planet must have been squashed flat here, there was no other explanation). A few Indians who were perhaps especially skilful hunters began to walk round in circles staring closely at the ground, and then exchanged some words with Cafulcurá. In spite of the distance, Clarke could make out that the spokesman had put his eyes into a squint. He guessed he must be saying that this was a good place to find hares. The chieftain appeared to think for an instant, then shouted out in a loud voice that contrasted with his hesitant stammerings in private: "Ñi Clarke!" Silence spread still further, like a shock wave. The Indians around Clarke looked the

other way in such a childish fashion that it was comic. He supposed the cry must mean something like "In honor of Clarke!"
Several riders sped off in a line, which others joined at the end.
Their leader took only a couple of minutes to reach the horizon. The bulk of the hunters fanned out, also at top speed, in
what appeared to be a random dispersal. Cafulcurá was among
them, and Clarke urged Repetido on in a direction more or less
parallel to that of the chieftain. How they galloped! There was
something hare-like about these lean, tireless horses which knew
nothing but how to run. It took only a short time for them to disperse all over the vast prairie. When they reached a certain point,
which must have been measured more by time than by place,
the Indians turned round and sped back the way they had come.
Obediently, Clarke copied them, although no one had explained
the procedure to him. The mass of riders made up a moving grid;
this probably created, from the point of view of the cornered
hares, a closing circle which terrified them. Clarke even imagined he could make out the darting movements of the hares in
between the horses' hooves. But he would never have been able
to point to any one of them. They were the foreshadowings of his
perception, which never came to fruition. He racked his brains to
try to work out what the key to the maneuver was. Perhaps each
hunter simply passed the quarry onto the person who came after him in a lateral line, and so on the whole time. If that was the
case, it was like a game of checkers that was pure speed, with no
result. Although the result might be to exhaust the hares. Then in
the end, they would be able to catch them by the ears by simply
stretching out their hands, without even bothering to dismount.

That would be typical of the Indians. The faint line of the horizon, grown fainter than ever, always kept half of the participants hidden from view, while at the same time, each one was at the center of his own circle. Movement was everything; the earth slipped by in dizzying strips; the sun was first on one side, then the other. Space itself changed position with each sweep: it seemed as though they were watching it pass by upside down. Off they went! Back they came! But to Clarke they were neither coming nor going; his point of view not only accompanied them, but was transformed as he joined in.

The Indians were enjoying the exercise. As they rode by, they shouted to each other, but unintelligibly to him; this was the nearest thing to real laughter this melancholy people could achieve. Then a few of them dismounted and settled down in the grass to drink from small bottles; Clarke thought it was water and went over to them. Unfortunately, it was some liquor or other. He lay down for a while. Repetido was bathed in sweat, his own legs were soaking from the horse, and he himself had sweated profusely. He took off his hat and covered his face with it, lying flat on his back. The Indians' cries came from different sides and distances, seeming to follow a pattern, however mobile and changing. The Indians who had been drinking sped off again. It was as though after snatching a rest concealed from the others, they were now returning to their duty; but where had they been hidden? In sight of everyone? As Clarke continued to lie there, he began to feel that he himself was concealed, although the area the Indians were riding over had not changed. When he remounted, Repetido sprang off again, with more enthusiasm than his rider. But it is common knowledge that horses love to work up a sweat. Clarke had not completed a couple of sweeps before he heard a great tumult among the Indians. He thought they must have caught a hare, but it was not that. The cries were of alarm, of recrimination. They were all gathered together, screeching in a dreadful manner. Intrigued, Clarke went to see. Some riders headed like a streak of lightning for the encampment. When Clarke reached the other excited Indians, he gaped at them open-mouthed, unable to make out what was going on. He had never seen them so stirred up. They were making such a din he couldn't make out a word of what they were saying. Suddenly the ones bearing lances came toward him, with threatening gestures. Seriously threatening, Clarke realized with a horrible sense of shock that paralyzed the beating of his heart. Until this moment, everything in his relation with the Indians had been provisional, abstract, tentative. Even the courtesy they had shown him was in some sense preliminary. Suddenly everything had become serious—deadly serious. "They're going to run me through," Clarke thought as he gulped with fear, staring at the bamboo lances. The worst thing was not to have the remotest idea of what it was all about, or what he had to do with it. Yet they did not follow through on their intention to kill him. They shouted things at him which, in the confusion of his mental state, he was unable to decipher. They were brandishing their lances a few inches from his chest. They must have understood each other though, because after a brief shouted discussion one group shot off toward the east. It was when they started shouting again that Clarke finally realized what had happened: Cafulcurá had disappeared. His jaw dropped in astonishment.

He was trying to work out what few words he could say, some kind of expression of regret, when all the Indians' heads turned in the direction of their village, from where a bedraggled procession was approaching at full tilt. His own group headed toward them, forcing Clarke to accompany them at walking pace. What lungs those savages had! They did not stop shouting for a moment. But how could the chieftain have disappeared? It seemed impossible, on this panoptic plain. Although on closer reflection, there was nothing easier, if at every moment, depending on the position of the observer, there was another person just below the horizon. It should be borne in mind, Clarke thought, that the natural habitat of these races was in the mountains, where hiding places abounded; it was no surprise therefore that they should reproduce that scenery by multiplying the only element that the flat plains offered them, namely the horizon line. At any rate, Clarke could understand why the bodyguards were so nervous, if the old man had been snatched thanks to the simple expedient of lying in wait for him below the horizon. No "hare" could have been so easily caught. But who could it have been? He realized they had been keeping the details of their political problems from him, even though it was true that he had not asked them any questions either. And why did they put the blame on him? He tried to remember what he had been doing a moment before all this: he had been stretched out in the grass, resting, feeling good. Not much of an alibi! The sun fell vertically on bodies seething with frustration. The horses snorted in disgust, deprived of their exercise.

Among those heading out toward them were the chief shamans and the entire council of ministers. Their faces bore such expressions of dismay that they looked ugly and menacing. There was some heated discussion on horseback, then the first practical decision they took was to send Clarke back to the encampment under guard. On their way, they passed several groups of warriors hurtling off at top speed to the scene of the disappearance. They shut Clarke up in a tent along with a perplexed and furious Gauna, and left two savages inside the tent and another pair outside to guard them.

"What's got into these lunatics?" the tracker asked him.

"Don't shout at me, I've had more than enough of that."

Clarke was only just beginning to get over his bewilderment. The first thing he did was to sit down on the leather rug, take his hat off, undo the buckle of his uncomfortable belt, and ask for a glass of water. The Indians paid him no attention. Gauna went to sit by Clarke, and stared at him with his crazy paranoid look.

"It's incredible," began the Englishman, "the way events have started speeding up."

At that moment the Indians outside called to their friends in the tent, and they went out. The two prisoners (Clarke holding up his trousers with one hand) crept to the entrance slit to see what had happened. It was nothing. The men were all happily chatting to some Indian women about this and that. Further off though there seemed to be lots going on. They had been put in a tent almost on the outskirts of the capital, no doubt so that they would be close at hand but not in the way: if, as seemed likely, the news had got out, the center of the camp would be swarming with people. The two of them sat down again, and Clarke went on with the story he had barely begun:

"It appears that Cafulcurá—and don't ask me how—has gone up in smoke."

"What? He's exploded?"

"No, please, it was just an expression. I believe the Indians think he has been kidnapped."

"And what have we got to do with it?"

Clarke shrugged his shoulders, in a gesture typical of Gauna. He was busy weighing the possibilities: for example, that the Indians thought they were traitors. All of a sudden, a thought occurred to him:

"Where can the boy be?"

"Which boy?" Gauna asked.

"Alzaga Prior."

"How should I know?"

"Where did they capture you?"

"I spent the whole morning talking to some old men, and was still with them when those madmen arrived."

Clarke had a dark foreboding about the young man's fate.

"They were expecting something like this," Gauna said.

"What?"

"An attack on Cafulcurá. Didn't you see how they were guarding him?"

"That's what Mallén said last night," Clarke confessed, "but the truth is, I didn't notice."

They sat a while in silence.

"What will they do with us now?"

"Nothing, of course. Have we done anything wrong?"

"As if that would stop them!"

Clarke was not so skeptical as to the savages' sense of justice, or at least of etiquette.

"Don't worry."

"I'm not worried. But I'd be sorry to die as a result of the vagaries of their internal politics. Especially now, when I'm so close to ..."

"Close to what?"

There was no reply, because at that moment their two guards came in again and they thought it better to keep quiet. That was how things stayed for about an hour, when someone arrived on horseback. Thanks to the infallible intuition of people in danger, they knew at once it was for them. And indeed, they were led out of the tent. Some Indian worthies they knew only by sight dismounted in front of them, with forced smiles on their faces.

"We must offer you our most heartfelt apologies for any unnecessary inconvenience. For a short while it was feared that our chief had been the object of an attack, and it was decided— somewhat hastily perhaps, though with nothing but the best of intentions toward you—that you should be kept in preventive detention. As you were the only outsiders in our capital at that moment, we were afraid we would not be able to guarantee your safety faced with any unforeseen emotional reaction from our people. If in the initial confusion we overlooked any of the requirements for your comfort, we hope this has been remedied. Now that the matter is over and done with, you may go about your normal activities, and we beg you to forgive any lack of politeness on our part."

"Am I to understand that Cafulcurá has reappeared?"

"What has restored the most serene tranquillity to our people is the news that our benevolent emperor had never in fact disappeared. It was one of those all-too-common misunderstandings. In the middle of the Hareathon, he had gone off in search of water, and stayed talking to an acquaintance he met by chance."

"I must admit," Clarke said, "that I also felt quite thirsty during the hunt. Next time I'll take a bottle of water with me."

While this exchange was going on, they had mounted up and were heading for the center of the camp at a walk. For once Gauna, who never directly addressed the Indians—at least not in front of Clarke—spoke straight out to them:

"How foolish," he observed, "to spread panic like that on an unsubstantiated piece of news."

His falsely polite tone was so charged with sarcasm that Clarke became worried. He could not understand how Gauna could be so foolhardy, after the danger they had been in. But his fears proved groundless. The Indians, who could be so subtle when they had a mind to, were impervious to anyone else's irony. He himself felt sure of nothing. The gaucho's words made him think that this latest denial could well be nothing more than a lie designed to restore calm. He hadn't thought of that before. Moreover, he preferred not to ask after the young watercolor artist. If he turned up, and if it proved to be true—something he very much doubted—that they were free to come and go as they pleased, then the three of them would leave Salinas Grandes at the first opportunity.

In the wide central avenues of the camp, the situation seemed under control. They went straight to Namuncurá's tent, where they parted company with their escort. The young nobleman's wives were there as always. They asked them for something to eat. It was already late for them to cook, but they brought cold meat and salad, and a jug full of wine mixed with water.

"Don't tell me you believed them this time as well," said Gauna.

"Listen, my good friend," the Englishman replied, taking his time, "you'll have to forgive me if I don't ask you to explain your theory. I've no doubt you have one. But on this occasion, to be quite frank, I'm not interested. I already have enough things to worry about. All that concerns me at the moment is finding the boy, and then getting out of here, if they'll let us. All right?"

The gaucho withdrew into a hurt silence. Clarke went outside to smoke a pipe in the fresh air. From his tent entrance he could see the back of Cafulcurá's tent, where there was a regular to-ing and fro-ing of women. Further off, on the horizon, he could make out several parties of Indians. He had no idea whether this was normal or not.

Obeying a sudden impulse, and without telling even Gauna that he was leaving, Clarke climbed onto Repetido and set off for the creek, thinking that was where he was most likely to find Carlos Alzaga Prior. He patted his mount's neck: with everything that had been going on, he had badly neglected him. He hadn't given Repetido anything to eat or drink, had left him in the sun the whole time, and now he was making fresh demands of him. The least he could do was go at a walk, and so he did. He promised himself he would bathe Repetido in the stream.

Getting there proved no easy matter. Apart from the fact that

all the emotions and riding had left him with his head spinning
and feeling drowsy with exhaustion (he had got used to a siesta,
and it was exactly that time of day), he had no idea where this oa-
sis was. The previous afternoon he had simply followed Gauna.
Now, on his own, every direction looked the same. Of course, in
the absolute flatness of the salt pans, all he had to do was to discover which direction to take—then the shortest route was obvious. But, as happens with every line, there were tiny deviations,
and these inevitably produced far-reaching effects. In reality, on
this plain, any one point was always elusive. The brightness of
the air, added to the horse's painfully slow progress, also made it
hard for him to calculate how long it was taking him, and in the
end he felt completely disoriented. He decided to follow a broad
curve, which despite being longer, was more reliable. It was not
for nothing that the Indians had adopted it for their settlements.

Eventually, some children riding plump mares gave him the
clue. Since his snail's pace wanderings had taken a couple of
hours, the heat was dying down by the time he saw the riverbank
trees, and the bathers were already out of the water. He rode past
the beach without dismounting, glancing at the lazy groups as
he passed by. He was thinking that there were many things to
envy in the Indians' way of life. They confined themselves to the
delicious task of being happy, doing nothing, and having a good
time. They ate till they burst, slept like logs, played cards, and let
the years slip by. They must know a secret.

He led his horse in among the willow osiers, dappled in the
sunlight like giant green and yellow shards. The river followed
its fanciful course, with quiet backwaters, deep pools where the

water was darker and its bed was covered with tall waving weeds, tiny waterfalls cascading over pebbles, an entire hydraulic system whose charms kept everyone entertained. Who could tell how far this linear labyrinth extended: and it seemed that there were Indians all along it, placed there like ornaments, their skin glistening with water, their black eyes half-closed as they followed the procession of the hours with snakelike patience.

Clarke had taken the same direction as the day before, riding upstream, which seemed to be the one people preferred. But he went a long way with no sign of the young painter. The groups of Indians began to get scarcer, apart from an occasional fisherman dozing to the sound of the birds. Clarke gave up hope of finding Prior in this direction. Perhaps he hadn't even come to the stream. If he didn't find him now, he would have to ask their hosts for help, although they seemed to have forgotten he even existed. There was also the possibility that the opposite was true, and that they were keeping Prior shut up somewhere.

Whatever the case, Clarke gave up the search. He found himself alone on a kind of grassy beach, surrounded by overhanging trees. He dismounted, removed Repetido's saddle and led the horse into the water, making sure beforehand to take off his boots and trousers. The cool sensation of the current immediately gave him a feeling of calm. Repetido drank his fill, then stood quietly with the water halfway up his legs. Clarke was sorry he did not have a bucket to wash the animal with. He cupped his hands and splashed water onto the horse until it was completely wet. What he did have, in one of his fine red leather saddlebags, was a brush, and he set to work energetically. Clarke had always

adored horses, and this one General Rosas had lent him was a
fine beast. Serenity in a living being is always an admirable quality. He wondered what it was about horses that made everyone
admire their beauty. Could it be merely habit? For someone who
had never seen a horse, could it seem like a repugnant monster?
He could not imagine such a person.

It was the empty hour of the afternoon. A bird sang above
his head. The swishing of the brush and the murmur of the water round his feet dulled his senses: He could hear the cry of a
lapwing in the distance ... the horse snorting, the monotonous
chirrup of the crickets ...

When he had finished the grooming as well as he could without soap, Clarke sat on the bank to smoke a pipe. Repetido left
the stream and began to browse on some weeds. Clarke thought
how good it would have been to have a cup of coffee with his
pipe. He tried for a while not to think of his problems, nor of the
Indians at all. That the Indians had become part of his problem
was nothing more than a stroke of bad luck. His chief concern
was Nature, or should be anyway. Apart from a couple of fat Indian women who had appeared while he was washing the horse,
had stared at him for a moment, then gone back to wherever they
had come from, nobody passed by. Clarke wondered if he was
at the far end of the Indians' bathing area. As he thought about
it, he became curious to see what lay beyond. Considered as a
line of water that dissected the plain, the stream was a homogeneous whole, whose attractions were interchangeable, but moving along it, it changed without changing, in direct proportion
to the distance traveled.

Clarke stood up and, just as he was, without shoes or trousers, walked on about a hundred yards. A different aspect of the stream and its banks presented itself to him, novel despite being vaguely predictable. It was a kind of reworking of the same elements: water, the riverbanks, trees, grass. Fascinated, he walked on further, in the midst of complete silence. All the charm of the place lay in its linear aspect, the way each of its segments was hidden from the previous one: the very opposite of what happened out on the open plain. As he had thought, there was no one around. Even the distant sounds of voices and noises he had heard from time to time on the little beach no longer reached him. The river was a series of secret chambers, following on from each other as in an Italian palace. As he crossed a number of "thresholds," the mechanism of increasing distance led Clarke to feel he was entering a world of mystery, a self-contained nothingness that invoked the infinite.

All of a sudden, he heard something: a quiet, stifled moan, a kind of private crying that was directed at no one in particular, but which had something of a call for help about it. It came from beyond him: to reach it, Clarke would have to cross into another invisible zone. He did so, and was transfixed with shock. All alone on the riverbank sat Carlos Alzaga Prior. He was weeping disconsolately, his head in his hands.

The sight came as a great surprise to the Englishman. He couldn't recall ever having seen a man cry. It was true the water-color painter was still almost a child, but there was something adult and definitive about his sobbing that touched Clarke deeply. He was confronting pain, and this brought out a feeling of nostalgia in him—although that was hardly a strong enough word to describe the mixture of anxiety and distress it caused him.

It was as if Clarke saw the youth cut out in a vacuum, in silhouette. Despair produces this kind of vacuum around one. Robbed of all points of reference, the figure could have been either near or far away: he could be a thousand leagues off, and be a giant, or only five inches away, and be a miniature. But he was only a few yards away, and Clarke had to trust to his eyesight, to the normal correlation of size and distance. This inevitability made the scene a cruel one. He thought he saw before him an emblem of his own life, and it terrified him. The terror came from being English, educated, reserved, from being unable to cry in public (or in private), from living inside a bubble and not allowing himself to feel any emotions. His emotional life had dried up years earlier—when in the first flush of his own youth, he had lost someone he loved who might have taught him how to cry. From that day on, he had never felt the sense of dread that is a natural part of life: he could see this now, when he was least expecting it, but in someone else.

His first impulse was to turn and run, but he thought better of it. He went closer. As he had no boots on, he got all kinds of thorns and sharp stones stuck in the soles of his feet. Carlos neither looked up, nor took his hands from his face, nor stopped crying for a second. Overcome with pity, Clarke put his arm round his shoulder. When he tried to speak, words failed him. He wanted to console the boy, but did not know how to. The most natural thing seemed to him to take Prior somewhere else, to go and fetch his horse at least, to get on with his plans and forget about the Indians. He wanted to concentrate on one thing and forget the other. His mind was in such a confused state, however, that the two impulses became entangled.

All the same, the youth allowed himself to be led along a few steps without protesting, sobbing all the while. They had hardly gone a few yards when a shadow fell across them. Clarke was the only one who lifted his gaze. A horseman stood out against the setting sun, mysterious as yet, slightly threatening because of his position above them and because he had stopped and was staring at them. "What's he going to think?" Clarke immediately wondered. The lugubrious voice that rang out clearly showed him that it wasn't a question of thinking anything.

"I was looking for you."

It was the voice of Mallén the shaman. A voice from beyond the grave, filled with concern: the voice of a man with a serious problem. Clarke let go of the youth and stepped to one side so that Mallén would not be against the light. He was taken aback by his face: he seemed to have aged twenty years in a single day.

"What's wrong?"

"I have to talk to you."

He used none of the usual circumlocutions. The Englishman realized the seriousness of the situation, and did not keep him waiting.

"All right, I'll get properly dressed." Then to Carlos: "I'll be back right away." He walked on a few steps, but then felt the need to add something more, so said: "Try to calm down."

Clarke returned to the grassy beach as quickly as he could, with the shaman behind him. He put his trousers on, rubbed his feet briskly to get rid of the gravel and bits of grass, and wriggled into his boots.

"I'm all ears," he said, facing the Indian.

"Come with me, please. Let's find somewhere quieter."

It was difficult to imagine anywhere quieter than the spot they were already in, but Clarke mounted up anyway and followed the shaman, who headed off at a walk in a direction perpendicular to the stream. They were soon in open ground. To Clarke's surprise, a hill appeared in the distance. It was a gentle one, but well-defined, perhaps in contrast to the flat plain all around. They rode up it. When they reached the top Mallén, who so far had not opened his mouth again, dismounted and invited Clarke to do the same. It seemed strange that by climbing such a little way, they could see so far, but that was a natural property of the prairie: each yard climbed represented a hundred leagues. They sat down in the grass, their faces turned toward the sun. As the Indian still said nothing, Clarke decided to take the initiative with something neutral:

"It's a fine evening."

"Would you believe I'm so worried I hadn't even noticed?"

"You must have your reasons."

"I'll say I do." A fresh, prolonged silence. But the Indian had got started, so Clarke contented himself with waiting. Sure enough, with the lines on his face deepening and his eyes turning even blacker, Mallén began to explain. "What I most feared has happened."

His words had a special resonance for the Englishman.

It was the kind of expression which, when examined logically, did not make sense. Yet it was the second time in the space of half an hour that he had heard it, in one way or another.

"As you well know," the Indian went on, "in spite of all the precautions taken, Cafulcurá has disappeared."

"But hasn't he appeared again?"

"Don't tell me you believed that official denial! If you did, you were the only one to do so."

Yet again, this scorn for his naivety. Obviously then, it wasn't just Gauna. Clarke decided not to let it upset him.

"The fact is, I didn't stop to think about it. I accepted what I was told, as a matter of course."

Emerging from his pessimistic daydream, Mallén stared at him as if he were seeing him for the first time that evening:

"Of course. I'd forgotten they suspected you at first. How absurd." He waved his hand, as if dismissing a triviality. "Well, yes, our chieftain has been kidnapped. And everything appears to indicate there is little chance of getting him back alive. All we can hope is that for some reason or other they postpone his execution. There's also the fact that his son Reymacurá, who went off in pursuit of his kidnappers, has not returned. As you can see, we only have a slender thread to hang on to."

"Couldn't he have disappeared of his own accord?"

"Don't talk rubbish."

"So who could it have been?"

"Everything suggests it was our most bitter enemies, the Voroga."

"Why shouldn't they kill him immediately?"

"Mister Clarke, I have decided to confide in you. You'll soon see why. To my mind, there's a black-hearted, ferocious woman behind all this. Have you ever heard of Rondeau's widow?"

"No."

"A few years ago, Cafulcurá defeated a Voroga chief by the name of Rondeau, and quite logically, put him to death. Among the reparations that were then paid to the defeated tribe (because we have the generous custom that it is the victor who pays) was an offer of marriage to the chieftain's widow. That woman, who is not even a Voroga by birth but a complete stranger, had the audacity to reject the proposal, and fled with a group of her followers. Over the years, a lot more have joined them, so that today she has a fearsome power."

"What does she have against Cafulcurá?"

"Nothing, and that's what is most disturbing. It's not because he killed her husband, because she herself tried to do that on more than one occasion—she hated him. In fact, she doesn't seem to have anything against Cafulcurá or anyone else in particular; she's happy just to be bloodthirsty and to survive."

"Why do you suspect her?"

"Because she is the only person daring enough to carry out a raid like this, and the only one with so little to lose (she doesn't even possess any territory) that she doesn't fear any reprisals. Even so, she must have realized she was going too far, and that is why I suspect she has reached an understanding with the current leader of the Vorogas, that hypocrite Coliqueo, who is the one who stands to gain most from Cafulcurá's death. My whole line of thinking is based on that hypothesis: if Cafulcurá was taken alive, it must have been her, with the intention of keeping him and threatening her associate with returning him to us if he does not fulfill his promises, whatever they might have been. In that way, she secures her position."

"I see."

"I wanted to ask a great favor of you, Mister Clarke."

"At your service."

"Will you go to Coliqueo's camp and try to discover his intentions? I don't know if that makes sense."

"But I've no idea how to do that!"

"Oh come now, don't be so modest. If anyone knows, it's you."

"How would I get there, with all the tension there is in the air?"

"But you are precisely the one who would have the least problem doing so. How did you get this far?"

"Well . . ." said Clarke, who in reality had never seriously asked himself that question, "I suppose it was due to the skill of my tracker, and good will on your part. . . ."

The shaman looked at him again, this time in genuine astonishment: "You mean you don't know about the horse?"

"Repetido? What has he got to do with it? Rosas lent him to me, that's all I know."

"And where did Rosas get him? Haven't you seen Cafulcurá's horse?"

"Yes, it's similar. . . ."

"No; it's identical."

"Well, I wouldn't go so far as to say that. . . ."

"Yes, it is! But this is incredible! You mean to say you came here blindly, trusting to your good fortune?"

"Mister Mallén, do me the favor of enlightening me."

Choosing to ignore the Englishman's irritated tone, the shaman collected his thoughts.

"In our humble way, we like to breed our horses to produce the piebald effect we admire. Why do we like it so much? Because we can read the language of the different patches of color, and this is very practical for us. Repetido is a horse which exactly reproduces the same patches as Cafulcurá's favorite, or what might be called his 'official' mount, and it is for that and no other reason that you succeeded in reaching Salinas Grandes unscathed. The two horses are twins, foals born at the same time from the same mare, and that mare was the granddaughter of the famous Fantasma, the horse in whose kidneys was found the blue stone which is Cafulcurá's talisman. Apart from the stone, the legend, and the resulting play on words, Fantasma was the source of a line of twin horses. Your Repetido was a gift from our chieftain to Rosas on the occasion of an eternal peace treaty they signed a few years ago."

"I had no idea."

"I'm not surprised. There's so much we do not know.... Well, not to waste time, will you help?"

Clarke only needed a moment's thought: "Agreed."

Their conversation was at an end. From their slight elevation, they could see the encroaching night gradually veiling the splendor of the evening sky. Flocks of pigeons rose into the heavens. Everything seemed to invite them to stay a while longer. Then a question occurred to Clarke:

"But, according to what you said, you were expecting something like this to happen, or am I mistaken?"

"Yes and no. It would take a lot of explaining."

"Then please do so. We have the time. And I wouldn't want to leave without knowing, it might be useful to me."

"No, it won't be useful in the slightest. If experience has taught me anything, it is that the less one knows, the more effectively one can act. But I'll tell you anyway, because we do have the time. You should start out tomorrow morning."

He lapsed into silence for a while, organizing his thoughts. "Let's think where I can start. I should say at the outset that there is a lot of absurdity in the whole thing."

"That's the least of my concerns."

"I'm very glad to hear it. Well, it's true we had taken all kinds of precautions to guard Cafulcurá, but not for any real reason. There's a paradox for you, seeing that in the end what happened was something real, all too real. Years ago, some hired shamans carried out who knows what oracular maneuvers, as a result of which there emerged the prophecy that on the day our chieftain celebrated his seventieth birthday, he would suffer an accident similar to the one that had happened thirty-five years earlier, when he reached that age. On that occasion, the birthday celebrations were complicated because they coincided with Cafulcurá's wedding, since he was finally to be married to the great love of his life, the marvelous Juana Pitiley, whom he had yearned after for more than a decade. The celebrations were extraordinary: a week-long feast, with the inevitable over-indulgence in drink— you can imagine the state we were in by the end. At midnight on the final day, a small band of Vorogas had not the slightest difficulty in penetrating right to the heart of our encampment, picking up Cafulcurá like a bundle of dirty linen, and making off with him. In those days, the Vorogas were nothing like what they are today, except in their evil ways. They were nomadic groups, who could not get used to the plains: anarchists, in a word. Nor were we exactly what we are nowadays. Cafulcurá was young, somewhat dissipated, and our organization in times of peace left a lot to be desired. All this is to explain why the kidnapping caused such disarray in our ranks. It took all Juana Pitiley's ardor to achieve the miracle of rounding up a party to set off after the Vorogas, and to pursue them for weeks without losing their trail. It was an entire small tribe which had carried out the kidnapping. They went at a good pace, and by pure instinct headed for the southern mountains. We never found out what they intended to do with Cafulcurá, but the fact is they kept him alive, drugged with herbal drinks. Since they knew they were being followed, as they believed by a large force, they spread out and holed up in the mountains, keeping their captive well hidden. When our warriors arrived, there was a series of skirmishes, in which all the ten or more brave Huilliches were killed off one by one, until only the heroic Juana Pitiley was left alive. She was determined to recover her husband or die in the attempt. From this point on, her feat enters the realms of legend. Nobody will ever know what she actually did, but I'll tell you what has become the accepted version. A different kind of intelligence (now proverbial) came to life in her, a sort of animal instinct, which guided her like a sleepwalker who has the use of reason. Alone, naked, without weapons, she succeeded in getting into the *sancta sanctorum* of the Vorogas, which in fact was not a cavern but a circle of steep peaks about a league in circumference, at the center of which was a pierced rock, known as the Cerro de la Ventana. One evening she managed to climb up it without being seen, and then, as the sun set, the last ray threaded through the 'window,' and on the far side she saw the flight of a hare, later known as the Legibrerian Hare. By now we're in the realm of pure fiction, for which I apologize. The path the hare followed showed her the way to Cafulcurá. You probably realize that all this could have a perfectly reasonable explanation: how often has the innocence of a tiny wild animal led to the discovery of a secret place? That same night, Juana rescued Cafulcurá all by herself, and the two of them climbed back up the Cerro de la Ventana, where she was sure the Vorogas would not search for them (their natural strategic response would be to disperse, once they discovered that their prisoner had been seized). At dawn, when Cafulcurá came round, they consummated their marriage at the summit of the pierced rock. The next day their escape and the pursuit began. It lasted a whole year. There have been many conjectures about their prolonged flight, but all we really know is that at a certain moment, when Juana Pitiley was about to give birth to the son she had conceived on the night of the rescue, the two lovers separated. As for the duped Vorogas, legend has it that they went to live beneath the earth like armadillos. Cafulcurá returned alone to our tents, and then two months later Juana Pitiley appeared, safe and sound, with a child in her arms: Namuncurá. Since that day she has been the foremost of the chieftain's thirty-two wives, and a powerful political force in our court. By the way, tomorrow a deputation is to go to Carhué to inform her of the unfortunate occurrence. Her reaction could be fearsome."

Clarke was no longer listening to him. The mention of the

Hare in the Indian's story had left him on tenterhooks. It was exactly what he wanted to find out about, but he judged this was not the right moment to press Mallén with questions, especially since it was unlikely he had anything important to say on the subject. He also had to give himself some time to reflect on what he had heard. It was bitterly disappointing that this information was coming out just when events were gathering pace around him. Following a very English (but mistaken) line of reasoning, he considered he would be able to think more clearly in peace, away from everything.

"What about Namuncurá?" he asked. "I heard he was on a trip. Has he been told as well?"

All of a sudden Mallén seemed much less self-assured.

"I don't think it would be easy to find him.... Anyway, we'll see."

He stood up and went to mount his horse. Clarke did the same. By now it was almost night. They headed for the encampment at a walk.

"Tomorrow," the shaman said, "you can leave with the riders going to Carhué to see Juana Pitiley. You could accompany them for that part of your journey, it's on your way. I suggest you go to sleep soon, because they're thinking of leaving very early."

"At what time?"

The shaman gave a typically Indian reply.

"At three."

4: *Carhué*

CLARKE WAS HAVING DINNER WITH GAUNA AND NAMUN-
curá's seventeen wives when all of a sudden Carlos Alzaga Prior
burst into the tent, beside himself with excitement. Due to the
unexpected turn events had taken, the Englishman had completely forgotten him.

"I've come to say farewell," the youth said.

"What? Why?"

There was a silence. Gauna had not even raised his eyes from
his food. Following their invariable custom, the Indian women
had acted as if nothing had happened. Clarke was waiting for
some explanation, but Prior simply said:

"Could I speak to you in private for a moment?"

"I'm eating, and I would prefer to finish doing so: in peace, if
at all possible."

"I'm sorry, but I'm in a hurry."

What an adolescent he was! Clarke decided to teach him a
lesson.

"Sit down."

"But I'm in a hurry!"

"Sit down and eat!"

"No, I'm leaving!"

"Could we have a partridge for Mister Alzaga Prior, please?"

"Yes, Mister Clarke, coming right up."

Grudgingly, the boy sat on a leather mat. He was served some meat, and began to nibble at it, an expression of disgust on his face. Clarke kept up a pretense at conversation, out of a stubborn regard for form. The Indian women answered every one of his remarks politely (in fact, it cost them very little effort). Namuncurá had not shown a well-defined taste in choosing them: they were of all kinds. At least, that was what Clarke imagined, if he put himself in the shoes of an Indian husband, because to him they were all the same: Indians, with slanting eyes, black tresses, their bodies covered in grease down to their toes, and that somewhat savage docility that concealed a sense of menace.

"And now," Clarke said when they had finished, "let's hear what the problem is."

He stood up. The youth seemed to have lost a good deal of his initial urgency. But he livened up once they were outside the tent. A grave frown returned to his face, although during the meal his childish disposition to be cheerful had led him to relax. The role he had given himself was too important for such an attitude, however, so that by the time the two of them stood outside, he was serious once more, brimming with impatient anger.

"Well then, what's all this about?"

"Mister Clarke, at this point I must take my leave of you."

"In what sense?"

"In the only sense possible. I am in love, and I am pursuing my only chance of happiness."

Clarke said nothing. There was no need. A young person in love always feels obliged to offer lengthy explanations. And, as it proved, he did not have long to wait.

"Yñuy has run away, and I propose to set off in pursuit."

"Yñuy?" A sudden doubt assailed Clarke. "Would that be a female?"

"Of course! Who do you take me for?"

"You're right, I'm sorry. Who is she?"

"A girl I met when we arrived, and who I fell in love with."

"In a single day?"

"In a single moment. What's wrong with that? Time is irrelevant. What matters are feelings."

"Agreed. And this girl has run off?"

"The thing is, she has problems. I don't think I was explicit enough about my intentions, and now I want to put that right. What I'm trying to say is that she ran off because she has problems, which are nothing to do with me; but I don't think she understood that I was willing to help her."

"What sort of problems?"

"She's pregnant, and detests the man involved. She's not married. I don't know who he is, and I don't care. I want to offer to marry her."

"And the child?"

"I'll give him my name, and love him as though he were my own."

It was all so typical. Clarke did not know whether to laugh or cry.

"What do you think your parents will feel about it?"

"I don't have any parents."

Clarke was disconcerted.

"I'm adopted," Carlos said.

"That doesn't matter. You'll be giving the bastard the name, or names, of your adopted parents."

"And I've every right to do so!"

There was a lot to say, but Clarke preferred not to say it. Especially as it would be of no use.

"So what do you propose to do?"

"To go after her, of course. To find her. Tell her that ..."

"Yes, yes, all right. Which way did she go?"

"I don't know. But I'm certain I'll be able to find her."

"First things first. Are you sure she's actually gone?"

"Yes, she left me a farewell message with her best friend. It was a real blow for me."

"I can imagine."

Clarke felt the story did not fit together, but once again refrained from expressing his doubt. He thought for a moment. In fact, this foolishness offered an almost ideal excuse to remove the boy from the circle of friends he had become so caught up in. He would not even have to exert his authority: a bit of persuasion should suffice.

"Look," he said, laying his hand on Prior's shoulder, "for a variety of reasons which I'll explain to you later, I have to leave Salinas Grandes, and it so happens that I'll be heading south, along the only route that people can take out of here. So I see no reason for us to separate. You'll be safer if you are with me and Gauna, and we could even help you in your search. Do you agree?"

Carlos looked at him suspiciously.

"You're not doing it just to keep an eye on me?"

A classic young person's line of reasoning, to believe that the world revolved around their own silly problems.

"We'll be leaving before dawn," Clarke told him. "Let's get some sleep."

Carlos did not seem very convinced. This coincidence had spoilt most of the effect of his amatory heroism, but he could find no excuse to refuse their company. Clarke took hold of his arm:

"Tomorrow you can tell me about this girl ... what was her name again?"

"Yñuy."

"What a nice name. And what do her parents say?"

"She doesn't have any. She's adopted."

"Ah, yes? Her too?"

"That's the reason I identified so closely with her misfortune. She is so alone ..."

Clarke cut him short before he could get into full flow.

"I should tell you I am adopted too."

"I don't believe it!"

"Why not? It happens in England as well, you know."

"So you must understand ..."

"Yes, yes. Now go and lie down. I'm going to smoke a pipe. These savages will be waking us up at three."

"At three! They're going to have to drag me along. I mean if I manage to sleep. But I doubt I'll be able to close my eyes."

"Get along with you." Clarke pushed him inside, sorry he

was exposing him to Gauna's mocking gaze. But the boy was so sleepy he would not even notice.

Clarke lit his pipe and stood watching the bonfires and the Indians riding slowly by in the night. He was thinking, but had no real idea what about. He was sleepy as well.

A short while later, with the night still dark, the three travelers—of whom Gauna was the only one really awake—left the encampment accompanied by half a dozen silent Indians. The cold of dawn was intense. The lack of sun made itself felt. The stars shone in all their splendor, each of them in sharp outline against the black sky, like shimmering drops of liquid crystal. To anyone who could read them, every possible direction must have been clear in their twinkling. The earth was an ocean of shadow. A few strands of grass captured the dim astral reflections. Apart from that, everything was the purest black. The feeling of space dominated all, without being oppressive. It was a portable grandeur. Clarke, who suffered badly from the cold, had left his gloves in Buenos Aires, and stuffed his hands into a sort of improvised muff he had made. It was an ingeniously adapted piece of eiderdown, that kept him snug and warm. The increasing humidity made the cold seem even more biting. At last, they could hear a bird singing, and from that moment on the whole process of dawn unfolded, with exasperating slowness. A poppy-red sun appeared above the horizon, and soon the world was bathed in a warm glow. Everything had come to life again, that is, distances were defined once more—distances filled with nothing. An azure sky all around. The dark green of the land slowly took on its hallucinatory coloring. From time to time Clarke stared at the Indians, hermetic in their impenetrable silence. Then, when he was least expecting it, one of them spoke to him, to ask if he would care to have breakfast. He agreed, and they soon came to a halt. As if by magic they lit a fire, and in no time at all were drinking tea. Thinking it the least he could do, Clarke had added a handful of the fine Ceylon leaves he carried in his saddlebags. When they had drunk their fill, all the Indians stood up and urinated at great length in unison, starting and finishing together, as though this were their way of thanking him. To see them like that, in a line against the rising sun, was for the Englishman one of those picturesque and unforgettable experiences which give travel all its charm. The daytime part of their ride provided no more dialogue than the nighttime had, although at least there were things to look at. Clarke fell into a highly complicated reverie which took his mind off to the most distant parts, so that when the first partridge started up in front of him he was so shocked he almost had a heart attack. He almost fell off his horse as well, which caused Carlos Alzaga Prior to burst out laughing. Gauna was more sympathetic, perhaps because beneath his bitterly cynical shell he also was a dreamer. After this, Clarke tried to be more observant of his surroundings, but this also required an effort of concentration, so that the second partridge had the same effect as the first, or even worse, because he thought he was prepared for it.

It must have been seven or half past by the time they spied the outskirts of Carhué, the famous thermal spa. Some hills and valleys added spice to the landscape, as they rode down a route or track the Indians had made in their constant pilgrimages to the lake. There were no trees, but lots of agave plants, some of them huge. When they reached the seasonal tents the summer visitors put up, they separated. The Indians finally opened their mouths to wish them a good journey. Now the three of them had to rely on Gauna's judgment. The night before, the tracker had claimed he knew the way from here to Coliqueo's camp perfectly, and Clarke had no other option but to believe him. They said farewell and headed off to the left, while the Indians made for the tents.

The track climbed, and suddenly on their right they could see the lake, the color of tarnished silver, very still and endless. Far off in the middle stood an island. In spite of the early hour, or perhaps because of it, there were a lot of bathers on the lakeside or splashing about in the water. When they emerged, they dried off in the sun, and the salt caked on their bodies, leaving them looking as white as ghosts.

They could see that the Indians they had come with were trotting along the lakeshore. As the three of them continued to climb their high ground, they watched them head for a group of women further off. When the Indians reached the group, they dismounted and began to talk ceremoniously, puffing out their chests. As the three white men came level some distance away, Clarke paused out of curiosity. The Indians were talking in front of a woman whose companions had stayed a few paces behind. This was Juana Pitiley: Clarke was sure of it, even though he had never seen her before. She was naked, and was covered from head to foot in dried salt, which gleamed in the sun like diamond dust. Despite her years, which could not have been less than sixty, she was a beautiful, imposing woman, and so tall that the Indians opposite her looked like squinting dwarves. She was very still. She must have already heard the news, but said nothing. There was something tragic, or indifferent—but in either case, sublime—in the way she stood immobile. Clarke could not take his eyes off her, or continue on his way. An inexplicable fascination drew him to the sight. It seemed to him as though she raised her eyes, sparkling with salt crystals, to look in his direction. When they finally got going again, she had still not moved. In his confused state after seeing such a vision, Clarke was sorry he had been unable to talk to her about the famous Hare. Yet at the same time he realized it would have been useless to try to do so directly. She did not seem the kind of woman who responded to questions. In fact, she did not seem the kind who spoke at all to mere mortals.

5: *Traveling South*

THE JOURNEY LASTED A WEEK, AND TOOK THEM ALONG one of those straight lines that are so perfect as to be unrepeatable, though this was undoubtedly pure chance, because all Gauna did was calculate the equinoctial line and follow it. They had good weather: tranquil suns, breezes that did not ruffle the shade, a landscape accommodating all the shifting hours and minutes. It was like meeting beautiful women at every step—except that there were no women, in fact there was nobody, which meant they also managed to avoid all the pitfalls of reality. Even the relationship between the three of them remained reasonably unperturbed. Gauna was wrapped up in his own world, and paid no attention to anything or anybody, apart from his whistling, which was a monotonous but harmless accompaniment to their trip. "To think I didn't bring the dog!" he exclaimed whenever a partridge appeared. He had a theory that a dog could hunt a partridge on its own, without help. And one of his dogs, called Concuerda, was an expert at this. The number of flocks of birds they startled was remarkable, and Clarke often practiced his marksmanship. Whenever he aimed at one partridge in flight and hit another, he invariably admitted it: so much so that his telling of the truth itself seemed suspicious. It was as if he had good but off-kilter marksmanship, something beyond mere skill. Gauna had made it a rule to fetch the game himself, which gave rise each time to a joke the Englishman muttered to himself: "To think I didn't bring the dog!" Then once when Gauna was retrieving the bird, he quite tactfully let it be known he had heard the Englishman: "She's called Concuerda, or rather that's what she was called, because she was trampled by a bull, and I am sorry not to have brought her, truly sorry, and doubly so, because I could not have brought her since she's dead." Clarke felt ashamed, and never repeated the joke again. Like all English people, he put the love of animals above everything else.

"Mister Gauna," he said to him some while later, "you perhaps consider it unjust that I should have made it a condition of your employment that you not carry a weapon. Especially since I brought my own shotgun. But elementary security reasons led me to impose that condition. I won't be so hypocritical as to claim that if I had known you as I do now, I would have allowed you to come with your gun. It is a matter of principle, which knowledge, that is to say the before and after, does not affect in the slightest."

The gaucho agreed as if it were so much water off a duck's back.

There was also the possibility that they were heading in anything but the right direction. Every now and then they caught sight of Indians, but only in the distance, and were unable to exchange information. Once, a lone rider who remained in their sight for hours caught their attention. He was traveling along what was for them the skyline, and his trajectory seemed to be moving from one side to the other, not in the manner of a normal zigzag (in which case they would have noticed him moving closer then drawing further away) but rather as if the whole space between observers and observed were tilting. Things like that gave Clarke food for thought, and of late he had been thinking that in fact he was not cut out to be a naturalist but something else, for which he had no ready name. What was he? He did not know, but then everybody was in the same situation. The wanderer with his intriguing course was a reminder of all the varying positions of life.

The alarming thing was that they saw him again two days later, but this time at a completely different point, separate from the horizon. Since it was improbable that an Indian would be going round in circles for the fun of it, the only reasonable conclusion was that it was they who were going round in circles. Clarke became worried:

"That wanderer . . ." he said to Gauna, drawing a diagram with a twig in the dust when they stopped to camp. He was trying to work out how the rider's position had changed, but contradicted his own calculations when he tried to include the tilting in space he thought he had detected on both occasions.

"When are you going to stop pestering us with that blasted wanderer of yours?" Gauna eventually protested, and from then on Clarke kept his drawings to himself. After all, he could still put his trust in luck. Even if they ended up somewhere far from the Voroga encampment, it would still be a measurable distance from them. Perhaps the best thing would be to keep away from the Indians altogether. Except that, in addition to his curiosity,

Clarke was one of those people who pride themselves on achiev-
ing what they have set out to do, even when they have no clear
idea what that was.

Besides, all these and many other details of their journey were
of minor importance compared to what turned out to be its main
attraction: Carlos Alzaga Prior's loquacity, which reached unsus-
pected extremes. He was an extroverted, self-assured, expressive
type; all that was needed was to pluck the string which would set
him resonating indefinitely, and this apparently was what Clarke,
or life itself, had done on this occasion. The strange thing was
that the Englishman shared this same peculiarity, in spite of the
difference in their ages; he felt as though he were looking at himself in a mirror, but twenty years younger. And as his traveling
companion's conversation came to life, so did his own, with the
result that there was a perpetual dialogue between them. Gauna
seemed happy to take the opportunity to chew over his own
thoughts. The glances the other two shot in his direction, inviting him to join in, fell wide of their mark. He whistled, and
amused himself staring at the clouds, the grass, or simply into
the transparent air.

One morning, the second or third, they set off with the sun already high in the sky, because they did not like to get up early. Or
rather they did, but only when there was a pressing need to do so.
They had dined and breakfasted on fish, the result of Gauna's ef-
forts with a rod in an attractive stream they had crossed, and Carlos, no doubt because of the morning cold, felt ill and eventually
was sick. Immediately afterward, he felt fine again, better than
before the incident: his cheeks were rosy, his eyes shining, his

smile as white as milk in his chubby, pleasant face. He brought his horse up into step with Clarke's.

"Love," he declared, "is a wonderful thing."

"So you've already told me."

"But what happened is that I thought it again. I believe you can always think more, with greater intensity, when ..."

"I'm sorry to interrupt you, but something has occurred to me, and if I don't tell you now I'm sure I'll forget it. As you know, I was brought up in the countryside, in Kent; but in a countryside very different from this one, almost the opposite in fact; the kind of countryside to go for a walk in, inhabited by lots of people. But I've also lived in London, and what this desert we are going through reminded me of was in fact London, the greatest city in the world. Strange, isn't it? They would seem to have nothing in common, and yet the effects are the same, even down to details. If you head in any direction, either along its streets or out into this endless wilderness, the sense of being in a labyrinth where there's no labyrinth, of everything being on view, of homogeneity, is exactly the same."

"To me, as someone who hasn't traveled, Buenos Aires is the greatest city in the world."

"Well, for me there is a complete reversal: Buenos Aires is like Kent, and the pampa is like London."

"So you are in the position of the hero in that book of Swift's, who goes from this world to an upside-down world."

"Have you read Swift?"

"In a Spanish translation adapted for children. I'm afraid all the sexual references were left out."

"There aren't all that many of them, believe me."

"Books should never be adapted. As a reader, you start thinking of all the changes they must have made, and you don't enjoy the book."

"I completely agree. It's a crime. But a translation is already an adaptation. That's why it's necessary to learn languages."

"Despite that, in my opinion what matters in Swift is the general idea, which comes across in any language, because it's so strong."

"I'll say it is."

"How can he have got the idea?"

"What one should ask oneself is how the idea didn't occur to any writer before him."

"It may be that something prevented them from conceiving it. My governess told me that Swift was inspired by a scientific theory which proposes the coexistence of infinitely small and infinitely large worlds."

"Your governess must have taught you some English. The Argentines are such anglophiles...."

"Very little. Words rather than sentences."

"But that's ridiculous!"

"Surely. She was an old maid, a virgin. But words, even random ones, have their meaning, and allow you to form some idea of the psychology of different nations."

"How splendid that such a young man should have reached that conclusion. Can you give me an example?"

"There's the English word 'game,' which means 'pastime, spell of play.' But at the same time it means 'a hunted animal,' doesn't it?"

"Yes, like the French 'gibier.'"

"But in French you don't say, 'I'm going to play a gibier of chess!'"

"No, of course not. And what national characteristic do you deduce from this double usage?"

"A transfer from cause to effect. For you, hunting is a 'spell of play,' because it involves 'fair play.' Fine. But the word also signifies the dead animal, which has been killed not according to the rules of sport, but thanks to a sure shot."

"Are you trying to say we English are hypocrites?"

"It's not the moral judgment which matters, Mister Clarke, but the form. And in this case, the form that I can see is the continuum created between the reality and the result."

"Everything you have just said is complete nonsense, but what's striking is that you've ended up agreeing exactly with something Cafulcurá said to me the other day."

"Oh, by the way, what happened to that crazy old fellow? Has he disappeared?"

"That's a real mess, their own business. 'For them to deal with,' as Burke would say."

"Mister Clarke ..."

"Yes?"

"How about if we stopped for some tea?"

"Why? Are you still feeling queasy?"

"No. What I'm feeling is an empty stomach."

"I'd like nothing better. But what will Gauna say?"

Since Gauna had heard every word, it was he who invited them to dismount on the slope of some small hillocks. They had covered an enormous amount of ground while they were conversing. And it was always possible to make up lost time. The second half of the morning ride was even more productive in terms of leagues traveled, which gave them a perfect excuse to take a lengthy siesta beside a wooded creek. The species of tree were somewhat exotic for this latitude, which led Clarke to believe they had been planted by Indians who had emigrated from further north. It seemed very odd that people should emigrate taking tree seeds with them, but after all, it was more practical than taking furniture. They ate scraps. Then the three of them lay back in the shade and fell asleep. Following the Indian custom, which they found very convenient, they left their horses (they had twelve in total) loose to graze: the curious thing was that the animals appeared to have understood the way they were being treated. Clarke was awakened by cries from Carlos Alzaga Prior. When he opened his eyes, he saw the youth sitting upright in the grass, bathed in sweat, his eyes staring wildly. He had had a bad dream. Gauna was busy adjusting the stirrups on three of the horses. They set off again after a drink of coffee to help them wake up.

"I'm sorry about your dream," Clarke said to Carlos when they had got under way and their horses had fallen in step so that the two men could talk again.

"Nightmares are the worst thing imaginable."

"Do you think so? I wouldn't go that far. If nightmares become real, yes. But when you still have the possibility of waking up ..."

"How clever of you, as always! What you say is true, I'd be the last to deny it. But at the same time, I'd say there's another truth.

One can think one is always in the middle of a dream, precisely because of the consistence of reality, because it continues and keeps on going, though we have no idea how or why."

"Yes, but sometimes reality is not such a continuum. Sometimes it can be interrupted."

"Always!"

"What are you trying to say?"

"I don't know … don't ask too much of me."

"You're a typical empiricist."

"What's that?"

"It doesn't matter. Might I ask what exactly you dreamt?"

"I'd better not tell you." Prior blushed. "I'd rather tell you what I am dreaming now, but you already know what that is." He gestured toward the vast expanse of pampa.

"Are you enjoying the outing?"

"It's as if I had just started to live. There's Yñuy, there's you…"

"Thank you."

"Think nothing of it. But there's an example for you: Yñuy disappeared, and that whole line of reality was interrupted. It's as though she passed from one state to another, from one dream to another."

"We'll find her."

"Of course. There's a bridge: love."

"That wonderful thing," Clarke said, quoting his young friend with gentle irony.

"Don't you think it's a great wonder that something should exist which can infallibly link the discontinuities of life?"

"Not everybody loves."

"Yes, everyone."

"Ah, Carlos, Carlos, if only I were still fifteen like you."

Their conversation took many unexpected twists and turns. While they talked, the miles slid under their horses' hooves like a ribbon that could have included everything, not just the ground, but all the rest as well: their thoughts, the sky, the weather. Fifty yards ahead of them, Gauna went on whistling his tune, paying them not the slightest attention. They saw a rider in the far distance. He was no more than a dot, so distant they could not tell whether he was moving or not.

"Can it be the wanderer?" Clarke said. This had become his obsession. He called to Gauna and pointed to the dot in the distance.

"I've already seen it," said Gauna.

"It's an Indian on horseback, isn't it?"

"What eyesight you have," the tracker said.

"He's a real eagle," Carlos Alzaga Prior declared.

"Can it be the wanderer we saw before?"

Gauna shrugged and turned to stare in front once more. When he had got his usual distance ahead of them, Clarke whispered to his companion:

"Gauna seems French."

"Why?"

"Because of that habit he has of shrugging his shoulders. The French have inherited the gesture from the time of the Revolution, out of fear of the guillotine."

Carlos burst out laughing. "That's a good one! I'll tell it to Federico, who does the same."

"Who's Federico?"

"My best friend. It's a shame he didn't come."

"You'll have lots to tell him when you get back."

"I'll say! When he sees me turn up married, and with a child too! He's not going to believe it!"

"We're going to have to have a serious talk about that."

"Why's that?" Carlos became defensive.

"We'll talk later," was all Clarke would say.

"As soon as you meet Yñuy, your doubts will vanish, believe you me."

"I've no doubt she must be an extraordinary girl. But it doesn't do to rush into things." Before the youth could let fly with the vehement denial that was on the tip of his tongue, Clarke went on: "I know what you're going to say. That's why I'd prefer to drop the subject until later—until you have something to say which might surprise me."

"Perhaps I never will. You are far too clear-sighted."

This might have been ironical, but Clarke let it go. So that Carlos wouldn't take offense, he asked him to tell him about his family.

Immediately, Carlos was in his element! He loved talking, and always assumed the other person was interested. Since this was of course a mistake, he could not avoid taking it to its extreme and showing a particular pleasure whenever he talked about himself.

"Since I am adopted," he began, "it could be said I am all the family I have."

"That's a grave error on your part," Clarke said. "There are many ways to have a family. But it's typical of you: I've never known anyone so aware of the circumstances of their birth. As I've told you, I also am adopted. And I think I've never recalled the fact in my whole life. It's you who have reminded me of it, and even so, I can't attach much importance to it."

"I on the other hand even think I can recall the moment I was born."

"That's impossible. Nobody can."

"Mister Clarke, we always come back to the same thing. You are such a rationalist, but you don't realize that reason itself can prove you wrong. Tell me, what is there to stop someone recalling their whole life, right from the beginning?"

"You won't deny that if you ask a thousand, or a million men that ..."

"That wouldn't prove a thing, as far as reason is concerned. Answer my question."

"All right, it is possible. Where does that get you?"

"Do you admit then that everything possible is possible?"

Clarke did not reply: he did not want to get caught up in the byzantine adolescent arguments his companion was so fond of.

"You're a distant relative of Rosas, aren't you?"

"Some great-uncles in my family are in-laws of his. My adopted family, I mean of course."

"Yes, yes. Can't you ever forget that?"

"Well, I think it's important."

"Have you no idea who your real parents are?"

"None."

"Haven't you tried to find out?"

"No. Why?"

"How absurd you are! If it's so important to you, wouldn't it be logical for you to go to that trouble at least?"

"Did you?"

"I adopted my adoptive parents from the start, and completely. I don't recall ever having mentioned to anyone that I am a Clarke by adoption."

"Everyone must do as they think best."

They rode for a while in silence. Eventually it was Carlos who took up the conversation again:

"In fact, I did make some inquiries. The person who knows is my mother."

"Of course."

"But she's always been very reluctant to say anything."

"I'm sure it's for your good."

"I made her promise that when I am eighteen she will tell me."

"Do they have other children?"

"I've three brothers and three sisters."

"Do you get on well with them?"

"More or less."

"I suppose they never get at you for being adopted?"

"Never. They'd pluck their tongues out first. They're too well-brought-up for that."

"Too good-natured, you mean."

"Their upbringing is enough for me."

"My parents never had children," Clarke said, then laughed at the way the phrase sounded. But Carlos had not even heard him. He was preparing to carry on talking about his own situation:

"The fact is that my mother ..." he began, but then he paused, interrupted by something amusing that was happening in front of them—or rather, in front of Gauna, who as usual was some way ahead. A little bird kept landing on the ground in front of the gaucho's horse, and just as the latter's hooves were about to crush it, the bird would fly off and settle again a few yards further on, only to repeat exactly the same action a few moments later, like a metronome. Even though Gauna had stayed calm, it was clear that the bird's obstinate hopping was driving him crazy. He had gone so far as to stop whistling. Clarke spurred on Repetido so that he could get a better view.

"It's a roadrunner," he told the tracker. "It can spend hours doing that."

"Get your shotgun out," Gauna growled.

Carlos laughed. He maneuvered his horse so that he was in the lead, and the bird immediately adopted him. The other two fell back, listening to the young painter's laughter each time the roadrunner repeated its senseless gesture.

"Birds of a feather flock together," said Gauna.

"That's exactly what I was thinking," Clarke replied. "Have you never seen a roadrunner before?"

"If I have, I didn't notice. I've had more important things to do."

"Don't imagine that to observe Nature is simply a waste of time, Mister Gauna. It can also be a profession, as in my case."

"So you knew what it was?"

"Yes, and all the species in its family ..."

"Well then, what did you learn by looking at it?" his companion interjected.

"... the family of the '*caprimulgidae*.'"

"Fascinating," Gauna drawled laconically.

"It's more fascinating than you might think. There are experts who have devoted their lives to studying this one family."

"Incredible! What a way to waste their time."

"They are nocturnal birds...."

At this, the gaucho burst out laughing, which was unusual for him. He was genuinely amused. It was after all broad daylight.

"The roadrunner is the one which comes out earliest, before sunset."

"I can see that."

Annoyed by now, Clarke said nothing more. He was a patient man, but he had his limits. Suddenly the bird flew off, with a plaintive cry. Carlos dropped back, and Gauna took the lead once more. The sun began to set. They did not even think of coming to a halt. This was the best time of day for riding. In addition to the refreshing coolness, the light took on a new luster; as it grew dark, the air became more crystalline, and distances defined themselves more clearly. As happened every evening, a glorious pink wash of color spread across the sky. The silence became deeper, denser. Even the two inveterate conversationalists fell quiet. They must have ridden on for a further two hours, until the day gave way to night and the stars began to shine. Stillness reigned. They made camp out in the open, gathering together fossilized straw and strips of quebracho wood for a fire, which Clarke lit with his British tinderbox. As every night, they were exhausted, and moved like slow clockwork figures. It seemed incredible to them that the grass was no longer running backward, two and a half yards beneath their eyes. The horses formed a friendly group around them. They gave them water to drink from a small barrel, then fed them. Afterward, it was their turn: they made some tea, and roasted some small partridges, speaking only in monosyllables, then made ready for the night. All this was done quite rapidly, so that it was only now that the night was losing its final glow in the west. Well fed, relaxed, and with a refreshing tea soothing their aching bodies, their spirits rose again. They could hear the steady breathing of the horses around them. Gauna lit a cheroot, which for him was a sign of good humor.

"I'd go for a bit of a walk," Clarke said, "if it didn't seem impossible to do so here."

"Off you go," Carlos replied, "just pretend you're in London."

A snigger, then they both lay down flat on their backs on their blankets.

"What an incredible number of stars," the boy said.

"It's an impressive sight, isn't it?"

"Each one in its spot, every single night. It's incredible how they don't all get mixed up."

"It makes you feel so tiny looking up at them, so insignificant."

"People always say that."

"The thing is that faced with Nature, the obvious is the only thing to say."

"How do you mean, Nature?"

"I mean, the world."

"I thought Nature was things like the grass."

"No; it's everything."

"Us too?"

"Us above all."

"I wouldn't change myself for anything or anybody."

"You've spoken the first and last law of Nature. The stars aren't replaceable either. Nor is a single blade of grass."

"But I also think that anything in the world would really like to take my place. And in fact, I think they do so at every minute, without my even being aware of it."

"You've hit the nail on the head again. It's as though Nature were to speak through your mouth—and perhaps it does."

"It's strange you don't say 'mother Nature.'"

"Is that the expression in Spanish as well? I didn't say it, but I was thinking it. I thought it might sound odd in another language."

"You shouldn't be so worried. It's much nicer if you just let yourself go."

"What's that?" Clarke said, sitting up suddenly and staring at a huge white circle rising above the horizon.

"The moon," Gauna said drily.

They watched it emerge in silence. Once it had risen above the horizon line, it seemed to shrink to its normal size.

"Mister Clarke," Carlos said, "tell me something honestly: are you an atheist?"

"Yes."

"Me too."

Gauna threw them a withering look as if they had both gone mad. The Englishman's face dropped, and he said nothing. He felt strangely content at the youth's admission, although he was convinced it was nothing more than a coincidence: he was an atheist after thinking it through, Carlos before having done so.

But that was also a kind of coincidence, perhaps all the more striking for not being on the same level.

At that very moment, in the deep silence of the night, they heard a dry barking sound close by.

"What was that? Did you cough, Gauna?"

"It's a fox," the gaucho said.

Clarke picked up his shotgun.

"Let's see if I can bag it."

He set off in one direction, but Gauna pointed him in the opposite one. "He's over there."

"Let's see."

The plain was bathed in moonlight. Everything was an ashen gray color. The Englishman raised the gun to his shoulder in a classic gesture. With a loud "click," he cocked the gun: something moved about twenty or thirty yards away. He fired. Carlos went with him to examine the result.

"I knew you wouldn't miss him," the boy said when they came to where the dead fox was lying, its bushy tail covering it like an eiderdown.

6: Clarke's Confession

THREE OR FOUR DAYS LATER, THEY WERE IN EXACTLY the same situation. The distances were as huge as ever, the sky changed colors on cue, they swapped horses regularly, the weather continued stable. Gauna was still morose, Prior irrepressible. His way of conversing was in itself irrepressible, consisting as it did of tiny, meaningless sallies thrown out at every step and at any excuse. He had begun to address Clarke familiarly, both out of sheer exuberance and because, as he said, he considered they were twin souls. At times, Clarke was unsure whether the youth's remarks were mere absurdities or deliberate mockery, as when Prior showed himself both inquisitive and disbelieving over the question of Clarke's bachelorhood:

"You're thirty-five already, Clarke! What are you waiting for to get married?"

"In England, no one marries before they're forty."

"Don't talk nonsense! How can everyone get married when they're old! No, no, in your case, there's something very special going on."

"What's that?"

"I don't know. I rack my brains over it, but I can't find the explanation."

Clarke could not help but laugh.

"I've traveled a lot ..."

"All the more reason to marry. When you got back from your journeys, you'd see how your children had grown. Can you imagine the satisfaction? Thirty-five! You could be a grandfather already."

"Don't exaggerate."

"But I'm being serious! You could have a child my age."

"Er ..."

"No, you say? But if you'd married at ..."

"All right, all right! How about changing the conversation?"

"Can't you see you're scared stiff? You could at least tell me if you intend to get married, even if it's in your extreme old age."

"Yes, I'm going to marry. Are you satisfied?"

"Do you think you'll reach old age?"

"How will I get married otherwise?"

"No, it's a serious question. I'm certain I'll reach a hundred. Would you believe it, my great-grandfather is still alive? Old man Alzaga Gonzalez, known as 'three Zees.' He's ninety-six and as strong as an oak. And his wife, a comparative youngster, is ninety-four. They had eleven children and only one of them died—and he was drowned, it wasn't his health that failed him, no chance. And on my maternal side ..."

"Wait a minute: didn't you say you were adopted?"

Prior suddenly remembered. He burst out laughing:

"I'd forgotten. You see, I'm not so dogmatic about it. In fact, I didn't forget, I said it to see if you'd remembered."

"Don't be such a hypocrite! Admit you had forgotten."

"No, seriously, it was to test you."

"Admit it!"

"I swear!"

"Admit it, or I'll leave you here staked out on the ground!"

"All right! Don't be so gleeful, just because you were right for once! Are your grandparents still alive?"

"I don't have any: I'm adopted."

The youth's laughter rang out across the empty plain hour after hour. Clarke was slightly ashamed of these absurd conversations because of Gauna, but apart from that, he was thoroughly enjoying himself. Life does not often give one the chance to revel in all the childishness one has inside.

"What kind of woman do you like?" Carlos asked him some time later, returning once more to the theme that so fascinated him.

"I don't have a definite preference."

"You mean you don't want to tell me, which is different."

"All right, I don't want to tell you."

"Just as long as they're not the sort with mustaches and tattoos."

"Is that the kind of thing the priests teach you at school?"

"Do you like them educated?

"...!"

"Well, you're such an intelligent fellow, so well-read."

"I like the silent type."

"Oh, Clarke, Clarke, you're so mysterious. The more I know you, the more you surprise me. How many times have you been in love in your life?"

"Only once."

Clarke responded so quickly that his reply sounded a serious note in the midst of all their idle chatter. Carlos could not help but notice it, and this immediately awoke a real, generous interest in him. Once his curiosity was aroused, it was overwhelming. Clarke regretted his involuntary confession. There are times, he thought to himself; when it is much better to keep one's mouth shut. But he was sufficiently honest with himself to recognize that it had been his own fault. In all these years, he had not opened himself to anyone about this painful episode in his life. Perhaps now was the time to do so. Carlos was the same age as his silence. There was a certain poetic justice about it all.

"One of these days," he said, "I'll tell you about it."

"No, right now."

"I promise. Don't be impatient. You're bored, and want to be entertained. But in this case, it's not a question of just talking for the sake of it, at least not as far as I'm concerned. We adults often have unhappy memories, which mean a lot to us. For some reason, we store them up. And it can cause us still more pain if we confide them to inattentive or mocking ears."

"Don't insult me, Clarke. I do have some idea about life."

"Very little."

"And what does that matter?"

Clarke smiled at him.

"You're right. What does it matter? I promise I'll tell you, and you'll be the first to hear it. Just give me some time to make up my mind."

"No. Now."

Clarke did not want to continue the argument, so he said nothing. But after their lunch and siesta, when they were riding out again in the fine afternoon across the empty wastes, the sad poignancy of the hour brought the words flowing naturally to his lips:

"It was many years ago...."

"What was?"

"What d'you mean, 'what was?' What happened to me. Didn't you ask me to tell you?"

"That's right! I'm sorry, I was thinking of something else."

"Carry on then, don't let me interrupt you."

"No, please, tell me."

"I'm not going to tell you anything now."

"Clarke, you're driving me crazy! I'm sorry, but don't be so touchy. My mind was elsewhere for a moment, but now I'm all ears."

Clarke sighed, and began again:

"When I was young ... when I was your age, my greatest dream was to come and discover this part of America. My father had always spoken so nostalgically of it as a land of fable that it had made an indelible impression on me. My father had been a sailor, a trader, even a soldier. He traveled in Patagonia, Chile and Peru, in the days of General San Martín's expeditions. His wanderings ended abruptly and without explanation; one fine day he returned to England and his wife, whom he had not seen for ten years. They adopted me, and he never left Kent again. All my adolescent dreams revolved around his years of adventure in America, made more poignant by his mysterious decision to come back home. So that when I was eighteen and had the chance to travel, my dream of getting to know these lands became reality. I went to Valparaiso, where I worked for a year and a half in an import-export house. I made numerous trips into the interior, if that is the right word in a country like Chile, which is so narrow people always walk sideways as though they were in an Egyptian frieze. I visited the northern desert, crossed the Andes a couple of times, and even ventured in a ship to the frozen south. Eventually, I headed south again with a small group which was exploring the possibility of settling there. We traveled overland, and reached the region of the fjords in a glorious springtime. In a shack on the coast I fell in with a compatriot, an aged adventurer who was waiting for the spring thaw to set off into the mountains to discover heaven knows what. He was a geologist and a widower, and was accompanied by his daughter, the wonderful Rossanna Haussmann, with whom I fell head over heels in love. Since she reciprocated my feelings, I said goodbye to my companions and set off with Professor Haussmann and her, who themselves had for company only four Indians and a black Chilean (an extraordinary thing, a black Chilean), by name Callango. Following the professor's plans, we headed east as soon as the passes were clear. And so began for me a bewitching adventure, in which love and nature came together in one moment and one place, something life does not prepare us for, and which unfortunately is never repeated. Rossanna's father was interested only in the mountains, in their composition, their mass, their complex relations with the earth's gravity. Years later, I realized he was a scientist ahead of his time. At that time, his words went in one

ear and out the other, while Rossanna's words of love stayed forever in my heart. We discovered a confirmation of our love in
every demonstration of nature's power. And I can assure you that
nature, in those latitudes, is in itself a confirmation. I don't know
of what exactly, but it is. We came upon mountains of black ice,
which moved in front of our eyes; forests of giant blue pines,
where deer as tall as horses grazed; valleys where every last inch
was covered in flowers, while above them hung gigantic cornices
of snow carved and polished by the wind; lakes as still as mirrors,
winds howling awesome melodies, marble cliffs as lofty as pal-
aces. It was all a delight for us, we felt 'at home' with every detail,
no matter how big or small. But wherever we went, Callango's
insane eyes followed us. It was he who caused me the worst moment of my life. The man was out of his mind, though this was
far from obvious on first acquaintance with him. He was unctu-
ous, clinging, tenacious. By an incredible stroke of misfortune,
he had also fallen in love with Rossanna, but in the way that
black men fall in love with white women, that's to say without
much hope beyond a sort of perverse devotion; and devotion
can never be wholly spiritual, because it is an intensification of
desire. I would be lying if I said that was how I thought in those
days (I had not even read Hume yet), but I was aware in some
obscure way of the danger, and went to talk to the professor. He
made excuses for Callango, telling me he had known him a long
time, and was aware of the somewhat morbid fascination he had
for his daughter, but felt it to be harmless. In his view Callango
was a hysterical primitive, with feminoid tendencies. He even
suggested he might soon fall for me instead, and then we could

all have a good laugh about it. I'll never forgive myself for the easy way I let myself be convinced by his explanation. One of the reasons was our meeting with a mountain tribe. They were an extraordinary group of Indians, who provided the professor with a lot of material for his notebooks. A little farther on, somewhere on the eastern slopes, we came upon a magnificent wood of myrtles, and made camp there for a while. Nearby was a towering glacier which lent itself perfectly to study as a model of tectonic displacement, and Professor Haussmann proposed to make a detailed examination of its composition and movement. In addition, the local Indians had told him a great number of legends related to this mass of ice, which he said contained quite a few profound truths he wanted to verify. Nothing could have pleased Rossanna and me more, because the little wood was the most wonderful thing we had seen, the place that most stirred our tender feelings; in the midst of those slender golden trees, whose bark was like human skin, but icy to the touch, like no other tree in the world (European myrtles are warm), we rediscovered our love, writ large. We spent our days there, while the professor and the Indians were on the glacier, taking measurements, examining samples, constructing hypotheses. Callango alternated between the two, as though he were everywhere at the same time. More than once, in our transports, we suspected his eyes were spying on us. Of course that strange wood, which in fact was a single tree since all of them shared the same root (how could we or he hide, behind just one tree?), with the diamond of the glacier close by, were enough to create that impression. And also, I was twenty years old, and in love; my ardor prevented me from thinking straight. All I wanted to do was to contemplate Rossanna, who seemed if anything to have grown still more beautiful during the weeks of our journey. It was like having perfection in one's grasp. Until one day . . . that fateful day when, during a dark, torrid noontime, with the sky full of heavy clouds and a humid electricity in the air, the terrible event occurred. Howling and half naked, a tribe of unknown Indians fell upon us, without the slightest provocation. We were having lunch, in the doorway of the improvised hut where we slept. Spears came raining down, fortunately without doing us any harm, but they were followed by a more dangerous volley of rocks and lighted rags which set fire to our roof and scared off the mules. Our own poor Indians were petrified with fear. The professor and I fetched our shotguns, losing precious time while we loaded them, then fired almost at random. It was only at this point that we realized how vulnerable our camp was: it was in a hollow, with no easy escape routes. We had given it no thought, as there had been no indication we might be attacked. I gave my revolver to Rossanna and told her to withdraw in the direction the mules had vanished in. I thought I could frighten off our attackers with my gunfire, then follow her. You can imagine my distress when I heard shots from the revolver behind my back. Meanwhile, our attackers had come dangerously close. Our four Indians were dead, and there was no sign of Callango. As soon as I could, I left my position and ran after Rossanna. I met up with more Indians, who gazed at me with a crude bloodlust, or so I imagined. It was only the sound of my shotgun which kept them at a distance, a distance which kept changing, not only in extension but in position. In such a labyrinth, and bearing in mind the rocky terrain, it's hardly surprising that I lost my sense of direction, especially considering the agitated state I was in. I don't know how I was not killed. The fact is that a long while later I met up with the professor, beside himself and half-crazy, who was also trying to find an escape route. We were both alive and unharmed, but our shared concern was for Rossanna. I had a feeling which was almost a certainty: the savages had abducted her and then, satisfied with their booty (what more could they hope to gain from us?), they had pulled back. It was true we could no longer see or hear them. I swore to myself that I would find her, even if it took years to do so. I consoled myself with the thought that it would not be too difficult. The professor though was in despair over his daughter's fate. We found the path back to our camp. The Indians had disappeared, taking their dead with them, and leaving the bodies of our assistants. They had stolen a few small things, as though to keep their hand in, and of course they must have taken our horses with them. There was no sign of Rossanna. Still less of Callango. We began a disorganized search. I dragged the old man into the myrtle wood. The daylight had faded although the storm had never broken, and we were in half-shadow. In fact, several hours had gone by without us noticing it, and nightfall was upon us. Our beloved wood seemed threatening and ugly. We crossed it without seeing a soul, while vague thunderclaps rolled round the mountains. Finally, I came to a halt, distraught, my mind a blank, with no idea what to do or where to go. The professor, who was in no better state than I was, suggested we make for the glacier. His words sounded strange. I didn't really understand him. But he set off walking, and I followed...."

At this point, Clarke fell silent, and did not resume his story, because at that moment they met up with a band of Indians who were apparently heading at no great speed in a direction that cut across their own path. There were fifteen or so of them, all men, with a few heavily-laden spare mounts. Clarke and his companions had not spotted them because despite appearances they were in fact traveling quite quickly. The Indians shouted greetings that inevitably sounded rather wild, but generally friendly. They circled round the three of them.

"Who can they be?" Clarke wondered. Gauna had pulled up, to let him take the lead. There was nothing else for it.

He pushed his horse forward at a walk. None of the Indians responded, but there was one who seemed to be the center of the group. It was to him that the Englishman addressed himself, using common Mapuche: "Good afternoon."

"And a very good afternoon to you," the supposed leader replied. Then they fell silent for a moment. That was the problem on the pampa: it was almost impossible to ignore other people if you met them, but often there was nothing to say to them. Eventually the Indian, in a remarkable display of courtesy, deigned to ask: "What are you up to?"

Clarke of course chose to tell the truth:

"We're going to visit Coliqueo's camp."

"Ah."

Another silence.

"What about you?"

"Hunting."

"Congratulations. Did you get anything?"

"A little and a lot."

No doubt he would explain. And if he didn't, it was neither here nor there. There were no introductions. After a brief consultation with his companions, the Indian invited the white men to make camp with them, as they were thinking of halting for the night at any moment. Clarke in his turn made a pretense of consulting Gauna. The strangers seemed fairly normal, sociable even. Everyone dismounted. Within a few minutes they had started a large fire, and were sitting talking. Next to Clarke were the Indian he had spoken to, who said his name was Miltín and claimed to be an anarcho-huilliche leader, and his brother. They had glasses, which they handed round and soon filled with a potato liquor. After a couple of initial toasts, Gauna and Carlos went to watch the Indians slaughtering some wild calves for dinner.

"Now tell me," said Miltín, "where have you come from, if it's not indiscreet to ask."

"From Salinas Grandes."

"Ah, is that so? Were you with that crazy old man?"

"With Cafulcurá? Of course."

"What news is there of his son?"

"Namuncurá? He wasn't there."

"I reckoned as much. He's so inconsiderate!"

"In fact, they didn't say much about him, although we were staying in his tent."

The glasses were refilled, and Miltín changed topics:

"And what has brought you to this wilderness, Mister ..."

"Clarke."

"You're British?"

"That's right. A naturalist. I'm carrying out a field study."

"Of?"

"Animals."

"How interesting. Let's drink to your success."

They carried on in this vein for some time. The meat was brought to the fire, and the smell of grilling beef accompanied the glow of sunset. This hour of the day, usually so slow and silent for them, flew by in noise and hectic activity. Clarke, who by now knew a thing or two about Indians, was sure that the hunting they had spoken of was nothing more than a white lie: this was a group of liquor smugglers, who were returning loaded down with their merchandise, not a drop of which might reach its destination.

The ribs were served very rare, and there was no bread or other accompaniment. They were well seasoned though, to the extent that the salt formed a charred crust they had to crack open with their teeth. Clarke called to Carlos, who was chatting animatedly with some of the Indians, his cheeks ablaze from the alcohol, and asked him to fetch his canteen: if he did not calm his thirst with water, he would have to do so with liquor, and he couldn't guarantee his reaction.

Night had fallen and they had all eaten their fill of meat, when Miltín, who was beginning to demonstrate the characteristic stubbornness of a drunk, insisted on showing off for his white guests the strange talents of one of his followers, whom he described as a shaman in the making. This fellow was a short, plump, unexceptional-looking savage, with a slightly darker skin than his companions, and who was smeared in a thick coating of grease.

"This man," Miltín said, once he had persuaded Gauna and Carlos to sit next to Clarke, "has the incredible ability to enter into a trance whenever he wishes, in an instant, without having to prepare himself." He paused, to give them a chance to swallow their disbelief, although in truth they had no idea what he was talking about. "Come on, show them."

The Indian in question glistened immobile in the firelight. From behind him, a drunken voice shouted: "Ready ... steady ...!"

Miltín silenced up with a curse. Then he said to the fat man: "Carry on."

At once, they could see him go into a trance. Not a hair on his head had moved, but it was plain that his mind had flown a thousand leagues from them in the twinkling of an eye (not that his eye had twinkled either). He did not stir.

"Did you see that?"

"Incredible," Clarke said. He cast a sideways glance at Gauna, fearing one of his sarcastic sallies, but the gaucho looked not only as bad-tempered and gloomy as ever, but also seemed drunk, and was not paying any attention. Young Carlos was looking on, open-mouthed.

"Now watch," said Miltín. "Wake up!"

The Indian came out of his trance.

"Do it again!"

The same thing happened.

"Wake up!"

The same trick was repeated four more times. Clarke asked if the man saw visions.

"Who knows," the chief said.

"It's very likely he does."

"Undoubtedly."

The Indian returned to his companions, and Clarke and the chief resumed their talk. This shifted imperceptibly from paranormal phenomena to the subject of love, and the names of some of Cafulcurá's children were mentioned. Clarke thought it was the right moment to find out more about Namuncurá. Miltín was not one of those who make a secret of what they know, quite the contrary:

"So they didn't tell you where he had gone? I bet you didn't ask the right person."

"In fact, I didn't ask anyone."

"Ah, always the same delicacy, like all Europeans! I can't see the point of it, because you're still curious. I ask everybody everything, even how much money they have! What I've heard is that the good-for-nothing Namuncurá is chasing a woman, and his father must have gone white with fury when he learned who it was. Do you know?"

"No."

"The headwoman of the Vorogas, the widow of the famous Rondeau."

"You don't say! Rondeau's Widow!"

"Do you know her?"

"Only by reputation."

"I congratulate you for never having met her. She's a harpy, one of the most dangerous people loose on the pampa."

"And Namuncurá is in love with her?"

"Who knows what is in a man's heart? The fact is that for years he has pursued her, preferring to forget the fact that she spurned

Cafulcurá himself when she was widowed."

"Yes, I heard about that."

"But that's no more than scratching the surface of the story, the 'gossip' part. The background is historic. I don't know if you're aware that Cafulcurá, son of the famous Huentecurá, was a twin. His brother died young, but by all accounts they were identical, to the point where no one could tell them apart. So when one died, it could have been the other, couldn't it? Anyway, that's unimportant. The Huilliches though have made a mountain out of that molehill, enthusiastically promoted by Cafulcurá himself, who has gained political advantage from each and every one of the curious events that have occurred in his life. As things stand, one of the long-lasting foundations of his prestige is this line of twins, or multiplication of identity, which he is supposed to represent. I know you're a civilized man, but please don't think we are idiots. Consider our historical position. Faced with you white people, we Indians represent the survival of the human race, as against its extermination. So a myth, a symbolic or poetic element, can be of real importance. Now as you know, twins do not normally themselves have twins: Cafulcurá, who has had around eighty children, never had any. But his children should, and not just for purely biological reasons, but for the politico-magical dimension as well. Curiously though, none of them has. It's in this context that the struggle for succession between Namuncurá and Alvarito Reymacurá has to be seen. Their reputation as womanizers is based entirely on their grotesque pursuit of these twins. Namuncurá has always held the advantage, because no woman can resist him..."

"Really? Is he very good-looking?"

Miltín threw him a look which combined a hint of sarcasm and something darker, but merely said:

"In your style."

Clarke, who knew he was not particularly handsome, said nothing. Then he asked:

"Yet it seems that the Widow ..."

"So it seems. Namuncurá could be playing a double game. On the one hand, it's said that a long time ago, before her marriage to Rondeau, she had twins. That kind of predisposition is very valuable. It's also possible that the rumor in fact started after Namuncurá began to pursue her. On the other hand, he could be after what no Indian leader has had before: a warrior queen, someone who is a political force in her own right, which could make up for the lack of twins—because when it comes down to it, that is nothing more than a shadow game."

"It all seems rather far-fetched," Clarke commented.

"Even so, it has a rational basis. You should judge by results, not by intentions."

"But is it certain that Namuncurá is with the Widow? There were other versions circulating in Salinas Grandes about where that woman was, and what she was doing."

"Ah, yes? What were they?"

As Miltín himself had said, he made no attempt to hide his curiosity. Clarke thought it wiser not to give him the latest news: he would surely find that out from another source, and he had been recommended to keep silent.

"I'm not sure, but as far as I understood, I think they were even afraid she might attack them."

"Bah! they always say the same. As if the great Mapuche empire had anything to fear from a poor woman and her band of
madmen. What is certain is that this time Namuncurá is risking
everything, because word has it that the Widow is preparing for
her final withdrawal to the Andes, where she came from originally. It seems she considers her time on the plains is drawing
to a close."

A loud snort from Gauna distracted Clarke. It seemed the
tracker had been paying them close attention, and Miltín's final
words had startled him. But they were unable to continue their
conversation, because a sudden argument had broken out among
the Indians around the fire. The din was infernal. While Clarke
had been talking, part of his mind had been following the stages
of the Indians' increasing drunkenness. He had heard them go
through the "how much I love you, brother" stage; now they had
reached the inevitable aggression and insults. Miltín had also
continued to drink while they talked, and when he went to me-
diate in the dispute, he was every bit as inebriated as his followers. His intervention only served to make matters worse. By now,
all of them were shouting in hoarse, slurred voices. The firelight
added an extra glow to bodies which were already starting to lock
in conflict. The funniest thing (or rather the only funny thing, because everything else was so sad in its degradation) was that they
kept accusing each other of being drunk: "pie-eyed Indian! pie-
eyed Indian!" they repeated like maniacs. And Miltín, the drunk-
est of all: "pie-eyed Indians!" They were taking it out on one man
in particular, as drunk as the rest of them, who apparently had
said something insulting about the tribe's team—because the

original argument had been about hockey. The outcome of the quarrel was as rapid as it was unexpected, and for the three white men as terrifying as a bad dream. A knife suddenly glinted among all the shining greased muscles, then its blade opened a wide slit in the throat of the arguer. It seemed that the killing was something that agreed with their chieftain, who was shouting and reeling about. The shock paralyzed Clarke, but not the Indians. In a further frenzy of meaningless violence, they repeated the slash (and even its shape) in the round, inviting belly of the dead man, then plunged their hands into the wound and began to pull out his intestines, with shouts that ranged from fury to amusement. The Englishman leapt up as if activated by a lever. He was overcome with an irresistible urge to re-assert humanity. He wanted to cry out something earth-shaking, but all he could manage, in imitation, was "Pie-eyed Indians! pie-eyed Indians!" Carlos and Gauna tried to hold him back, but unsuccessfully; he was also in his cups, and the alcohol made him reckless. He pushed his way through to the dead body, howling all kinds of insults against the killers and profaners; as best he could, he snatched the slippery guts from them and clumsily tried to stuff them back into the wound; since he was seeing double, he pushed some ends into the gaping throat. Fortunately, the Indians thought this was just another joke, otherwise they might well have stabbed him too. Miltín raised a glass above the scrum and called a toast, but Clarke, raging like a madman, knocked it from his grasp.

"What d'you think you're doing?" muttered the drunkard.

"Animals, wild beasts!"

"What are you saying?"

The pair swapped the grossest insults. Luckily, neither of them could hear the other, because the Indians were shouting even louder than them. Clarke kept feeling at his belt in search of a revolver he had not worn for fifteen years; Miltín slipped and fell to a sitting position and stayed there, howling like a banshee.

Happily, outside the circle of violence, Gauna had retained a minimum of sangfroid. He sent the boy to grab Clarke, while he himself went to round up the horses. With the greatest difficulty, seeing he was in no great shape himself, Carlos succeeded in dragging Clarke some distance from the fire, where Gauna caught up with them and made them mount up.

"Animals, animals!" Clarke shouted, among other things.

The Indians did not even bother to prevent them leaving. Perhaps they were in no state to do so. What they did do was launch all kinds of scabrous taunts in their wake. One in particular, a man with a formidable voice, shouted after them for a long while. Clarke was sobbing with indignation and nerves. It was the moon which finally calmed him down. They rode on for two hours, at random of course, the main thing being to put distance between themselves and the camp. They halted when Carlos fell straight off his horse with a dull thud. The chill of the night had cleared Clarke's head a lot, and he was worried by the fall, but the boy lay fast asleep and snoring on the ground. They spread out their things there and then, and, surrendering themselves body and soul to the mercies of the night, slept like logs.

The next day, as was only to be expected, their timetable was turned upside down. They slept all morning: since it was cloudy, the sun did not wake them. Then they rode for a while, their heads throbbing and their stomachs churning. What few comments they made were about the disgusting murder and how savage the Indians were. Gauna was even more taciturn than usual; it was obvious that he was obsessed by some idea. They were fortunate enough to come across a picturesque stream, where they bathed to refresh themselves from the heat of a gathering storm, then they drank a hasty cup of tea, and took a siesta. The rain woke them. Sheltering beneath the trees, they waited a long while for it to cease, and when it eased to a drizzle, they set off in the gloomy dusk. It continued to rain off and on, but since they were neither hungry nor sleepy, they continued to ride until, around midnight, the sky cleared and the moon came out. Immediately, they halted to make a fire, then, in marked contrast to the previous night, spent a short time sitting round it in silence, and soon fell asleep.

The next day was one of brilliant sunshine and gentle breezes. Their spirits lifted, the bad dream was left behind. The air was so clear that the horizon, perhaps the only thing to be seen, stood out with a special clarity. They could almost make out the far side of it, as if the line had become crystalline, a prismatic extension that divided the visible from the invisible, and broadened perspective beyond the normal. And it was precisely at this point that they saw the wanderer whose changing position had given the Englishman such cause for reflection.

"There he is again," he said to Carlos.

"I can see him, I can see him."

"Is he coming or going?"

"That I couldn't tell you!"

"Let's see ... if he is moving from left to right, that means he's traveling in the same direction as us; if it's the opposite, then he's bound to cross our path without our realizing it, so that we'll see him on the other side, on any other side, because that depends on where we are at the time.... What a mess! We should draw up a timetable, plot our relative positions in black and white. It makes me afraid we're lost. I think I'm going to have to have a serious talk with Gauna." He lowered his voice as he said these last words, but fifty yards ahead of them the gaucho's shoulders shrugged visibly.

In the meantime, the wanderer had vanished again, like a speck of dust drifting out of a sunbeam.

"Who can it be?" said Clarke.

"Some Indian or other."

"Of course. But where is he going? What is he thinking? Isn't it intriguing to ask oneself that kind of question?"

"All questions are intriguing, Clarke: if not, they wouldn't be questions."

"Do you know what it made me think of, a moment ago? Of Natural Man. There was a time when I read about nothing else. In the last century it was an intellectual fashion ... it still is, in fact."

"Natural Man?"

"Yes. With a little philosophical effort, you can imagine the characteristics of a man stripped of all the prejudices of reason, culture, customs, and so on. It's similar to building an automaton, but by taking bits away rather than adding them. In the end you're left with the essence, the naked heart ..."

"But that's very poetic!"

"And scientific as well. Getting to know distant and exotic peoples, like the Indians we see here, fills one with ideas about Natural Man. Or at least it does me, who lacks imagination."

"But we are always creating people in our fantasies."

"Rousseau, one of the inventors of the idea of Natural Man, says that the creation of one man by another is the most obvious sign of a failure of education."

"In that case, he was the one with no education."

"He did die mad."

"Really? That often happens to philosophers."

"That's the way of the world."

"Isn't it rather repugnant to create monsters?"

"If you think about it properly, yes. But that takes us back to Natural Man by another route. From the outset, man is a kind of monster, an improbable conjunction of mind and body."

"What about those Indians we were with the night before last? Would you say they were natural or artificial?"

"Both things."

"But which side would you say they were closer to?"

"What would you say?"

"Natural, in spite of everything."

Clarke suddenly remembered his responsibility—however fleeting and accidental—as the educator of a young mind. He thought of the inevitable failure. This led him along tracks that took him back into his own past, and his autobiography (as he knew better than anyone) bore a mysterious relation to Natural Man. He spent the hours and leagues until lunchtime pondering these thoughts, while beside him Carlos Alzaga Prior was equally wrapped up in himself. Shortly after their siesta, toward the end of the afternoon, they came across a flock of ostriches, and soon afterward met up with the men hunting them, who turned out to be from Coliqueo's tribe. When these Indians heard that the white men were intending to visit them, they put on a show of great amazement at the (nonexistent) coincidence, and escorted them to their camp, forgetting all about the ostriches—who, to judge by the speed they were traveling, must by now have circled the globe.

7: The Duck's Egg

"THE DUCK'S EGG IS THE MOST EFFECTIVE OF ALL,"
Coliqueo declared with an air of finality.

Clarke felt completely overwhelmed by the situation, out of
place, struck dumb. The tent was full of women, children, dogs,
and a fire where water was constantly being boiled for tea. Despite the fact that two of the leather sideflaps had been rolled
up to allow air to circulate, the tent was still thick with smoke,
so that Coliqueo and Clarke's eyes were as pink as if they had
been weeping profusely over the death of a loved one. And that
in a sense was what Clarke had been doing, because he had sat
vigil all afternoon over the dead body of Truth. Coliqueo was
the prototype of the dishonest Indian, which might be comical
at first, but became increasingly depressing as time went by. For
his guest, that time had been and gone a long while since.

The way they had arrived at the duck was tortuous in the extreme, even though with hindsight it seemed not only direct,
but even over-hasty. All the Indian's lies and deliberate mislead-
ings came together as if they were part of a deliberate stratagem.
Of course there was no plan: Coliqueo did not have the brain
for that. But on reflection, the twenty-four hours that the three

white men had spent in his camp were nothing if not predictable. As he began to listen to the story of the duck's egg, Clarke was at pains to go over in his mind what had happened up to that point. He did this quickly, but in a detailed fashion, because the secret of his fatalistic acceptance lay in the details. It did not matter that there was a gap in the conversation; there had been others before that, and with less reason; besides which common courtesy, to which he continued to pay tribute even among these savages, owed him this respite. His interlocutor could put up with a silence. In all fairness, it was the least he could do.

Coliqueo was a tall, thin, ungainly man, as black as an African, with the face of a Chinese gangster and flowing locks lightened by chamomile. He wore a filthy army uniform that revealed his skinny grease-covered frame (the Indians were so brutish that they used grease even when dressed in clothes). Like all the rest of them, Coliqueo drank; he had that animal, cruelly cunning streak that the Indians got from habitual drinking. Although he was supposed to come from the most blue-blooded Mapuche aristocracy, he had no manners whatsoever. Clarke was surprised to find himself put out that Coliqueo indulged only in the briefest of squints when he sat down to talk with him. After all, he told himself, what did it matter to him. The Duke and Duchess of Kent, whom he encountered in his own country, did not turn crosseyed on formal occasions, and nobody thought any the worse of them for that.

The chaos and promiscuity of Coliqueo's encampment were in stark contrast to the courtly disposition of Salinas Grandes. In fact, it was a provisional settlement, or rather a seasonal one,

as in the winters these Indians took advantage of the hospitality
of their white allies. Although they were totally influenced by
the white man, they were no less Indian for it; on the contrary,
some of their peculiarities were spectacularly exaggerated. They
had chosen to spend the summer in an area of low hills, through
which a narrow, treeless river ran.

The previous night, when the three white men had arrived,
the Indians had been in the middle of a feast. They were celebrat-
ing the wedding feast of Coliqueo's eldest son, a youth who atop
a magnificent body had the same head as his father. Coliqueo
was proud that his fifteen sons all looked like him. He made them
line up in the bonfire light for Clarke to inspect: and it was true,
they did all have his features, some more, some less. Some indeed had almost none; but here imagination and goodwill came
into play, plus their progenitor's assertion.

There were both drawbacks and advantages to arriving in the
midst of an Indian feast as they had done; among the latter was
the fact of being able to mingle almost unnoticed among the
uproar and to observe without themselves being the object of
unwanted attention. And the savages lent themselves almost excessively to observation, smothered in grease, turned into mirrors. They even performed a dance, in which the men came together, moved apart, formed circles, lines. They performed it
as if against their will: holding themselves rigid, pretending to
be clumsy, to be drunk, slow, or forgetful. In order to represent
drunkenness, they drank like fish; the rest followed naturally.
The women of the tribe meanwhile stood apart in their own disheveled group, screaming at the tops of their voices. Once the

men's dance had finished, they began to sing. A chorus of victims of the worst imaginable tortures could not have come out
with a more terrible noise. Then after these attractions, everyone drank and screamed some more. They had all eaten unbe-
lievable amounts of meat. Several cows, doubtless specially fat-
tened for the occasion, had been slaughtered. The three white
men stayed close to each other and refused as much as courtesy
would allow, making their ribs of meat last as long as possible,
merely wetting their lips in the mugs of liquor that were passed
round. Even so, Carlos turned green and had to go and be sick;
after that, he went from fire to fire and group to group, looking without much hope for Yñuy. Gauna, who on this occasion
was very careful with his drink, fell in with some relatives of the
chieftain, while Clarke had to put up with the latter's ceaseless
chatter until it was almost morning. He could never have recalled
half of the senseless stories the Indian had told him. Coliqueo
spoke incoherently, not so much due to the drink (which was
to blame only for the general stupidity of his talk) but because
he thought this made what he said sound more serious, more
impressive. He did in fact possess a quite logical mind, but for
some reason Clarke could not fathom, he believed that this quality was for second-rate people, or only to be used for domestic
purposes. He created monstrous sentences, joining the subject
of one with the predicate of another, in order to increase their
vagueness. The Voroga dialect lent itself to contortions of this
kind: indeed it seemed as though it had been specifically created
for them. Eventually, the fires went out (they were fetid, made of
dry manure) and in the vague daylight the Indians looked bleary-

eyed and gloomy. So everyone went to sleep. On his and the others' behalf, Clarke turned down the chieftain's offer of his tent. He said they were accustomed to sleeping in the open air, and found it healthier. Since Gauna had asthma, and had suffered an attack during the feast, his little lie sounded convincing. The result however was that Clarke could not get a wink of sleep because of the daylight. Instead, in a state of indignant stupor, he went over Coliqueo's endless nonsense in his mind. The Indian chief had not even asked him what his name was, or where he came from. He had spent the whole time talking, and about what? About what, good God? The worst of it was that he created the same sort of monsters from his topics as he did from his sentences. It was the method of a born liar: in that way, he did not even have to commit himself to his lies. And as for the other matter, the one which had brought Clarke to the camp, the tribe did not appear to be interested in war in the slightest, and their leader still less: but then, it was probably best not to put too much weight on the previous night's impressions. Carlos was sleeping on his gear, his mouth wide open. Gauna had gone off on his own to join some other white men he had met among the Vorogas, one of whom he knew from before. Clarke had shared no more than a few words with them, but promised himself he would sound them out during the day, if Gauna had not already done so in private.

The Vorogas got up very late, and Coliqueo did not appear until one o'clock. Clarke and his companions were given some sticky cakes for breakfast, washed down with a bitter boiled maté. Clarke and Carlos spent a long while staring at Indian men and women, who were busy doing nothing. There was no one for them to exchange a word with. The white men in whose company Gauna had spent the night did not seem much more promising. Gauna introduced them to his former friend, a half-caste by the name of Aristídes Ordóñez.

"What do you know about Cafulcurá?" Clarke asked him point-blank.

"Who?"

Clarke turned to Gauna: "Can he really not know who Cafulcurá is?"

"Don't you know who Cafulcurá is?"

"No," said Ordóñez.

"Have you never heard of him?"

"I don't get involved in Indian matters, boss."

"What do you do, then?"

"I write."

This was enough to awaken Clarke's dormant interest.

"You're the chieftain's scribe?"

"That's right, by your leave."

"And who on earth does that madman have to write to?"

"He dictates endless memorandums, all of them addressed to Rosas."

"Since when could you write?" Gauna asked him, with his habitual suspiciousness.

"A priest taught me."

"Which one?"

"The one who used to stay in the houses ... the one with the pigs, you remember?"

"Ah, that one," said Gauna.

"What happened to the pigs?" Clarke asked. Gauna did not even deign to reply, but stared into the distance. Ordóñez answered on his behalf: "He bought four pigs, and they all died of the evil eye."

"That priest," Gauna condescended to comment, "was the dumbest person who ever drew breath."

"By the way," Clarke said to Ordóñez, "what's the matter with Coliqueo? Is he smoking too much?"

"No more than normal."

"How about drink?"

"Yes, of course. He likes a bit of everything."

"He says things that are hard to interpret."

"You're right, he is a bit odd. But he's not a bad sort."

Clarke kept his thoughts to himself. Aristídes Ordóñez did not appear to him to be a particularly good sort. Who could say what he was escaping from among the savages? And if Gauna succeeded in getting any useful information out of him, he would not tell Clarke—the two of them appeared to have come from the same mold, but at least Clarke was used to Gauna by now.

Soon afterward, Coliqueo sent for Clarke to come to his tent, and so the unbearable interview began. Clarke went alone, sending Carlos off to have a dip in the river.

"I gather," the chieftain started by saying, focusing his eyes normally after the briefest of squints, "that your honor has come from Salinas Grandes."

"That's right. Last night I didn't have the chance to mention it, because in fact it seemed rather a mouthful."

"Because your mouth was full of half a cow at least!"

Clarke sighed: his intended joke had fallen flat in Voroga. The Indian went on:

"So my distant cousin Cafulcurá—the more distant the better—has vanished into thin air?"

"You knew about that?"

"I heard about it the other day, by chance."

"And what did you make of it?"

"I split my sides laughing."

"Don't you think he might be in danger?"

"What kind of danger?" Up to this point, Coliqueo had tried to be reasonable, but this was too much for him. Before the Englishman could reply, he raised his arms in protest: "I had nothing to do with it! I knew they'd try to pin it on me! I'm sick to death of those charlatans!"

"If it's any reassurance, I can promise you that nobody in Salinas Grandes suspected you of having anything to do with it."

"I should think not! To get me mixed up in their fantasies!"

"But this isn't a fantasy. The man has vanished."

"And what do I care?"

"Aren't the Vorogas enemies of the Huilliches?"

"We have signed a treaty of everlasting peace. It's a dead letter, but I'm happy enough with it. My concern is my people: production, development, foreign affairs. Within my modest domain, I aim to be a model statesman. They on the other hand live from stealing, from lazing about, from extortion. They're empty-headed and envious. That madman Cafulcurá has raised the new generation in such an atmosphere of fantastic beliefs, I wouldn't be surprised if one day he ended up dead thanks to some prophecy or spell or other. Serve him right."

"You're not mistaken, Mister Coliqueo, at least as far as I am able to judge. I saw some of it in the few hours I spent in their court. But the picture you paint is too gloomy: the Huilliches seem happy enough, superstition or no superstition."

"Good for them."

"They have a particular devotion to personal hygiene."

"To me, politics comes first. Hygiene is secondary."

"Well, it all depends on what your definition of politics is. For example, I interpreted your earlier words as denigrating the weight that the politics of magic has for them."

"That's not politics, it's hocus-pocus!"

"What if it works?"

"Don't make me laugh! Do you think it means it's effective, if their chieftain disappears into thin air in front of his subjects' noses? They're condemned to live in a system which is constantly feeding his lunacy. I'm sure for example that this latest episode has given rise to a whole series of laughable exorcisms by his shamans. They'll climb yet another rung of the ridiculous. It's effective in a kind of way, I agree, but it's absurd. But tell me, who is it they suspect?"

"They weren't blaming ghosts, I can assure you. They presumed—I have no idea with what degree of accuracy or truth— that it had been a woman ..."

"Rondeau's Widow! I don't believe it! They really can't see beyond their own mad ideas, can they?"

"Is it such a remote possibility?"

"There is no possibility at all. To accuse the Widow is no more than hot air. It's like saying that a story can become real just like that, because they say so. That's a good example of their 'effectiveness' for you. They're so far gone they take their own fantasies seriously."

"What makes you so sure in this case?"

"Because the Widow came through here about a week ago, and she is concerned with other things; if her body—and I can swear to it—never came within a hundred leagues of Cafulcurá, her mind has been a thousand leagues away of late. She was going to join her daughter to celebrate her fifteenth birthday. And it's not that I'm trying to excuse that viper, much less be her accomplice. On the contrary, I'd be more than pleased if they accused her, pursued her, and wiped her out. It would be one less problem. If I ever get my hands on her ..."

Clarke thought Coliqueo was contradicting himself, because he had just asserted that the Widow had paid him a visit only a few days earlier. He made no comment. Coliqueo had started up again, this time with one of his leading questions:

"Do you want to know what happened to Cafulcurá?"

"Of course."

"One of his sons killed him: Namuncurá or Alvarito Reymacurá."

"Well ... Namuncurá was not in Salinas Grandes."

"Where else could he have been? He must have been hidden. They spend the whole time saying the same thing: that the 'princes of peace' chase women, that they pursue shimmering illusions like migratory storks.... It's all lies. That farce about twins. The duck's egg. The hare. The blue gallstone. Pure bunkum! That poor old man is probably paying for his sins buried somewhere on the outskirts of their camp. And his sons are about to gouge each other's eyes out. What an edifying spectacle that will be!"

"Whose side will you be on?"

"Me? Nobody's. It's for them to sort it out."

"Begging your pardon, your Majesty, but you said you were interested in foreign affairs. That's quite logical. All the more so considering the fact that the Mapuche federation is in a state of organic equilibrium from Tierra del Fuego up to Córdoba. I don't understand therefore how you cannot be concerned about the key element in that equilibrium, which is Cafulcurá."

"That's because I base my effectiveness on other premises. To be concerned about one individual thing is to lose sight of the whole. Take you, for example, what is it you do?"

At last he's asking me, thought Clarke. "I'm an English naturalist."

"A contemplative person?"

"To some extent. It could be said I practice an active kind of contemplation."

"What area do you work in?"

"Animals, mostly. Although it's impossible to rule out everything else, because Nature, as you just pointed out, is a whole."

"Did I say that? Look, what do you think about the duck?"

"What duck?"

Coliqueo thought for a moment. Eventually he said:

"Cafulcurá is full of animal stories. He must have told you lots."

"Some, but not all that many. One of his shamans told me more ..."

"Which one?"

"One called Mallén."

"Is that cheap charlatan still around? I can just see him, forever peddling his stale repertoire of worthless tricks. Goodness, what a sad lot they are. They're caught in a mechanism where they can't change any of the parts, because none of them is real. You're a scientist: you see one animal for example, then another ... you make a note of the first, then the second, you think about it, you trust in the grandeur and variety of the world. But them ... what a difference!"

"They're different cultures."

"No, sir. That is to use the concept of culture as an excuse to sanction mediocrity, to persist in superstition and brutishness. They are like children, fascinated by their toys."

By this point Clarke, a victim of his companion's supreme self-deception, had come to regard him as wise and thoughtful. He yielded to this optimism:

"My position as observer, Mister Coliqueo, allows me to take advantage of whatever perspective the people I meet have adopted. The Huilliches' is one of many. Yours is another, much more rational one...."

"Look, you and I understand each other. You wouldn't have time to do a spot of work for me, would you? I could pay you well, and I'm sure your studies would benefit from it."

"Well ... I'm in the middle of an investigation."

"You aren't looking for Cafulcurá, are you?" the chieftain asked jokingly.

"What work is it?"

"It concerns everlasting peace, no less. You would be performing a true service for these lands, with little effort, and at the same time it would remove you from that circle of nonsense which, whatever you may say, your Huilliche friends must have ensnared you in. I'm talking about reality, tangible things, things that can be thought about without a sense of shame. I suppose you have heard about the question of everlasting peace. The Mapuche federation, which has fought within itself for centuries, has finally brought the clearest of its logic to bear on that radiant point which is everlasting peace: the end of time, the dawn of life. Do you believe it's possible?"

Clarke did not know whether to say yes or no.

"I'm glad you're hesitating," Coliqueo said, "because in fact the reply lies elsewhere. Did you believe those animal legends that Mallén told you?"

"Of course not." How stupid of him! Clarke thought afterward. He had walked straight into the trap.

"Good for you. One of those legends is that of a duck's egg with two yolks, from which will come two identical ducks, who will swim at dawn on a secret southern lake: and that will be the day of everlasting peace."

A silence. Clarke had not the faintest notion of what was coming next.

"Well, the job I had in mind is for you to get that duck's egg for me. With all your knowledge, and with time at your disposal which I don't have because of all the problems I have to contend with here, and above all with a mind like yours free from prejudice, you'll find it in no time. And then I'll be the true emperor."

Clarke's astonishment was like a mental earthquake. He suddenly realized that everything he had been listening to, with such naive consideration, was nothing more than the ranting of a complete madman. What a waste of time! It was then that Coliqueo proffered his final sentence from on high:

"The duck's egg is the most effective of all."

"I need to get some air. If you'll excuse me . . ."

Clarke stood up.

"Yes, off you go. We'll meet later. Think it over."

Clarke left the tent taking great gulps of air. Nobody likes to be made a fool of, especially when faced with the demanding jury represented by the inner scruples of an Englishman with a good education. Together with the air, Clarke sucked in all the images around him, to clear his mind. The Voroga camp seemed less miserable than it had that morning. The blue of the afternoon sky, the children's cries, the constant to-ing and fro-ing of the loose horses, the glances of the Indian women—everything drew him back to a normality he had momentarily felt tremble beneath his feet. He walked toward the gully where they had left their troop of horses and their gear. Aristídes Ordóñez was sitting keeping watch. Clarke asked where Gauna was.

"I don't know," the gaucho said, "he left me to look after things, but that was a long time ago. He's not come back, and I have to leave."

"Yes, off you go. Many thanks."

Clarke was left on his own. A few minutes went by, and he began to regret having come to replace Ordóñez. He was stuck there now until nightfall, because there was little hope that Gauna and Carlos would interrupt whatever they were doing to come and see if he needed them. And if he so much as budged, everything would be stolen, down to their stirrups. He decided at least to enjoy his solitude. He lit his pipe, and began to smoke staring at the river, which flowed past beneath him. It was a small, treeless stream; the little water it contained was far from clean. At the top of the riverbank lay the untidy assortment of tents. Many of the Indians had come out like him to enjoy the fresh air. The Vorogas looked exactly the same as the Huilliches, except that they spoke a different language; once out of earshot, this distinguishing feature naturally disappeared. And yet it was still there. Since in reality nothing is imperceptible, thought Clarke, the difference was absolute, and involved their entire appearance. And the difference could be summed up by saying that in Salinas Grandes the Indians lived outside life, whereas here they were inside it. He had landed directly in the realm of fable, which he had taken to be real; now he had to get used to the idea that this fable was merely an island in the ocean of normal life. Plebeian and westernized, the Vorogas were a reminder of the ordinary things in society. To be completely ordinary, all that was needed was for them to work. Of course, there was no danger of them making that sacrifice, not even for aesthetic reasons.

Something in the river caught his attention. Something whitish was floating downstream at the leisurely pace of the murky current. He found himself unable to tear his gaze from the undulations of this large, soft object. It was only when it passed in front of him that he realized what it was: a man's shirt, its arms slowly waving almost as if it were filled with a drowning body. It drifted on down the stream and disappeared round a bend, still in the center of the current, as slowly and as inexplicably as it had appeared. Clarke wondered if it might not be a passive kind of washing, by distance rather than by scrubbing.

His thoughts spread to more general considerations concerning the aporias of sight. The way the Vorogas reflected current society coincided with the river current, and in both cases the idea coincided with what he had been looking at, and the time span his gaze had created. Two young Indian girls walked past him arm-in-arm, staring at him provocatively, then started whispering and giggling in a hysterical manner. A short while later, they were back; on this occasion they asked him the time, but without waiting for his answer, began to whisper and giggle again. One of them turned her head ... they could not have been more than ten years old, but they were already behaving like experienced streetwalkers.

A dog came up to Clarke, a skinny mongrel which sniffed at him as though he were an object.

It was at this moment that Gauna appeared. He was in a hurry, and had his usual morose look on his face. When he saw Clarke sitting among their gear, he slowed down, and his face darkened still further. He sat down beside Clarke, and stared into the distance. Clarke wanted to ask him how he had met Ordóñez, but did not have time: Gauna came straight to the point:

"We're wasting our time, don't you think?"

A thousand ingenious and philosophically intriguing responses flashed through Clarke's mind, but something told him it would be better not to risk any of them. He had found that this kind of reply only took the conversation away from what really mattered. What had come to seem most important, given all the philosophically intriguing events that had happened to him, was the need for action. He was therefore willing to hear what the gaucho had to say, because he sensed that thanks to him they might finally begin to act. And indeed it was on this point that Gauna, without seeming at all put out by the lack of response, now insisted:

"They could go on talking to you here for a year or two, and you'd still be stuck where you were at the start. The hare, as they say, leaps where least expected—always supposing that you're expecting something, however little, in reality. And you're looking for a hare, aren't you?"

"Yes, Gauna."

"You'll be surprised to hear that I am too."

"Yes? You didn't tell me."

"You didn't ask. You were so busy chewing the fat with the kid that my intentions were never mentioned."

"That's easily put right. As I've said often that it's become second nature to me: I'm all ears."

"But we've had more than enough talk! What I'm suggesting is that we leave here today, right now."

"Heading where?"

"Heading after the Widow. I've found out that she's close by, three or four days' ride to the southeast, no more. She came through near here less than a week ago, and apparently she was in no hurry."

"Coliqueo told me something of the sort. I agree it's probably true—but what's so important about the Widow that we should go in search of her? I don't think she kidnapped Cafulcurá."

"Nobody has ever believed that."

"But Mallén ..."

"You're so naive! You've swallowed everything you've been told, without exception. And then you say you don't believe in God!"

Now it was Gauna's turn to bring in philosophy. Clarke deliberately did not follow him down that track:

"Well then?"

"The Widow has got the Hare. Or will be getting it in the next few days. It's as simple as that."

(Clarke supplied the capital "H" in his own mind, and could have sworn it was there in reality.)

"Explain yourself, I beg you."

"You don't believe me?"

"I can believe anything, as you've said. But I prefer to know what it is I am believing in."

"It's not something that can be explained in a couple of words. It's a long story."

The summer afternoon had merged into an extraordinary purple sunset. As if shot like arrows, huge flocks of parrakeets flew past toward some tall violet-colored cliffs in the far distance. Bands of dark blue began to spread above the horizon. The shadows of the two men lengthened down to the water's edge.

"I belong to one of the families," Gauna began, "who have most right to own land in Argentina. I am a Gauna Alvear. Does that surprise you? Vast, immeasurable estates, cattle as plentiful as the blades of grass they eat, salt meat factories, accounts in English banks, and even a decisive political role—all of this should be mine by right, were it not for the fact that unfortunate family complications have prevented it becoming a reality. That is why you have come to know me in this ragged guise of a gaucho exposed to the hazards of a tracker's life. The entire branch of the Gauna Alvear family I belong to—the richest one—has been affected by illegitimate births. None of my grandfather's three daughters were married; all of them had children. Throughout my childhood I thought I was the only son of a devout, melancholy woman. But this was not the case: another offspring, female this time, the fruit of as fleeting a relation of my mother's as I myself was, had come into the world. In her case though, her father—an adventurer—had not only recognized her, but had taken her with him. It was only as an adult that I learned of the return of this half-sister of mine. She had even for a brief while been in Buenos Aires, before setting off for the interior, where she had created a very curious position for herself. A great beauty, she had seduced many idle indigenous leaders, and ended up married, apparently against her will and in payment for her dissipated life, to a chieftain called Rondeau ..."

"The Widow!" Clarke exclaimed, unable to believe his ears.

"That's right, the Widow. At least, that's what I've deduced. I've never actually seen her, nor found out anything concrete about her. A few garbled words my mother said as she lay dying have allowed me to reconstruct the story. My aunts died at almost the same time—all of them, including my mother, the victims of a strangely simultaneous (and highly suspicious) illness. It was then, around the time of Rondeau's death at the hands of

Cafulcurá (a death which no one will convince me was not due to some act of treachery by my half-sister) that the Widow's representatives became extremely active in Buenos Aires. The claims on the inheritance, which had been undivided during my grandfather's lifetime, became more strident. Of course, no one person could claim legitimacy against the others. This was the chance that snake in the grass De Angelis had been waiting for—perhaps inspired by dialectic effusions emanating from Salinas Grandes. He it was who gave Rosas the idea of enjoying the usufruct of all the possessions of my grandfather, General Aristóbulo de Gauna Alvear, while our quarrels went on—perhaps for ever. You should also know that we descend in direct line, albeit a collateral one, from the Hapsburgs, and one royal legacy has continued to figure in all our family's papers: a large diamond, unique in the world due to its elongated form and the highly unusual way it was cut. Tradition had it that the diamond was handed down by the distaff side, but our logical tendency toward endogamy meant it had more or less stayed in the family, at least until the generation prior to mine. But my grandmother, its last legal owner, died before the eldest of her daughters had reached the age of fifteen, the date established for handing down the stone. Supposedly, presumably at least, it was my grandfather who handed it to his eldest daughter when she reached fifteen, but here comes yet another strange mystery: nobody ever knew which of the three sisters, my mother or the other two, was the eldest. Apparently there were exactly ten months between each of them, and since their mother had raised them hidden away in the nursery of one of our old patriarchal mansions, nobody could say which was which: they themselves must have known, I'm sure, but they never said a word. Did my grandfather know? He never made any comment either, and he was such a drunk and crazy old man that no one would have believed him anyway. The fact is that he died, and they, I am sorry to say, after living lives of easy virtue in their youth, turned into sanctimonious old maids. When they died there was no sign of the jewel. Everyone thought our grandfather must have given it to one of them, even if he had chosen at random. But that wasn't the case. I should clarify one other small point: as a result of their amorous adventures, the sisters had given birth only to boys, with the exception, discovered much later, of my half-sister: the now infamous Widow. Are you following my drift?"

"I'm following it perfectly. Although, if this were a novel, I'd take the trouble to reread that last paragraph as carefully as possible. So, we'd reached the point where Rosas ..."

"Rosas, or rather that reptile of an Italian who advises him, used the fact that the legal inventory was incomplete because of the gap left by the diamond, to declare the inheritance proceedings frozen. It's a common trick among us. What they were after in this case was to suspend matters until they could produce one of the female relatives with the diamond in her possession, so they could negotiate with her ways to divide up half the province of Buenos Aires between them. That's all the facts for you. The rest is easy enough to guess."

"I assure you it's not so easy for me. Couldn't you give me a helping hand?"

"It seems to me obvious that the jewel has been in the possession of the Indians all these years. It was just what they needed to extort any number of advantageous treaties from that monster of Palermo. When you appeared, the time for the great sleight of hand was ripe; and you were as good an instrument as any to set the whole thing in motion. Why else would Rosas have lent you his best horse? Repetido was the password that you innocently took with you to Salinas Grandes. Once you were there, while they were putting on a great show of pretense, things became more complicated. I have no way of knowing for sure what actually happened, but I have my suspicions. It's likely there were arguments in the court about handing over the diamond, especially from the faction supporting Juana Pitiley. Leaving themselves without the stone could bring down Rosas's greed on their heads, and perhaps even speed their own extermination (even though they must be getting a sizeable cut from the deal over the inheritance). If you remember, we saw, or almost saw, the supposed flight of a 'hare.' Well, the shape of the diamond precisely recalls that of a hare. As for the 'legibrarian' part of it, which I must confess was a surprise to me, it can be explained by the legend of its extraordinary shape. It was cut by an unknown Jew in Amsterdam on the orders of Emperor Charles the Fifth, to fit into Erasmus's right superciliary arch so that he could use it as a monocle to overcome his astigmatism, for him to be able to 'read,' 'read' the 'legible,' if you follow me: a gift from the Emperor which was never sent as a result of the philosopher's death."

"Very original. So according to you, up in Salinas Grandes someone stole the stone?"

"Or faked stealing it."

"What about Cafulcurá's disappearance?"

"I haven't managed to find an explanation for that yet, but you won't deny it's linked."

"There are important holes in your story, Mister Gauna."

"What's important aren't the holes, but what remains. If you look closely, it's all holes, but the evidence to cover them is there. You must have heard that the Widow is preparing to move on. They say it's to the Andes, but I have the feeling it's to somewhere else: once she's got her hands on the ill-gotten gains, she won't stop until she's reached Paris. And today I heard she's preparing to celebrate the fifteenth birthday of someone who is supposed to be her daughter...."

"Yes, that's what Coliqueo told me."

"What he won't have told you is that when she came through here she tried all she could to buy any fifteen-year-old girl available ... that can only mean that things have got out of control and she wasn't ready for the playacting. What I don't know is where ... But she didn't take any girl from here, because Coliqueo refused to sell her one—not out of principle, of course, but to force her to stop somewhere else to find one, so that he could gain time. I'm sure that lunatic has also smelled something odd going on, and is trying to find out what it is. That's why I think we should follow her traces now while we're so close to her...."

"It seems to me that you're using the plural a little too lightly, Mister Gauna. What has your family quarrel got to do with me?"

"But my 'family quarrel' is what it's all about! All the rest is simply idle chatter! Do you want the hare? Do you want Cafulcurá?"

"I'm not ... convinced."

"Well then, just listen. There's more. My half-sister, the Widow, is in fact ..."

At that moment a deafening noise cut their conversation short. Night had fallen while they were talking, and the Indians had lit their bonfires. There were so many of them, and they were so close together because of the confused huddle of the tents, that the whole camp was lit up like a city. In fact, the profusion of bonfires had brought forward nightfall artificially, and it was not yet completely dark. The sky still gave off a viscous glimmer of light, which made the intervals between each fire a dull gray rather than black. Even the distances floated, mysteriously visible, a while longer.

The shouting was coming from all around them. Clarke, who was always startled by the least little thing, leapt up, his head spinning like a top. Gauna understood what was going on before he did:

"An attack!" he shouted.

And indeed a surprise attack was taking place. A disheveled rider passed close by them, along the top of the riverbank. He was the typical Indian warrior: spear in one hand, stone bolas whirling in the other, his naked body covered in grease, hair streaming in the wind, his face contorted in a ferocious war-cry, his mount galloping flat out under him, plunging forward without reins. The horse's features were a picture of pure terror. The two men stood paralyzed at the sight, but it was gone in a flash. Fortunately the warrior had not spotted them, but it might be very different with the next one (leaving aside the fact, unimportant as ever in the darkness, that they had nothing whatever to do with what was going on). They rushed to find shelter. As he ran, Clarke looked back and saw other attackers streaming past at the speed of imaginary blinkings of an eye. They were charging along the same path, which must have been chosen by the enemy strategist as one of the lines of attack on the camp. From their new vantage point, he and Gauna could see the upheaval going on there, where only a few moments before the Indians had been peacefully awaiting the arrival of night. The camp was a seething mass of writhing bodies: hideous-looking centaurs launched themselves on howling groups of women; men stood stock still in the center of deadly circles of stone bolas, whose dreadful whirring could be heard even above all the uproar; leaders gesticulated, hoarse from shouting orders into empty air; bodies jerked upright until they reached the height to have their throats cut; children and dogs scrambled desperately amid the horses' hooves; even the hens were trying in vain to take to the air in fizzing gaggles. And the campfires were reflected in a thousand moving dots, in the sinews of every muscle: the Indians of the camp may have been surprised without their weapons, but not without their body grease — in this at least they were equal to their attackers. A wave of Indians swept out of the camp, then swept back almost at once on horseback.

The lack of space became increasingly evident: tents were knocked down by the flailing horses like houses of cards. The top of the bank on the far side of the river was clear, and the two white men at first thought they could take refuge there. But even as they looked, it filled with a motley gang of horsemen. The bank where they had originally been sitting was now empty, but there seemed no point going back there: their troop of horses had dispersed at the start of the raid. There was no escape. The band of marauders on the far bank charged down, shouting wildly, and Clarke and Gauna were alarmed to realize that they were the target. Clarke ran like the wind back to their things, and felt among the shadowy bundles for his shotgun and a bag of bullets. As he turned again, he saw the silhouette of a savage on the point of spearing Gauna. Clarke shot him and he fell from his horse. The other Indians charged on through a gap between two ridges, heading for the tents. Gauna waited for Clarke to catch him up.

"Are you all right?"

"Never better," said the gaucho, wheezing like a duck.

"What a disaster," Clarke exclaimed, gazing at the camp of Agramante that the Indian village had become. Everywhere, bodies had become fountains of blood, which darkened the darkness. Some of the bodies had fallen on to fires, and the stench of charred flesh added another dimension of horror to the scene.

Unfortunately for them, the battle flowed back toward them. A fierce combat was going on behind them. Clarke raised his shotgun and downed two Indians. He ran with Gauna until they were protected by tents. Then they were dragged by a mob of wailing, crazy women toward the very center of the fighting. The most dangerous thing were the bullets which, as usual with the Indians, were fired off at random. More than once they felt them buzz too close to their heads for comfort, like tiny nocturnal bees. All of a sudden, the two men became separated. It seemed as if successive moments of time were all being thrown together: there were women bending over wounded Indians to give them water, while a few steps away, another Indian was climbing on to a bloodstained horse and loosening his bolas.... Clarke wondered how on earth he had started out on the outside of the camp, and finished in the center, right where the fighting was at its height. The dust raised by the charging horses had mixed with the smoke from the burning tents to create a thick, impenetrable fog. Everywhere, people trod on dead bodies. Clarke had no time to worry about anything but himself; he tried to avoid any dangerous encounter, and ran first in one direction and then another, until he was completely disoriented. Even so, to his amazement, he still found himself in the thick of the combat, but his dodging kept him out of the way of the hand-to-hand fighting, and he did not have to fire any more shots, despite often being on the point of doing so. Horribly overexpressive horseheads kept looming through the walls of dust and smoke. The Indians' warcries constantly echoed through the confusion. Suddenly a rush of people carried him away with them. They plunged through the ruins of several tents, and just as he was trying to jump over the bodies of some wounded Indians, Clarke was astonished to hear ... laughter. There was something very familiar about it, and from the mist in front of him he soon saw emerge the figure of Carlos Alzaga Prior, together with a group of young Indians of both sexes.

"Clarke, I was so worried about you!"

"Throw that cigarette away!"

The Englishman's indignation exploded like a storm within a storm. He went up to the youth, seized his arm with his left hand (he was still clutching his shotgun in the other) and shook him, all the while dragging him away from the others. Carlos had a lighted cigarette between his fingers.

"How irresponsible, how thoughtless of you!" Clarke was choking with fury, and had to shout at the top of his lungs to make himself heard.

Carlos shook himself free. He wasn't very lucid. The bleary smile did not leave his face even when it was his turn to shout:

"Leave me in peace! You can't tell me what to do!"

"Come here!" Beside himself, Clarke raised the gun as though he were about to shoot.

Then something extraordinary happened: a horse that may or may not have had a rider (they didn't see one) galloped between them. Clarke was stunned, but Carlos carried on as if nothing had happened.

"Have a puff," he said, holding the cigarette out to Clarke between his thumb and his middle finger.

"No thanks," Clarke shouted, his voice shrill with nerves. He snatched the cigarette, threw it onto the ground, and stubbed it out with the toe of his boot in a rough, vengeful way. Carlos chose to give a dismissive laugh, as if to say: "who cares, I've smoked enough anyway." Clarke was on the point of slapping his face, when something else happened that prevented him doing so: a rush of air only inches from the back of his head as a stone bola crashed by. Clarke threw himself down just in time: the second bola cleaved the air where his head had been. "I would have slapped his face with my gray matter if I hadn't ducked," he thought. For the past few minutes, his adrenalin had been pumping. He was thirsty for blood. And more than the scandalous behavior of his young companion, it was something else, something unknown that was awakening in him. He raised his eyes and the shotgun at the same time. An Indian who, with his hair streaming out and his arms waving, looked like a woman, was bending from his horse to finish him off. Clarke fired without taking aim. The bullet struck the Indian full in the belly and lifted him into the air; they saw him do a somersault and land in a sitting position, his tongue lolling out. He was dead. Carlos had already set off running; Clarke followed him.

They came to a halt in a relatively dark spot from which they could look down on most of the battle. They decided to sit on the ground, in order to offer less of a target to any stray bullet.

"It's incredible!"

"It's barbaric!"

"They're Indians from Salinas Grandes," Carlos said. "I suppose you recognized them?"

So this was their everlasting peace as the fury that had gripped him subsided. Clarke was slowly returning to his normal self.

"I don't know how I could have shot that poor unfortunate ..."

"But it was in self-defense!"

"You're right. At least we escaped."

"Don't be too sure...."

"By the way ... what happened to Gauna?"

"I saw him go by on a horse a while ago. A horse he must have stolen from a dead man."

Clarke sighed, slightly ashamed of himself and the irresponsible adolescent by his side.

"I'm sure by now he's rounding up our horses. I hope he finds Repetido, or Rosas will give me hell. Gauna's a sensible person."

"He's a pillar of strength."

"Don't mock. I need to have a serious talk with you."

"Just look at that! Have they gone mad?"

Clarke looked—not very far, because the clouds of dust added

to the darkness of the night and the way his pupils had contracted
during his dangerous foray among the fires meant that he could
see nothing beyond about twelve yards. Even so, he could make
out a line of Indians riding past at walking pace, heading for the
center of the camp, obviously on a mission of peace. Although
at first it seemed like a hallucination, when Indians from the village came to a halt and stared at the newcomers, they realized it
wasn't. The two of them also went to see what it was all about.
When the peace ambassadors reached the center of the encampment, a remarkable scene took place: another procession, just as
formal and orderly as theirs, with Coliqueo at its head, came to
greet them. Fighting was going on all around, but they were at the
center of a zone of quiet. Even the dust settled, so that the bonfires
began to throw a fantastic half-light on the meeting. The effect
was the same as Clarke had noticed earlier, that of disconnected
fragments of time being superimposed on each other, as though
war disrupted the normal chain of events. Carlos, who was an
expert at recognizing people, whispered to Clarke that some of
the chief shamans from Salinas Grandes were among the new arrivals. Apparently there were to be peace talks there and then.
The two of them pushed their way to the front row of onlookers,
from where they could hear the speeches. A Huilliche who had
crossed his eyes elaborately was the first to speak. Without dismounting, of course. With no sign of urgency, he embarked upon
a complicated explanation of the state of mind of thirty-one of
Cafulcurá's thirty-two wives. Summing up a speech which lasted
a good three-quarters of an hour, it boiled down to the following:
these desperate wives had financed a punitive expedition, which

was bitterly opposed by the ruling council, who had ordered the dispatch of a simultaneous embassy, comprising the speaker and his companions, to beg forgiveness in order to restore the peace so heedlessly put at risk, etcetera. If the two groups had not arrived at their destination at the same time, this was due to the fact that the second one was distracted by the sighting of a lone rider in the distance ... then followed a highly complicated geometric-topographical argument, incomprehensible from the outset without a diagram, but in which Clarke discovered certain similarities to ideas he himself had formulated concerning the "wanderer," whom he had no doubt was one and the same person. Coliqueo listened to all this impassively. After the speaker fell silent, there was a short pause, in which more shots and cries could be heard in the distance, then in what seemed like a prepared speech, Coliqueo declared his acceptance of their apologies. The acceptance of this acceptance would doubtless give rise to yet another speech, but Clarke was in no mood to stay and hear it. He gestured to Carlos, and they pushed their way back through the enthralled throng.

"Let's get out of here," he said to Carlos in a stage whisper.

"Do you think that's wise?"

Riders were still coming and going inside and beyond the razed village. A number of terrified cows had strayed into the camp. There were loose horses everywhere, some of them lying prostrate, but where could theirs be? Clarke was prepared to mount any of them, provided they made their escape. He cocked his gun and led the way to where they had slept. Fortunately, they did not stumble onto any lingering combat. When they

were halfway to the river, Gauna appeared, leading two horses
that were as unknown to them as the one he was riding.

"Mount up," he said.

"Did you find Repetido?" was the Englishman's first question.

"Don't worry, he was the only one I looked for."

And indeed there he was, with a faint phosphorescent glow
to him, his flanks trembling ... together with ten other ponies at
least as good as the ones they had lost. They were already loaded
with their things, hurriedly girthed, but ready to leave nonethe-
less. Gauna had wasted no time, once he had spied the chance
to get his own way and make off after the Widow. Clarke did not
have the heart to reproach him for it. The best thing for all of
them was to get away. He would make an exception, and leave
without saying goodbye. They rounded up their troop without
dismounting, and within a few seconds were fleeing across open
country. When they looked back, the encampment was a mass
of glowing smoke, crisscrossed by bullets, spears, and speeches.
They said nothing, although they could all have admitted: "this
time we escaped by the skin of our teeth"; but it was difficult to
speak at full gallop. They soon lost sight of the scene of battle.
A welcome silence greeted them. For two hours, they traveled
through the night, lit only by a pale moon. Even as they fled,
Clarke still felt time had no meaning, because he had witnessed
a drama of simultaneity that seeped in everywhere. Might they
not be fleeing before the massacre had started? If that were so,
they would soon find themselves in the thick of it, killing and
dying—though not necessarily in that order. However, the ride
cleared the cobwebs from his mind. They changed once to fresh

horses (Clarke leapt on to Repetido's familiar back) so that they could continue for another couple of hours.

The moon traced a wide arc in the sky before disappearing behind increasingly dense mists. Above and below gradually became indistinguishable in the fog. It was only when they came to a halt that they realized how invisible everything had become. To go on would be suicide, because sooner or later one of the horses would fall into a gopher hole. And above all, they ran the risk of getting lost and heading back the way they had come. That was what decided them. They carried on a short while, more from inertia than anything else, and were surprised to find that they were on the bottom slopes of a range of hills. Some natural walls forced them to change direction, and there and then, they dismounted. They were so exhausted they scarcely had the strength to lay out their gear and wrap themselves in their ponchos. It was so damp, thought Clarke, that all his bones would he aching the next day. But there was no point in lighting a fire; because it was not cold. Nor had they eaten. So what? A leaden sleep forced his eyes shut.

8: The Underground

WHEN THEY AWOKE, THE SUN MUST HAVE BEEN HIGH, even though it was still invisible behind the fog, and cast little more than a diffuse white glow in the center of a bluish-gray expanse remarkable above all for its immobility. An immobile world was one without light, even in full daytime. Clarke was awakened by Gauna repeatedly shaking his arm: and although he always prided himself on being instantly alert, this time he was sunk so deep in a mindless stupor, that he had no idea who he was, or what he was doing there. This was explained in part by what had recently happened to him, but also by what was happening to him now. They were surrounded by a number of upright figures, who loomed through the mist. There weren't very many of them, although it took Clarke some time to realize this. He looked at Gauna, who as usual merely shrugged his shoulders. Clarke had sat on his saddle without being aware of it, and now searched for his boots. While he was pulling them on, his mind began to function. First of all in the past, reviewing the dreadful events of the previous night, then in the present. Naturally enough, he surmised that the present was a consequence of the immediate past, and that the strangers were, like them, fugitives from the disaster at Coliqueo's camp. But he only had to draw closer to them to see this was not the case: there had been a kind of break in the night, and these were new people, the product of new circumstances, who were coming to greet him. Objectively, this was a relief. They were four pale little men, Indian-looking but smaller and whiter, who wore no paint or grease. They were dressed in bright colors, and seemed in fact a little overdressed for the season, wearing caps as well. Clarke bade them good-day, and they replied, without much of a smile but without being too curt either. He asked who they were, and it was only when they replied that he realized they did not speak the same language. He was momentarily perplexed. The Indian who spoke did so for perhaps three-quarters of a minute; as Clarke had not grasped his opening words, he lost all the rest as well. He turned for help toward Gauna, who was a good linguist. There he met another surprise. The gaucho had gone as white as a sheet, his eyes had turned up and a wheezing moan came from his gaping mouth. He was suffering an asthma attack, which must have been hours coming on, although in that case Clarke was surprised he had not lit a fire to burn his medicinal powders. He offered to do so for him now, but Gauna shook his head firmly and gestured as if to say: "carry on, carry on," so Clarke turned back to face the Indians.

"Do you speak Voroga?" he asked.

"Of course. We *are* Vorogas," the man who had spoken earlier replied. Clarke understood him perfectly. He suddenly realized he had understood before as well. They had said: "Good day to you, we trust we have not interrupted your sleep, but it was hard

for us to contain our curiosity, because visitors here are so rare."
Why then had he imagined he had not understood? The logical
explanation was to blame the difficulty he had felt waking up,
but on reflection an illogical explanation was probably closer to
the mark.

The ten languages in the Mapuche family, which Clarke had
begun to study a decade and a half earlier, were distinguished
from the other languages of the world by one essential feature:
they were languages that were exquisitely deferential to foreign-
ers, and not because their speakers chose to be, but because of
their very structure, at least in their spoken form. When someone learns a foreign language, he inevitably commits all kinds of
mistakes, even after lengthy study and frequent practice. Native
speakers also make mistakes, except that they are not so much er-
rors as the natural deformations that a prolonged automatic use
of a language imperceptibly produces in such a delicate structure. Both kinds of distortion occurred in Mapuche, with the
result that no one who began to speak one of their languages
sounded like a beginner. Whether anyone else understood was
another matter.

That other matter was also an interesting curiosity. Mistakes,
bad habits, the stylizations of speech, all immediately appeared
as a manifestation of art. Art may be understood in many different ways according to different cultures and ages, but these
definitions all have one thing in common: art, the thing that is
art, is that which does not demand understanding, since it is
pure action whose meaning is a question of subjective choices.
Formalities, intrinsic translations, were at the very heart of all

the Mapuche languages. For this reason they had an old proverb which contained the key to all their behavior: "Do no more than talk." Crossing their eyes, staring at the ground, were only a minor part of their meaning. The rest came from their words.

This then was all that Clarke's misunderstanding amounted to: an instant. Fleeting as are all instants, even when placed end to end as it were, it passed, and he was now in animated conversation with the group of Indians.

"Do you live nearby?"

"Just down here."

"Which leader do you follow?"

"Pillán is the name of our present monarch. If you are not in such a hurry as to make a short halt impossible, we should like to introduce you to him. We receive so few visits!"

"Pillán? I have not heard the name."

"I'm not surprised. He's only very recently taken up the position."

"Ah, yes? Did he succeed to it?"

"After a certain fashion. In reality, I am sorry to tell you that we have suffered a power struggle, a civil war one might say—if that were not too grand a term for our tiny, submerged society."

"My condolences. A civil war is still a civil war, even if it takes place within a single family."

"By an extension of its very meaning!"

"If you like."

A silence.

"Well ... would you do us the honor?"

"As far as I'm concerned, there's no problem." At this point,

Clarke thought it desirable to introduce a note of democracy. "Wait until my friend here can speak, and I'll ask his opinion."

Gauna was still gasping for breath. The Indian who had been doing the talking made a suggestion which combined the most delicate courtesy with the most calculated sadism.

"Ask him now, so he can be considering his answer. After all, he can hear."

These words struck home. Gauna rolled up his blanket and slung it on his horse's back.

"To judge by his attitude," Clarke said, lowering his voice, "I would guess that he agrees. Where are your horses?"

"Nowhere."

"Pardon?"

"We don't use horses."

"What?"

"Well, it's nothing to be so surprised at. We don't need them, you see."

"I don't understand how you can do without such a useful animal if you live on the plains."

"That's just it: we don't live on the surface."

"Gentlemen, we'll go with you."

"Leave your horses right here. Josecito—" he pointed to one of his followers "—will stay to keep an eye on them, although it's hardly necessary. For your peace of mind."

"Let's go," Clarke said. Gauna came up, his eyes still bleary.

The Indian again:

"Far be it from me to give you advice, but I'd just like to mention that it seems one of your party is still asleep."

"Mister Gauna?" said Clarke, somewhat put out at what he considered an unnecessary dig at his tracker's continuing breathing problems. "Don't worry about him. I don't think he's sleepwalking."

"Right. I beg your pardon," said the Indian.

"Are you feeling all right, Gauna?" Clarke asked him, to draw the matter to a close.

"Perfectly fine."

"Just a moment," the Indian interjected, pointing to the gaucho. "Is this Gauna?"

"Who else could he be?" Clarke answered, by now exasperated.

"What's *his* name then?"

The Englishman followed the direction of the savage's gaze, and was not a little surprised to see none other than Carlos Alzaga Prior sleeping peacefully at his feet.

"Of course, Carlos!" he exclaimed. "I'd completely forgotten him. Just imagine. If you hadn't pointed him out, I would probably have left him here. I don't know where I've put my head today." He bent down to wake the youth up, but stopped halfway. "Look how he's sleeping. The sleep of the innocent. Isn't it a shame to wake him?"

"A real shame," agreed Gauna.

Clarke shook Carlos. He pulled his boots on sulkily.

"These gentlemen," Clarke told him, "have invited us to take breakfast in their tents, which just happen to be nearby."

"They are not tents," the Indian corrected him, "but we do hope our food will be to your liking."

"Well then, let's be off."

The savages asked them to follow. They walked a short way into the whiteness, and Clarke realized that the fog was not solid, but occurred in pockets. They climbed up among the rocks, not far, but probably just enough: it seemed that at any moment they must reach the ceiling of mist, but instead it appeared to climb with them. Suddenly, without any transition, they were walking in an interior. It was obvious they had entered a cave. As they were still surrounded by mist for a while, their eyesight had time to grow accustomed to the new surroundings.

Pleased with the surprise he had given them, the Indian, after nudging the companion he was walking alongside (the third Indian was behind, next to Gauna, at whom for some unknown reason he was staring with open admiration), turned and said:

"We live in here."

"How incredible!" exclaimed Clarke.

"You can have some beer and cakes as soon as we get there."

"That's all right, I'm not particularly hungry."

"Can you see?"

"More or less."

"We'll soon have torches."

Sure enough, a little further on, where the cave became narrower and really dark, the Indian took some small torches from the wall and proceeded to light them. Each of the three Indians held one and positioned themselves alongside the visitors, to shine it down at the floor for them. The ground was of a whitish stone, and was worn quite smooth by the tread of bare feet. It soon began to tilt downward, so that they had to take more care of how they walked. They turned bends, went down rough-hewn steps,

sometimes even had to jump. Up ahead and behind them, everything was dark. Clarke had viewed the excursion as something
perfectly natural, and far from worrying him, the unexpected turn
(or rather descent) events were taking seemed to him delightful.
Part of this delight came from the cruel satisfaction of knowing
that Gauna must be furious. This reminded him of the tale the
gaucho had told him the previous day. He had to admit it was a
very solid and plausible story, but that was entirely due to the fact
that it included all (or nearly all) the details of what had happened
in reality; by the same token, there must be other stories which
did the same, even though they were completely different. Everything that happened, isolated and observed by an interpretative
judgment, or even simply by the imagination, became an element
that could then be combined with any number of others. Personal
invention was responsible for creating the overall structure, for
seeing to it that these elements formed unities. Of course, Clarke
was not going to put himself to so much trouble ... but he could
swear, a priori, that apart from Gauna's version, there must be an
endless number of other possible stories. Moreover, between one
story and another, even one that was really told and another that
remained virtual, hidden and unborn in an indolent fantasy, there
was not a gap but a continuum. And the existence of such a continuum, which at that moment appeared to Clarke as an undeni-
able truth, created a natural multiplicity, of which Gauna's story
was shown to be merely one more example. But Clarke had no
intention of telling Gauna this, because that would be to run the
risk of no longer counting on his company. To Gauna, his story
was not simply one among many, but the only one.

Even though they were going deeper and deeper into the bowels of the earth, they could still feel currents of air, and from time to time crossed chambers with lofty ceilings. Then all of a sudden a light shone ahead of them. "We're almost there," their Indian guide said. Turning to his companion who was still admiring Gauna, he told him: "Llanquén, go and tell Pillán."

"OK," Llanquén said, and scuttled off.

"Welcome to our humble abode, Gauna, Carlos, and Mister ..."

"Clarke," said the Englishman, who had not previously introduced himself

"Equimoxis, at your service."

"What an odd name."

"My mother had a priest name me: it was taken from a book found in an ox-cart wreck in the Andes many years ago. The book was called *Memoirs from Beyond the Tomb*."

"I know it. By Chateaubriand."

They had reached the end of the passageway; in front of them opened a vast chamber, made to seem all the larger for not being completely lit; the hundred or so fires that were burning produced as much effect as a match struck in a cathedral. There was no smoke, a sure sign there must be fissures in the roof of the cave which provided air. The clear, dark atmosphere, like that of a summer night, the cool temperature, the silence free even of the sounds of birds or insects, offered them a welcome that was far more eloquent than Equimoxis's words.

"An underground city!" Carlos Alzaga Prior exclaimed in astonishment. "I never thought life would be so generous as to reward me with such an amazing discovery!"

"My dear young friend," Equimoxis told him with a paternal

smile, "it's not a city since, as you can see, there isn't a single house. It's an interior-exterior. And as for discovering us, I fear you aren't the first, far from it. Only last week, to go back no further, we had a visit from one of Rosas's officers."

They had set out on a stone path—or rather, they followed a line across the stone that they would have crossed anyway, toward a group of fires clustered together more closely than the others. A small party of Indians came to greet them. The Indians were naked (they must only wear clothes to go outside); a tall, white-skinned individual with fierce features stepped forward. This was their leader, Pillán.

"It's an honor to have you with us. Which one of you suffers from asthma?"

"I do," grunted Gauna, who hated any mention of his illness.

"Come over to the big fire; my wives are expecting you. I had a special preparation made up for you, from eucalyptus seeds, that'll ease the problem in no time."

Having done his duty in this way, Pillán addressed himself formally to Clarke, squinting as he did so.

"Words fail me...."

"Think nothing of it! We were in the area, and at a loose end. ..."

"Mister ... Clarke, isn't it? Your name sounds English."

"I am English."

"And what has brought you so remarkably far from your homeland?"

"Studies, nothing more."

"Historical studies?"

"Natural history."

"Botany? Zoology?"

"The second rather than the first."

"Then I must show you the little dogs we keep. But after breakfast, if you'll do me the honor of accompanying me."

They went over to the fires. These Indians had few possessions. Little more than blankets and clothing carefully folded on the stones, and some very artistic pots, all of them out on display, nothing kept in trunks or bags. As is the case with natural and fortunate peoples, they themselves were their only riches. Except that, although for the moment they seemed relaxed and contented, they bore signs of not always having been so. Their bodies were crisscrossed with great weals, scars that had turned pink and scarlet due to the lack of sunlight. Their chieftain was the worst in this respect, his skin offering a veritable showcase of knife cuts. The raised area next to the fire where Pillán brought the Englishman and Carlos was occupied entirely by men. The women were further off: plump, attractive creatures whose aggressively indigenous features contrasted with their white, barely ocher, skins. Apart from those who were fanning the concoction designed to help Gauna's breathing—which seemed to be doing him a world of good—the other women stood idly by. Clarke surmised that the Indians liked an easy life. He could tell simply by the way they moved. Not that they moved all that much, and besides, who could tell what was going on in the more distant chambers? There must have been about two hundred Indians sitting or lying about around fires that gave off a brilliant light but little heat (which was unnecessary anyway). The atmosphere was one of a calm evening get-together after a day's hunting or traveling, a reunion that was drawing to an end as everyone considered going to sleep, the only oddity being that it was ten in the morning. They were immediately served beer and cakes; the Indians limited themselves to watching them eat. When they had finished their meal, the conversation began.

"I envy you," Clarke said impulsively, "the calm you enjoy in the ... underground."

"It's not always this way," Pillán replied. "We're a very warlike race."

"How long have you lived here?"

"For countless generations."

That was too vague to be the whole truth. But the Englishman, who out in the wilderness had become used to pursuing the truth by roundabout means, let this comment pass.

"Have you not tried directing your aggression against external enemies?"

"The thing is, we don't actually have any enemies. It would cause too many problems. For a start, we'd have to go outside." Pillán paused for a moment, then declared in a solemn tone: "As far as the vagaries of fate are concerned, we prefer to follow the line of least resistance."

Clarke inquired about their means of subsistence. These were simple in the extreme: a little mining, some aphotic grains they used for making flour, a minimum of hunting and nighttime robbery. They obtained drink by bartering the high quality coal they dug from their caves. Their arts and crafts? These were reduced to two: not to tire themselves too much, and to congratulate themselves on anything that turned out well. They practiced a fair amount of gymnastics, and were comprehensively promiscuous in their enjoyment of sex. Most unusually for Indians, they had no interest in games of chance. They played music, mostly on portable organs such as Clarke had already seen in Chile. They did so very sparingly however, as any philharmonic excess might spoil what appeared to be their favorite social pastime: sleep. Recumbent bodies were scattered throughout the cave; all conversation was in low voices, and the dogs were silent. Occasionally a muted croaking could be heard: this was their edible frog farm, Pillán explained. Carlos was struck by the sight of several Indians gliding past them at ground level without moving a muscle, as though they were on a moving belt. The chieftain invited them to go and look: it was a stream of water on which small boats circulated. He told them that several of these streams crossed the chamber, as well as some freshwater springs. The Indians thought, quite reasonably, that the rock floor of the cave must float on a huge reservoir of deep water. The temperature was the same throughout the year. Gas never leaked out, nor were there any sudden seasonal falls in pressure. They could not recall any seismic activity—if there had been any, they would have left in a flash: for them, the caves had no mythical dimension, they were merely convenient, an effective way of living.

Thoughtful, Clarke stared up at the roof. The dark recesses cast back their blind gaze.

"Do you go outside much?"

"As little as possible. Some of us, never."

One thing intrigued Clarke. He had known many tribes of America, with an incredible diversity of lifestyles, but one thing was common to them all: their constant and vital relationship with the stars. He could not imagine a primitive culture doing without them. He said as much to Pillán, who paused for a moment's respectful consideration before giving his reply.

"Well now, Mister Clarke. There are two aspects to that question. The first is the relation we have to the truth, or more precisely to meaning. The reason you consider us primitive (no, don't worry, I didn't take it amiss) can only come from the fact that, unlike you, we do not have a God, or a monotheist system, to provide a general framework of meaning for us. We Indians 'still' find ourselves at the stage of potentiality: a sign is not guaranteed by reference to a meaning, but by its position within a specific framework. It is also the case, and I think this is the key to your puzzlement, that since the stars are pure perception, are purely visible without any possibility of becoming tangible, they need constantly to demonstrate their reality, if possible every night. That is the paradox of an imaginary system which needs to be real in order to generate all its images.

"Now, look at our own black, immutable sky, our rock. It's exactly the same. Points of darkness replace points of light. It is we who are the stars, the living memory of our lives, lived without days or nights on the margins of time. Meaning continues to exist however, whether or not there is a God or a sky. It may be that to go on believing in ourselves demands an extra dose of energy from us, but we do not regret it. We dream a lot, because we sleep so much."

He paused before continuing:

"As for the other aspect of the question, which as I understand it concerns happiness, I can offer you no such clear-cut reasons. Nature is man's happy passion, and the stars confirm that. That is all they do: such is their function. But here beneath the earth we are the most passionate of people, because we set no store by the conservation of life. It could be said that the sickness is the cure. Indifference contains within it one supreme value: the abandonment of everything, the infinite virtuality of the instant."

Gauna yawned ostentatiously.

"Excuse me for interrupting," Clarke said, "but you wouldn't know if a lady by the name of Rondeau's Widow has passed by here recently, would you?"

"Yes. That good-for-nothing … she was here a few days ago, asking us to lend her a young woman."

"Did you?"

"Not on your life. Do you take us for traders in human flesh? We asked her why she didn't turn to her relative Coliqueo, who is staying near here…."

"And what did she say to that?"

"That Coliqueo had suffered a devastating surprise attack and was in no state to conduct any kind of transaction."

"She lied to you …"

"I suspected that from the start."

"… because it was only last night that Coliqueo was attacked."

"I hope he was killed."

"When we left he was alive, trying to renegotiate everlasting peace."

"What a shame. I suspect that all this activity is because a certain diamond is due to change hands …"

Although Gauna did not move a muscle, his aroused wariness struck Clarke like a hammer blow. Pillán went on:

"… a diamond that belongs to us: the Legibrerian Hare."

"You know what it is?"

The chieftain gave a fleeting smile.

"Yes and no. Of course, the stone does not exist. Yet even so, it belongs to us."

"I don't understand. Could you explain?"

"It's quite simple. Doubtless in the distant past a tiny diamond was discovered in our carboniferous deposits—or perhaps not even that was necessary. What is beyond doubt is that one of our legendary tales concerns a hare that was fleeing across the plains to escape from a crazy horse that wanted to eat it, and it fell down a hole. Down and down it fell through the darkness, and its eyes puffed up more and more, while it saw scenes that are an important part of the story, but which I won't bore you with now; by the time it reached the bottom, it had been transformed into a diamond. A naturalist explanation of the story would involve the transformation of carbon into diamond as a result of pressure ... though now that I come to think of it, it's a good example of what I was saying earlier: the star in the bottom of the pit, the transmutation of the opaque into the transparent, the chase of words after meaning ... I don't know if that's made it any clearer for you."

The three men's stay in the cavern went on for an indeterminate length of time; it could have been a day, or a week. They ate, bathed in the placid waters of the springs, until finally they felt the need to depart. As they were taking their leave, Carlos asked the chief if he had ever heard of such and such a girl, pregnant, with a pretty face, who went by the name of Yñuy. No. They had never heard the name, or known of anyone by that description.

By contrast, they did know of someone else the three of them had described, and as luck would have it the men who were to take them back to the open air, led by the very outgoing Equimoxis, were on a mission to find out more about him: this was none other than the famous Wanderer.

"Who is he?" Clarke asked with interest.

"I wish we knew. He appeared a few days ago, and we're very worried by him."

This was surprising. How had they of all people become aware of this always distant and fleeting presence? And how could he affect them? Both questions, Pillán explained, could be answered together. Clarke reflected that it was only when guests had their hand on the doorknob to leave that the conversation became really interesting.

"The underground world," said Pillán, "is not strictly speaking autonomous (nothing is); nor have we ever lived under the illusion that it was. It is a temporary 'parallel,' whose worth changes daily according to its face value. That is why we are so alert to the changing circumstances outside, because to a certain extent we are those circumstances. And if it is true that news flies, it is no less true that it also sinks to the depths at an incredible speed. The 'surprise guest' is always a latent possibility. This strange Wanderer has come to fill a gap created not by the circumstances but by the system itself. I can't say that we were expecting him, but nor can I say the opposite. He would appear to represent a complex of speeds, distances, and directions inherent to the surface world, a world upon which, as I'm sure you understand, our depths depend. Please don't see us as excessively intellectual—

far from it!—just because we are so interested in what might seem a tiny, distant variation in the logical ordering of the plains; it's vital for us."

"Is there some relation," Clarke wanted to know, "between him and that ... gem?"

"As I think I told you, the gem does not exist. Our brothers in the parallel world are chasing, bedazzled, after a fiction."

"What do you believe then is really at stake in all this?"

"Don't get me started on philosophical explanations again ..."

"You're right, we'll say goodbye then. Farewell."

"Farewell."

"And thank you for your hospitality."

"Don't mention it. But we didn't even get to talk of speleology!"

Clarke burst out laughing. Carlos asked him:

"What's that?"

"I'll explain to you later. Farewell, farewell."

Equimoxis led the way up to the cave mouth. He was with another ten or so Indians, all of them warmly dressed. As they were leaving the great chamber, the three of them turned to give it one last look: as ever, it was filled with a calm grandeur. They started on the upward path. This time of course, it cost them more effort than when they had come down; before they had even reached halfway, the group was like a chamber orchestra of panting. They halted to get their breath back. Clarke asked Equimoxis who they were going to consult for information about the Wanderer. Equimoxis told him of some mint-growers who were their usual informants. They were normally to be found near the cave entrance, which made things all the easier for the Indians.

"In that case," said Clarke, "we won't be traveling together."

They renewed their climb, and eventually an intense light shone above their heads. It was daylight. They took the final stretch very slowly, so that their eyes could readjust. The light seemed to fade while they were doing so, and once they were outside they discovered that this was in fact what had happened, because it was late afternoon. By the time they were out in the open, the sun had set. Even so, the luminosity made them hesitate. Their horses were nearby: the Indian called Josecito said he had kept them in the shade and well-watered. As they were no longer accustomed to them, their horses seemed like huge, clumsy beasts. But they were soon in the saddle and ready to take possession of the pampa once more, as it stretched out beneath their feet—or rather, those of their mounts—in the gentle blues and pinks of the sunset. The Indians looked tiny. After the customary bowing and scraping, they said farewell. Then they were on the move again. Within a matter of seconds they had resumed their usual positions, with Gauna a hundred yards up ahead, Clarke and his young friend conversing as they rode side by side, and the troop of horses bringing up the rear. The pace was brisk.

"What did you make of them?" Clarke asked Carlos.

"I thought they were delightful. So simple, so open ... it's incredible that they should kill each other six times a year. Lucky we were there during a truce."

"Who knows whether that was true?"

"They didn't get all those scars from embroidering."

"Are my eyes deceiving me, or is Gauna getting further and further ahead?"

"He's in a hurry."

"He thinks he has reason to be. I'll tell you later the complicated nonsense he's got into his head. He was explaining it to me while we were with Coliqueo."

"Is it something to do with the Widow?"

"Correct: he claims she is his half-sister, and is planning to steal a family diamond from him ..."

"Ah, this time he really has gone crazy!"

"Let's change the subject. He might be listening to us, and his hearing's as sharp as a bat's."

"By the way, where are we heading?"

"After the Widow; where else?"

"Well, after all it could be an interesting experience. We've had forty already ..."

"And as the Widow is only forty-one ..."

They laughed like schoolchildren. The sky was turning a deep blue, the land was dark. A partridge gave Clarke a shock, and this brought fresh laughter from Carlos. The stars came out, like faithful old friends. They reached a spot where a skunk had fought an armadillo, and galloped on until they got away from the ghastly smell.

9: The Offensive-Defensive Alliance

AN INDIAN WAILING IN THE DARKNESS FILLED EVERY-
thing, although there was nothing to fill, simply a space stretching out in all directions. The sound was like thunder, but in reverse: it was high-pitched like a hysterical woman's, with throaty
reverberations, a real cry, as if trying to say something. The many
animals of the plain froze with terror when they heard it. They
were already nervous from the storm, which had crept up on
them as they waited for night; so that the darkness and the storm
became tangled up together. The shadows had closed in, heavy
with black clouds; the opaque, the voluminous, the quasi-sculp-
tural vied with each other in the sky; a strong wind that rose
as the air pressure dropped suddenly, only added to the effect.
Above the silence of the wind hung the fear of not being able to
see a thing. The constellations did not disappear. Reality did.
And then, these lamentations.

The three friends, who were about to go to sleep after their
dinner and tea, were also petrified. They were worried by the
storm, which threatened to flood them out: they could not believe their bad luck that this should happen on the very night
they had emerged into the open after their stay underground.

The weeping did not so much terrify them as take them aback. The Indians were always so reserved in these matters. And the sound was such a screech, so effeminate!

"What's that?" Carlos Alzaga Prior asked, casting uneasy glances into the shadows.

The other two did not reply. The sounds went on at a distance they found hard to judge. The fire they had lit blinded them to anything beyond it.

Then Clarke and Gauna both spoke at once, their words immediately revealing their different attitudes toward the world.

"Could it be someone wounded?" the Englishman said.

"Could it be a queer?" the gaucho said.

Both their suppositions were wide of the mark. The "ayayay" went on, seeming as though at any moment it might offer some explanation of itself. The howling wind forced its way into their perception, just as thunder began to roll slowly all around them. Everything became sinister. They could not, or would not, believe it, but the stranger was drawing closer. He must have seen the fire. The tricks the wind was playing had made it hard to tell which direction he was coming from, and they still did so. All at once there was a flash of lightning, followed by an incredible sizzling sound, and a boom that shook the earth. The lightning streak stood out quite clearly: a snaking thread that pricked the horizon. These dry rays were the worst thing imaginable. Gauna got up to cover the horses, whose manes had stood on end with electricity. The other two helped him without a word. When they touched the animals, they could feel small shocks run through their own bodies. They needed to think of covering themselves too, because huge drops of rain had started to shoot down like bullets. Still the wailing continued. Now, when they listened to it again after recovering from their shock, it sounded theatrical, unconvincing, unworthy of the moment, too private to be able to compete with a far greater fury. There was something of a call for help about it. Although none of them said as much, they felt it was a shame the lightning had not struck at what must have been a wide open mouth. Their fire began to die out, pulled by the wind into long, flickering tongues of flame. They sat without moving, waiting for something to define itself before they went to sleep. There was a rapid series of lightning flashes, and Gauna said he had spotted the stranger. He pointed out into the gloom. Then everything went dark again, and the first torrent of rain began to fall. Another flash of lightning, with another ray streaking downward, a multiple thunderclap that rolled on and on, and the others saw him too: a horseman who seemed motionless in the white glare, but then as darkness swallowed him up again, was definitely coming toward them. After one particularly loud howl, he subsided into sobs, a kind of shrill murmur. He was almost upon them. Clarke felt irritated: he was in no mood to talk, to ask questions, nothing. The rain was already soaking his head. The stranger was right next to them now, and by the dying glow of the sputtering fire they were astounded to see that it was none other than Mallén, Cafulcurá's favorite shaman.

"Mallén, what are you doing here?" Clarke exclaimed, without even thinking to help him from his horse.

A faint polite squint flitted behind the Indian's tears as he dismounted.

"Do you think we could heat some water to make him tea?" Clarke asked Gauna.

"That'd be rather difficult," the gaucho deigned to reply, staring down sarcastically at the puddle where their fire had been.

"Don't worry about me," Mallén said, choking back his tears, "I've already eaten. All I want to do now is die."

So Clarke would have to talk anyway. Around them the darkness was complete, but the frequent flashes of lightning allowed them occasionally to glimpse each other's faces. The Indian sat down, and Clarke went over until he was almost touching him, since otherwise the noise of the pouring rain would have made it impossible for them to hear each other. After throwing a blanket across Mallén's sunken shoulders, Carlos did the same. Gauna on the other hand wished them all goodnight, wrapped himself in his poncho and settled down to sleep. This lack of curiosity was entirely typical of him.

"My surprise," Clarke began, "comes not only at seeing you so far from Salinas Grandes, but at the state you're in. I take it for granted there's bad news: but what exactly?"

"Ah, Mister Clarke, a great misfortune has befallen our people, the worst misfortune. The worst, the worst."

"Have they all killed each other?"

"Don't worry, it will soon come to that." A loud sigh. Although usually so talkative, Mallén now seemed unwilling to speak. His dejection sealed his lips. They had to drag the words out of him. The external circumstances (the soaking they were getting, the claps of thunder, the cold) were partly responsible, but Mallén himself was more to blame, and eventually Clarke became impatient.

"Come on man, spit it out. If you don't, how can I find out what's wrong? Start from when we left. What happened then?"

"Nothing."

"How interesting. Didn't your chieftain reappear?"

"What d'you think?"

"Nor Namuncurá?"

"No sign at all. Not even Alvarito came back."

"We were in Coliqueo's camp when ..."

"Ah, yes. That too. Unfortunately Juana Pitiley also vanished, and she's the only one with enough authority to prevent that kind of rashness."

"So then you're more or less leaderless."

"Aha."

"Did you agree to a truce with Coliqueo at least?"

"Yes, but that treacherous rat is already preparing to break his word."

"How do you know?"

"What else would he do? All he has to do is think: 'So then they're more or less leaderless.' ..."

He imitated Clarke's accent perfectly, but the Englishman decided not to take offense.

"I can't believe it."

"He's rounding up all the warriors he can lay hands on."

"Well, at any rate you can make a stand against him, and successfully, I'm sure."

"What with? Farts?"

This vulgarity was so unusual in the polite shaman that it gave Clarke pause for thought. How fragile the Mapuche make-up must be, to disintegrate into such unpleasantness at the first obstacle!

"But I suppose you're also recruiting your friends. Cafulcurá's network of alliances can't break down just because he has temporarily disappeared."

Mallén gave another deep sigh, swallowing a mouthful of rain in the process, and made a visible effort to go on speaking:

"Yes, that was our idea. That was the reason for my journey, and I'm not the only one who set out. But everywhere it seems misfortunes have been leaping out at me like hares, so how could I not be depressed? My son, who was accompanying me, turned back with the excuse that he had other business to attend to, all my string of horses except this one met with accidents, and to top it all, I lost my knife and bolas somewhere and can't find them."

However hard he tried, Carlos could not contain his laughter.

"Go on, laugh," said Mallén. "But it is sad. Another time, I might have laughed as well. This afternoon, when I saw it was going to rain, I began to seriously ask myself: 'What for? What am I doing all this for? What am I living for?'"

He could not go on. Clarke snorted nervously. He could understand the shaman's reasons: he himself always found complications unnecessary, and thought simplicity should always prevail in life: otherwise, it really was not worth living. But at the same time, he was astonished at the shallowness of this man who quite possibly held the future of an empire in his hands, but who could allow such trivial external circumstances as a rainstorm to weaken his resolve. It was a truly breathtaking lack of responsibility. He tried to tell him as much without hurting his feelings. Of course, Mallén did not even want to listen. And since the storm was getting ever stronger, and the chattering of their teeth was becoming unbearable, they left the rest of their discussion for the light of day, rolled themselves in whatever ponchos they could find, and shut their eyes to try to sleep.

In spite of the wet, they managed to do so, and for more than a few hours. The next morning was still cloudy, with occasional drizzle, but they succeeded in lighting a fire thanks to a handful of the excellent coal the chief of the underground world had given them, roasted two chickens Mallén had brought, and made some tea, so that when they returned to the subject they were different men. Even the shaman, perhaps out of embarrassment, seemed more reasonable.

"Where were you headed," Clarke asked him, "before your ... depression?"

"To Colqán's camp."

"To seek reinforcements, I suppose."

"To activate the offensive-defensive alliance we have with him, which is something different."

"That's the way to talk!"

"But they could just as well give me a kick up the backside."

"Don't let yourself give in to negative thoughts again. Why would they do that? Isn't it in their interests as well to fight against Coliqueo?"

"How should I know! They may have made a separate peace with him."

"That's taking pessimism too far. We'll go with you to see Colqán. You sent emissaries to your other allies as well, didn't you?"

Mallén's explanations took on a technical slant. Given the complicated nature of the Mapuche confederation's politics, it could scarcely be otherwise. Although Carlos lost interest (Gauna had never had any), Clarke himself became more and more identified with the problem. Even the shaman roused himself, and became his old self. They had left the metaphysics of simplicity they had touched on the previous night far behind, but the Englishman found he did not regret it. Being based on a semblance of psychology (everyone not only admitted this, but took it as their starting point) the complexities of politics were resolved in a second process of simplification, this time a childish one.

When the rain came on heavily again, they set off. Before they did so, Gauna took Clarke to one side: he wasn't thinking of getting mixed up in this idiotic conflict, was he? That wasn't why they were there.

"And why are we here, Mister Gauna, if you would be so kind as to tell me?"

His Englishness came effortlessly to the fore. The gaucho did not insist. His story was falling to pieces: what was real was war, and his diamantine fantasies were relegated to the limbo they should never have left. As for the question of committing himself; Clarke felt as light as the breeze. He could take part in a

war as easily as he might play a game of whist. He was aware
that Coliqueo would do his utmost to enlist his white allies in
the campaign against the Huilliches. But to the white man, an
Indian was always an Indian, and deep down they did not care
who won. He did not care much either, but this only fueled his
enthusiasm: this opportunity to closely observe a war between
abstract peoples was too good to miss. And anyway, it made him
feel good, and that was enough for him.

So he mounted Repetido, got into step with Mallén's horse,
and the two of them rode off together, talking the whole while
about numbers, positions, distances, forces, deterrents and so
on. Feeling himself left out, Carlos showed his displeasure by
riding ahead to join Gauna.

They had hardly gone four or five leagues when they were surprised to find they had reached their destination.

About a thousand warriors had camped by a creek, making
shelters under the tree branches until the rain eased off. Mallén
recognized who it was from afar.

"They're Manful's men," he said. Manful was another of the
allies sought out by emissaries who had obviously proved more
effective than him. "Mister Clarke, before we arrive, I'd like to
ask a great favor of you."

Clarke knew what he meant: that he should not mention Mallén's moment of weakness. He reassured him politely in a roundabout way. A quarter of an hour later, they were sitting opposite
Manful himself; sheltered by oilskins and with the warmth of a
fire, discussing strategies as if they had never done anything else.
Manful was keen to fight; he had brought a large supply of cows

and gallons of liquor, which his troops were busy consuming as though the world might come to an end at any minute. He had also done something else, which he begged Mallén to forgive him for: he had sent a delegation to quickly inform Colqán of what was happening, so all they had to do was to wait for him.

"Yes," said Clarke, "as we were arriving we saw a small group of riders heading out. I suppose that was them."

"No," Mallén replied, staring after them. "Colqán lives in another direction, and my men left last night. The ones you saw, and who can still be seen—can you make them out?—are nothing to do with us."

They all looked: the group, made up of about twenty riders, was a dark stain on the rainswept horizon. The chieftain's next words took them by surprise:

"That's Rondeau's Widow."

Their eyes immediately became telescopes, though without the lenses; that is, they could not see any further or more clearly, but they did focus more closely: Gauna for his own reasons, and Clarke without knowing exactly why—from contagion, he supposed. Or for no reason at all. What he saw was an incomparable vision. That woman, whose existence he had been unaware of only a month before, had in such a short time become an integral part of his imagination. What if she really were Gauna's half-sister? He glanced sideways at the gaucho: he sat there in suspense, holding his breath, his eyes starting from his head. There was no hatred in his look, not even greed, but simply a thirst for adventure and knowledge which gave him a noble look despite his ugliness. Clarke had never perceived so clearly the need for the novelesque in life: it was the only truly useful thing, precisely because it lent weight to the uselessness of everything. Clarke turned to Manful:

"Why did you let her go just like that? Isn't she a Voroga?"

Mallén wanted to say something, but the chieftain got in before him:

"We are Vorogas as well."

"I'm sorry, I didn't know."

"Our loyalties don't follow strictly ethnic lines. There are a lot of crossovers. Anyway, she isn't strictly speaking a Voroga, and she's a sworn enemy of Coliqueo's."

"Where is she going?"

"She promised to join us in a few days, when she has assembled her subjects, who at the moment are all scattered."

This reassured Gauna.

"Now to our own business," Clarke said, by this time completely enthused by the preparations for war. A lovely rainbow was painted on the sky, even though it was still raining and there was no sign of the sun. They unfolded their maps.

10: Preparing for War

FROM THAT MOMENT ON, EVENTS GAINED MOMENTUM. The allies soon made their appearance. They all began to exist in a kind of perpetual symmetry, with emissaries coming and going the whole time. It was what the Indians most enjoyed, but only when they were about to go to war. In fact, it could almost be said that they used war as an excuse for them to find out instantly where the others were, what they were proposing, what direction they were heading in, at what speed, and so on. Not because they were really interested. The curious thing was that all these inquiries canceled themselves out as soon as they were embarked upon: by calculating the distances, they abolished them; by emphasizing the relative dispositions for movement as lines in a past crashing into the present, they put them all on the same plane of events, that of the flat pampas. They were not concerned whether something was near or far: an Indian would leap on to his horse to ride one league or a hundred. And they rode quickly, there was no doubt about that. At first Clarke thought they were pretending, not so much to deceive him as just for fun: from where they were to Salinas Grandes it must have been at least three hundred miles: and from one day to the next, a messenger traveled there and back, covering a distance that normally took two weeks. Yet they really did it: thanks to an ingenious system enabling the riders to snatch refreshment, and their mounts to rest and recuperate ... and above all, thanks to their knowledge of certain hills and viewpoints. What they succeeded in neutralizing in this way was precisely what they knew as if it were part of their own flesh and blood. Except that these Indians, in other words all Indians, did not seem to be made of flesh and blood but rather to be small, frantic machines. The sum of their passions unleashed or added together came to nothing, was simply a mechanical operation. Clarke found himself astonished at this paradox: inhuman as he was, he had thought when he first glimpsed the indigenous ways that he was approaching the truly human; but the more he became acquainted with them, the more he realized they were exactly the same as him. It was true that they could love, but had not he himself been in love? Although they did not so much resemble his past as an echo of it in the present. It was only now in the tumult of imminent combat that their starkest truth was revealed: a desire to leave and a reality of desire, a distancing by means of which the real both showed itself and at the same time vanished. The news from Salinas Grandes was reassuring: the break-up had been avoided, and some five thousand warriors were ready to leave at any moment, as soon as they knew when and in which direction. The creek where the three friends were camped, and which Carlos Alzaga Prior had baptized the Rainy One, became the nerve center for collecting and dispatching information. Two or three days were spent in this, during which time it never once stopped raining or drizzling. Truly this was a different landscape. Water everywhere, and everything gray; it was hard to recognize the pampa. Their situation had changed as well. Colqán arrived with his splendid warriors; two more chieftains also appeared, so that the numbers in the camp swelled, making it seem like one long wild party. They ate, drank, sent and received messages all day and night, as if they were in a transparent telegrapher's cabin. Spying was also commonplace: everyone was a spy, and it was impossible to tell if information came from allies or from their enemies. Coliqueo seemed to be fully committed as leader of the revolt. Clarke began to suspect that there were chieftains who were in contact with both sides; he had no concrete reasons for thinking so, but it occurred to him that nothing could have been easier, since it was nothing more than a matter of words shouted in the distance; without being cynical, he himself would have felt a natural impulse to keep in with everyone. Even among the leadership there was a sense of ambiguity. For example, they made as if they did not take Coliqueo seriously, laughed at him, saw him as the palest of phantoms of a true threat. But they had no choice. Were it not for the fact that Cafulcurá's disappearance was the cause of all this, it could have been seen as the reason for their uncertainty. Now he had disappeared, it was as if the opposing forces were inevitably drawn toward an empty zone.

The time flew by. The rain, the poring over maps, the consulting with emissaries all served to fill an improbable few days of inactivity. Gauna was pursuing his own aims (but the Widow did not appear), Carlos discovered countless amusements among the nations who were thus thrown together and having a wild time of it in the rain (though there was not a word about his Yñuy), and Clarke did not budge from the war council, soon becoming their chief adviser. He was irritated by the irrationality that governed the savages, but he had seen worse, and as long as they were not fighting for real, there was no serious harm done. He had only a slight problem with one of the chieftains, a short, almost dwarf-ish Indian by the name of Maciel, and that was over something extraordinarily silly. It so happened that they regularly held their meetings beneath a rectangular covering supported on four posts. The rain collected in the center of this awning, and they tipped the water out whenever it threatened to spill over them. They did not have to do this very often, as a fire lit directly under the bulge evaporated most of the water. This was a ridiculous system, but the Indians preferred it to the normal one of having a slop-ing cover, which they said would mean that water was constantly dripping off one end and splashing them. Once, when Clarke got up to ease the stiffness out of his legs after several hours of sitting down, he stood up so hastily that he bumped into the roof, which at that moment was heavy with water. His action caused a great stream of it to cascade down one side, so that a freezing jet of wa-ter struck Maciel full in the back. Since the savage was in a com-plete daydream at the time, the sudden soaking made him cry out in shock. He wanted to cut Clarke's throat on the spot, and it was all the others could do to calm him down. After that, as is so often the case, the two men became the closest of friends. As well as be-ing irascible, this dwarf was a habitual drunkard, and his drunken fantasies focused with a maniacal inevitability on Clarke, who he said reminded him of his father.

One other thing disturbed the Englishman, and that was the readiness with which the Indians executed spies. They went too far. Even the slightest suspicion led to yet another throat-slitting. The last straw was when they summarily sentenced to death a poor Indian caught some distance from the camp carrying nothing more suspicious than a sack of dahlia bulbs. Clarke made it his personal responsibility to get him pardoned. It was pretty obvious that the fellow was no spy or anything of the kind. But the savages around the leaders' fire insisted on cutting his throat. Although their reasons for doing so were nonexistent, when challenged they invented some. One of them came up with the idea that the bulbs were a coded message based on how many of them there were, their size, and even the bits of dirt they had on them (he could not prove any of this, because both bag and contents had been stolen). Another chief suggested it might be a delayed-action message: when the dahlias bloomed, the enemy might read its meaning in their colors. Clarke replied that was the most absurd idea he had ever heard. It made no difference. He fell back on an argument which he considered of central importance: saving a life with a view to the future. The Indians laughed wholeheartedly at this. They told him it was like prohibiting an Englishman from taking tea in order to save the parliamentary system. The argument was complicated still further by a spurious discussion as to whether it was more correct to use the word "bulb" (in Mapuche) or "tuber," which was more graphic. However ridiculous it might seem, they spent three hours of byzantine discussion going over and over this point. In the end, they cut the poor unfortunate's throat.

"Are you happy now, are you satisfied?" Clarke asked them angrily.

Yes. They were delighted. They even had the gall to add: "We discovered something interesting: bulb smuggling carries the death penalty."

At this, they all started to laugh, even Maciel, who until then had been the only one to take Clarke's side, not because he was convinced but rather out of a fantasy of friendship. Curiously, Clarke quickly got over the incident; at other times in his life he would have left, slamming the door behind him. There might have been several reasons for him not doing so on this occasion, but perhaps the main one was that there was no door to slam, nor indeed any "outside" for him to exit to. This made a great difference. To a large extent, it was impossible to blame the Indians. Not because they were innocent or stupid, but simply due to this lack of an inside or outside for his not inconsiderable intelligence to latch onto.

Due to the urgency of the situation and the prestige he enjoyed as a shaman and close friend of Cafulcurá, Mallén was the natural focal point for all the deliberations. These went on endlessly, largely because there was nothing else to do. But Mallén pushed Clarke to the fore with a constant stream of requests for advice. The Englishman adapted his counsel to what the Indians considered logical, but as he himself had a quite different logic, and as their pampa way of arguing was for him simply play-acting, something in him was plainly still *au dessus de la mêlée*, was ready, even if only in theory, to change opinion in an instant, to switch sides without the slightest reason; and this was precisely what the Indians most respected. Simultaneity brought the collapse of necessity. It was as though the narrative were being erased. All links between events were blown away. With the light of reason dimmed, all kinds of causal shifts took place, and they seemed to concentrate on one man, who was Clarke. An aura surrounded him. So much so that when after four days of waiting on the banks of the Rainy One the time was ripe for them to unite all their forces to crush Coliqueo, thanks to an almost silent decision, which seemed so natural there was no need to vote on it, the Englishman was invested with the rank and responsibilities of Commander-in-Chief of the allied armies of the Huilliche-Tehuelche confederation.

11: The War of the Hare

THE ENTIRE WAR LASTED NO MORE THAN A WEEK, AND ended with a sweeping victory for the Huilliches. Yet another triumph in the career of the legendary Cafulcurá, this time undeserved, one that fell into his lap gratuitously, but proof of his genius anyway: he had after all been the motive, the reason, the excuse for the war, and everyone knows that in war the be-all and end-all of strategy is to become invisible. According to rough estimates, subject of course to immense variations, one hundred thousand warriors took part in the struggle. Nobody even thought of counting the dead, but there must have been a great many of them, as the whole point of the war was to kill each other. From start to finish, the weather was atrocious, truly English: rain, fog, not so much as a glimpse of the sun, cold winds which heralded or mimicked winter in the midst of autumn. It seemed as though everyone was in a hurry to get the whole thing over with, just so that the weather could return to normal. Haste became the chief characteristic of what came to be known in the collective memory as the War of the Hare. The reason for the name was soon lost in more or less bewildered suppositions by everyone except Clarke, for whom it had a very precise meaning:

he in turn was dumbfounded as to how this meaning had somehow transferred itself from his subjective consciousness to a
general acceptance. In fact, this was the least of the mysteries
that went unanswered. Clarke got used to this being the case.
He came to think he was up against the apotheosis of the simultaneity of nonsense. He was the center and driving force of everything that happened, but since the outcome inevitably took
him by surprise, he ended up washing his hands of it all. He gave
in to the tumult of the instant so naturally that it seemed he had
been doing so throughout his life. From the outset, he rejected
the classic position of the general who hovers high above the
entire battlefield: he was no eagle, and anyway the pampa, with
its complete lack of topographical features, did not lend itself
to such a perspective. In itself it was pure terrain, a geometry:
it would have been superfluous to deliberately treat it as such.
Indeed, it would have been counterproductive, a waste. The
armies maneuvered in a space whose gradients they themselves
produced and instantly inverted. Everything was a question of
creating lines, as quickly as possible; lines of arrival and depar-
ture, which magically intersected each other at every point rather
than at any especially privileged one. It was like having to deal
with the most eternal aspect of war, as a natural epiphenomenon
of thought; to hasten life until it merged with death, and to keep
this action concealed from the adversary. The key was to imagine the grandeur of destiny infinitely compressed until it was the
size and shape of a rock crystal; the large and the small, the distant and the near, necessity and freedom. Quite how Clarke succeeded in doing this, to see clearly where anybody else would

have got lost a thousand times, could only be called a miracle. But not for him. He constructed his own system, adhered to the lines, the horizontals and verticals, to the poetry of destiny, and with cheerful insistence let things happen.

The first issue was the deployment of troops. Since no one wanted to take the initiative, Clarke called a war council. The different armies were drawn up a certain distance away. For them to deploy, it was necessary to actually move, rather than rely on the customary toing-and-froing of messages. Clarke's colleagues on the war council did not like this idea: in their view, it was tempting fate for bodies, the physical matter of human beings, to take the place of immaterial messages. They were afraid of seeming ridiculous. The Englishman would hear nothing of this, and so of course they yielded to him. One of their good qualities was that once they decided on something, or had it decided for them, they launched into instant, tumultuous action. So it was that in the twinkling of an eye the huge mass of some ten thousand Indians and an equal number of cattle got on the move. And at a gallop. The rain also helped drive them on. There was something slippery about the whole affair: no one could avoid tumbling into it. They went too far in their use of grease, which helped keep off the wet. It was amazing how much fat they could get out of even the leanest cow they slaughtered. They stored it, with a touch of unconscious humor, in big tins of English tea: every Indian had one to keep his supply in. Adept at practical matters, it took them only two minutes and two hands to renew their covering from head to toe. Then they shone like the outside of a window on a rainy afternoon. They invited the white men to do the same for practical reasons. Carlos Alzaga Prior had no qualms about stripping off and smearing himself all over. Clarke flatly refused at first, but the sensation of his wet, heavy clothing on his body the whole time, and the sight on the second day of Gauna anointed and glistening like a savage, finally persuaded him to try. It suited him. With his dark coloring, his black hair that had grown out of all recognition during the expedition, and his stocky build, he looked like any other Indian once he was smothered in grease and sat naked on his horse. He even rather liked the idea: it lent an air of carnival or masked ball to the whole affair; like every commander-in-chief, he was keen to make things seem a little less serious than they were, just in case. He borrowed the grease, and kept his clothing folded and dry in his own tea chest, ready to resume his identity as an English naturalist at any moment. Carlos even began to take lessons in how to throw bolas, the Huilliches' main weapon.

Their first march took them to the spot where Coliqueo's seasonal camp had been pitched. Coliqueo's men were no longer there (a fact which the allies already knew: according to their information, his army had withdrawn some fifty leagues to the north) but they soon ran into a large raiding party which was hastening to cut off their advance. The first battle was fought under a blanket of dense white clouds and drizzle. The combat itself lasted barely three or four minutes. There were no more than a thousand enemy troops, but in the general confusion their own superior numbers seemed unimportant. The two forces became completely entangled: as soon as they saw each other on their respective horizons, they charged straight at one another.

Both sides went clean through the enemy lines, and then scattered in every direction, fleeing but also fighting, caught up in extravagant chases that eventually formed one huge circle. The combat as such was over. The allies went to round up the cattle that had been scared off, then lit fires for dinner. A short while later, the Vorogas came to carry off their dead. The Huilliches buried their own in funeral ceremonies that same night. They committed the atrocity of skinning live horses to wrap the dead bodies in. Clarke was sure he would go on hearing the cries of those poor animals until Judgment Day. Everyone got stupendously drunk. The chiefs and the Englishman spent the night issuing and receiving messages. As baptisms of fire go, it had been passable. Gauna had stayed neutral, Carlos was unhurt and full of himself. Clarke had fired barely a dozen shots.

From that point on, Clarke began to understand something which reassured him completely with regard to simultaneity: it was subordinate to the narrative. It was this which gave it a structure, a perspective, made it comprehensible, and at the same time removed the terror of the moment from it. It confirmed the fact that it was unrepeatable, but made this acceptable. Deep down, it meant always contributing to the narrative, which became one long repetition. Although it seemed as if the Indians were caught up in the overwhelming present, they in fact relied on the goodwill of a narrator for their activity to exist in reality. The spectacle of the ducks convinced Clarke he was right. In order to see them, the idea had first to take shape in space, and this suddenly led the whole army to travel an incredible distance, without greatly changing the thoughtful calm that the movement emerged from.

This was the Great Sine Curve of the Mapuche armies, a line that would have exploded the maps if anyone had tried to trace it. In his youth, Clarke had been an enthusiastic student of the campaigns led by Charles XII of Sweden, Frederick the Great of Prussia, and of course Napoleon, which he knew by heart. He attempted to put what he had learned into practice, knowing full well that things would turn out differently on the pampas. And so it proved. Not even ten Europes laid side by side would have been sufficient to contain the Great Sine Curve. It was a movement that embraced all other movements, past and future. Without even catching sight of the enemy, they struck terror into them, they surrounded them a thousand times, they cut off all their lines of retreat, even ones they would never have dreamt of using. Finally there came a moment when their army touched the absolute tangent, the sea. This was such a novelty that they halted there for a full day. For many of the Indians, this was the first time they had seen the sea, and they were left awestruck, fascinated, even though the thick mists robbed the sight of much of its grandeur. If it had not been raining, they would have gone for a swim. They did so anyway. Several of them drowned, carried away unsuspecting by the pull of the waves. As night was falling, a party of Indians who had been exploring the shore appeared at the generals' bonfire and told them excitedly that something extraordinary was taking place on some nearby rocks. Clarke climbed on to Repetido and sent for Carlos, whom he felt obliged to show anything of interest. The youngster did not appear, but when Clarke arrived at the spot, he found him already among the crowd of spectators. They were all gathered at the top of some high cliffs, from the edge of which a small, inaccessible beach could be seen. On it were about a hundred grotesquely large ducks. Even allowing for the distance, they must have been at least five feet tall, like overgrown children. They were plump to the point of bursting, with snowy white down, huge blue eyes, and broad webbed feet that they planted firmly (they must have weighed at least one hundred and seventy-five pounds) into the wet sand. The first impression they gave was that they must be dwarves in disguise. But how on earth could a hundred dwarves be got together like that? And Clarke had never heard mention of any pygmy races on American soil.

"They're not ducks," said Maciel, who had ridden with him. "They're seagulls, which are quite similar."

"What about their bills then?"

"Well, they're spoonbill gulls."

Colqán, the aristocratic Tehuelche, burst out laughing. According to him, they were ducks all right, and not even particularly large ones; it was certain substances that the Indians had taken which made them see everything out of proportion. Clarke said nothing in reply, but he was convinced this was not the case. At any rate, even leaving aside the question of their size, the ducks were behaving in the most extraordinary fashion. They were walking very erect, like geese, with long, determined strides; even though there was no apparent pattern to their progress, there must have been a secret one. It was a shame it was so misty, because this meant he missed important details. The ducks were walking round and round. All of a sudden the onlookers could see an enormous white egg about the size of a feather bolster. It was obvious now that some kind of ritual was taking place. Although animals do of course perform rituals, and even highly complicated ones, this only increased the impression of artificiality. As soon as they saw the egg, the Indians stopped laughing and commenting. It was as if this colossal egg bewitched them even more than the sea had done. Clarke remembered some of the things Coliqueo had told him: the exact content of his ramblings was of little importance, it was enough to know that a duck's egg had been part of his grand scheme of things. Coliqueo, who like every emperor overdid the medicinal herbs, had made it seem like a hallucination; but it was in fact real, and Colqán was wrong.

The mysterious palmipeds, surrounded not only by mist but by the encroaching dark gray of a rainy dusk, gave little ceremonial kicks to the egg until it reached the sea, then dived in after it one by one. Defying the high waves, the sinister rumble of the tide, and the wind and rain, they performed stately circles around the egg, which floated in the center.

"It must be rotten, if it floats," Maciel said.

"What do you know about it?" another chief responded.

They left the scene lost in thought. They could have shot duck after duck (or at least the Englishman could have done so, and the few Indians who were good shots but never killed anyone because they never normally bothered to take aim, firing at random) but they would never have been able to recover their catch.

The second battle took place out of sight and sound for the naturalist and makeshift general, who learned about it only afterward, and elsewhere. The Great Sine Curve had disconcerted everyone, friend and foe alike. Half of their troops, previously grouped at Salinas Grandes, joined the Figure at an odd angle, and immediately ran into the Voroga forces. No one was killed, something so unusual that it led Clarke to think it had been nothing more than a skirmish. The person who described the action was a show-off from the Court who had become a messenger to see a bit of the world. He made a great show of standing on ceremony to utter complete banalities, lent himself airs, and prolonged his sentences interminably. In the end, he gave the impression he had no idea of what he was talking about, and that he was talking about nothing. And yet he said it with complete assurance, was totally convinced and convincing. Clarke's mind wandered as he listened to this babble. Something had occurred to him, and he preferred to follow the thread of his own thought than the Indian's grandiloquence, to which however the other chiefs in the war council were listening with rapt attention.

Clarke recalled one of the first explanations Cafulcurá had given him. The continuum, he had told him, was the key to everything for the Indians. Clarke could accept that, but where was this continuum? It was everywhere, including in Cafulcurá's affirmation: that was precisely what it was all about. It was a perfect passe-partout, an impalpable thread running through everything. Of course it was easy to say and even to understand, what was much more difficult was to find a practical example. Over the past few weeks, Clarke had often felt he was on the point of finding one, but he always shied away at the decisive moment, preferring to relegate the idea once more to the realm of abstract intuitions, which seemed not only correct but the only alternative when in fact it was the worst possible betrayal of the continuum. It was to completely negate it. The thought that had struck him while he was listening to the messenger was that war was the perfect opportunity to attain the continuum. Clarke felt he was ready to do so, and courageous enough. It was nothing more than a thought, like one of the hundred that flit through anyone's mind every day: he only had to cling onto it, and the continuum would start up. He could begin anywhere: at some random point in all the rubbish that the Indian opposite him was spouting, for example. But he did not even need to make that effort; he could begin at any point in the tendrils of all that had happened. For example, the Hare, in any of the intriguing or fantastic forms it had appeared in. The Hare was a good emblem for a strategic battle plan, because of its unexpected leaps, its elusive speed, its flexibility, the way it stared in fascination at the rising or setting sun (its indifference to whether it was sunrise or sunset mirrored the indifference as to victory or defeat that characterizes a true fascination with war). Then from the hare, he could and should move on to another element. The line. The horizon. The wanderer. The inversions of perspective. Everything else. And so on. But he had no intention of making a catalog of the universe. He had to force himself to make a break in the chain. It is always the same, there is nothing so true as the saying "it's the thought that counts." The break, which immediately became incorporated into the continuum, took the form (a form which also became part of the continuum) of a strategic plan which Clarke began to put into practice the very next day: the strategy of the Hare. As soon as he did so, the Huilliches' victory was assured. It was as simple as that. His only regret was not having anyone to tell all this to, but on second thought he had no need to regret it, because in this way the form passed wholesale into the content.

The next morning, using as his excuse the courtier's vague information, Clarke ordered a general mobilization in a straight line toward the shifting Voroga encampments. Enthusiasm ran like an electric current through the Indians, who were convinced, with that erratic fanaticism of theirs, that they were being led by a visionary. Everyone sped off. In mid-afternoon, whom should they meet if not Equimoxis. They were in such a hurry they would have butchered him on the spot had Clarke not got wind of it, and been inspired with yet another idea. What a splendid trap it would be, he thought, what an elegant way to go beyond the strategy of the Hare itself, if they used an underground passage from one horizon to another. When all was said and done, that was what this was about. The only thing the Hare provided was the idea. In reality, it was impossible. But in the narrative, the possibility arose, almost as a joke. Clarke recalled being told underground that the caverns had distant outlets on the surface: that was enough for him. After a brief conversation with Equimoxis, he decided to go underground with him and summon Pillán's help. No sooner said than done, and that night the twenty thousand Indians, plus all their horses and cattle, descended into the bowels of the earth.

On the other side, they emerged free from everything they could have wished to have left behind, except for the rain, which went on falling with relentless monotony. They joined up with the contingents from Salinas Grandes, and prepared to fall on

the rear of the Voroga army, which had not the slightest suspicion of where they were. Since their usual routines had been upset, they slept, marched, drank and made plans in one huge confused jumble. The final battle lasted two whole days and nights,
but could also have been said not to have taken place at all. It
was more like a big deterrent maneuver. Clarke and his "team"
camped by the side of a stream where messengers began to come
and go with the most contradictory reports. There was fighting,
or there was not. The foul weather got even worse. The second
night reverberated with thunder and lightning. At nightfall, worried by a number of reports that led him to fear his plans might
be going awry, Clarke set off with the ever-present Maciel and
four aides to the spot where the nearest camp was meant to be.
There were only a few Indians there, changing horses before they
sped off into the darkness again, but they assured him that Mallén was only a short distance away with the main army, so they
headed in the direction indicated. Instead of the old shaman they
ran into a group of drunken Indians sitting on a termite hill, with
no fire or shelter. Clarke dispatched two in one direction and two
in another with the task of getting some reliable information and
bringing it to him at his original starting-point, where he headed
back to with Maciel. The rain and the electric storm increased
in fury. Because he was so preoccupied, had not slept for several nights, and had so many things to worry about, Clarke had
not stopped to consider that Maciel was even more drunk than
usual. So drunk in fact that something happened which they say
never occurs to an Indian: he fell off his horse. The darkness
they were galloping through was so impenetrable that Clarke

would not even have noticed had it not been for the fact that with the continual rain the grease the Indians used to keep dry took on a slight phosphorescence. So what he saw was a kind of fetal ghost shooting over his head in a sleeping position. He was traveling so quickly that it took him about a hundred yards to rein in Repetido, and by the time he turned back to look for the Indian, Maciel's riderless horse, which had slowed and turned in the same way as Clarke had, led him off in the wrong direction, so that he could find no trace of Maciel. Clarke did not stay looking for long; he thought the Indian was bound to be all right wherever he was, because nothing happens to drunks in accidents; the worst he could suffer would be a bad thirst, that is, if he had not managed to cling onto his bottle during his feats of gliding. So Clarke galloped off; it was a miracle after all that had taken place that he did not get lost, but he eventually succeeded in finding his way back to the creek. A fire was lit under the trees; a couple of Indians were dozing beside it. He sent them to rescue Maciel, roughly indicating the direction where they should look. He decided to sleep until dawn, unless he was woken beforehand. It seemed strange to him that this series of chance encounters should represent the greatest battle ever fought between the Indian nations, but he was in no mood for speculation. His accumulated tiredness had reached crisis point. The thunder made him tremble, the lightning made him blink, and he needed a fresh layer of grease on his shoulders and back. For the past two days he had been living in a rectangular tent, built among the low branches of the trees by the stream; as he approached it now, he noticed the glimmer of a fire inside, the promise of a comfortable sleep. He drew back the flap that served as a door, took two steps inside, with his head spinning from exhaustion, his limbs quivering . . . and it was only then that he realized there was someone sitting by the fire. He could scarcely help recognizing him, and the shock sent his battered nervous system into a paroxysm of confusion.

There the man sat, and lifted his gaze to look at him . . . it was he himself, his perfect double, more like Clarke than Clarke himself, because he was wearing his clothes and smoking his pipe. An English traveler, a gentleman, whereas he stood there naked and dripping wet, looking like the most wretched of savages. He stammered out:

"What are you doing here?" What he would really have liked to ask was: "Who are you?"

"So you're the Englishman?" the man identical to Clarke said. The latter nodded agreement, more with his gaping mouth than with his head. "I must excuse myself for taking your clothes, but I couldn't find anything else to keep me warm. I'll give them back straight away."

"There's no need."

". . . But I'm warm now." So saying, he took off the clothes.

"I can see you're out on your feet. I'd heard you looked like me, but I didn't imagine you were identical. We can talk tomorrow." He stood up. The small fire on the ground threw up shadows on the tent walls flapping from the rain.

"You're leaving?"

"There's a battle going on out there! I've already lost enough time as it is."

The other Clarke came up to the first; his voice was deep, worried, almost inaudible in the thunderstorm.

"The Widow can't stand me."

Clarke collapsed on to the floor, so groggy that it was worse than if he had already been asleep. The other man went out. Clarke fell into a deep sleep.

By the time he woke up, it was all over. As he later learned, the everlasting peace had been reestablished, on terms detrimental to the honor and finances of Coliqueo, who fled to seek refuge among his white allies. Every chieftain left taking his tribe with him, without even bothering to attend the celebrations organized in Salinas Grandes. Clarke woke up thirty hours after he had fallen asleep, all alone, on a splendid morning with a clear sky and with the sun shining at last over the wet plain. In fact, it was the sun that woke him, because his companions had dismantled the tent when they left. He could see no trace of Maciel, but was not surprised: hastily made friendships were the first to dissolve. He woke up slowly, thoughts drifting through his mind. He was not upset about having been forgotten, quite the contrary. Apart from feeling slightly hungry, he was fine; Repetido and his other ponies were grazing nearby. He supposed that everything was over; he could well imagine the outcome, and all he had to do now was to decide which direction to head in. The most logical thing would be to make for Salinas Grandes, but the idea of seeing more Indians was wearisome. Well, he would see. For now, he went to bathe in the stream, scraped the remaining grease off his skin, dried himself while smoking a pipe in the sun, then got dressed. His clothes were scattered on the ground, which meant that some at least of the confused memory he had of the stranger who was also himself had not been a dream. Yet it still might be. A second pipe. The birds were singing in the trees. Idly, he picked up a stone and threw it at a tree trunk. A mouse scuttled off, terrified. Clarke allowed his mind to roam aimlessly. His main feeling was a vague sense of shame, not so much for having charged about naked and smeared with grease at the head of crazy hordes of savages, but for all the rest, all the improbable things he had witnessed and accepted: ducks as big as people, impromptu throat-slittings, a drunk flying over his head, a column of warriors riding through underground tunnels, his double rising to meet him at midnight ... man, he philosophized, can get used to anything ... because he starts by getting used to taking reality for real. What if he tried fishing? In the shady waters of the stream he could see the moving outlines of some fat, long-toothed fish. He had some hooks in his saddlebags, but he would wager that the Indians had stolen them by now. It would be easier to shoot a brace of coots, but then he would have to pluck them ... but of course, he would have to scale the fish in any case ... sometimes at least there was something to be said for polygyny, having thirty-two, or at least seventeen wives.

Clarke was mulling over his choices when he heard the sound of galloping close by. He got up to see who it was. A skinny Indian with a troop of magnificent ponies behind him. As he drew closer, Clarke could see he was wearing clothes. Closer still, and it was Carlos Alzaga Prior, with a smile from ear to ear, and one of those ears bandaged. They each raised a hand in greeting at the same moment, and laughed nervously together. It was a pleasure to see the boy, despite all his craziness and his endless chatter, especially because the pleasure was mutual, and sincere. Carlos leapt to the ground and gave him an extravagant embrace, even though they had seen each other barely three days before.

"Vale, vale, salutis, Clarkenius!"

"Hello there, madcap."

"Don't pretend to be so cool! You're a hero! You're being talked about everywhere! You're the new Hannibal!"

"Come off it. I've been asleep for I don't know how many …"

"You deserve it. And you haven't got a scratch, as far as I can see. Have you been hiding in a gopher hole? Hahaha."

"What about your ear? Did someone chop it off?"

"No, don't worry. They overdid the bandaging, that's all."

"But what was it? A lance? If it was, it just missed your ideas."

"No, no such luck. I'm ashamed to tell you. What happened was that I wanted to have my ear pierced so I could wear a ring, and the brute who stuck the needle in made a mess of it. You can't imagine how it bled!"

Clarke lifted his eyes to the heavens. The two of them sat down on a bank strewn with violets which, after a week's constant watering, gave off a strong perfume. It was then that the Englishman learned of the Vorogas' surrender, of the armies going their different ways, of the celebrations that must by now be going on in Salinas Grandes, even though Cafulcurá had still not reappeared. Carlos had heard that Namuncurá had turned up though, and had taken control.

"So they don't need me any more," Clarke said.

"They'll always need you, those blockheads."

"Where did you get so many splendid horses from?"

"There was an amazing share-out! I made sure I laid my hands on a few, because I reckoned that a bohemian like you would be on his uppers by now."

Clarke observed that Carlos was more grown-up, more self-confident, that he considered himself an adult, his equal, as he launched into his overwhelming stream of anecdotes.

"By the way, aren't you the slightest bit hungry?"

"Ravenous. When you appeared I was just thinking of hunting or fishing something."

"Don't be so primitive! Do you take this for the Stone Age? I brought some roast birds, and I don't know how I managed not to eat them on the way."

"How did you know I was here?"

"Some Indians told me. Just as well I believed them, even though I'd seen you head off in the opposite direction."

When he came back with the food, he asked curiously:

"Am I mistaken, or did you say you spent the whole of yesterday asleep?"

"That's right."

"How's that possible, when I saw you yesterday in that spectacular charge among the deer?"

"The deer?" Clarke was momentarily puzzled.

"I saw you clear as day!"

"Really? Do you know something? I think I have a double."

Carlos accepted the idea immediately, as if it were the most natural thing in the world. He described that particular combat, when a crescent of Tehuelche horsemen had unwittingly trapped a huge number of deer in front of them. The Vorogas of course had taken them to be demonic reinforcements, and had fled.

"It was there I met up with Mallén, who must also have thought it was you, because he said: 'That Englishman knows every trick in the book.' So you have a double … where did you/he come from?"

"How should I know? He turned up here, when I was about to go to sleep. I thought it must have been a dream, but now with what you're telling me …"

"He's entirely real, I can assure you. And even though I only saw him from a distance, I was sure it was you. The same face, the same bearing, that dandified look you have, but at the same time like a wise man, as if you're constantly thinking about Newton's binomial theorem."

Carlos fell about laughing. They carried on in a similar vein for some time. The birds were delicious. They made tea, then Carlos fell asleep. He said he needed to catch up. Clarke, who was if anything ahead on sleep, lay back smoking his pipe and staring at the sky through the foliage. He did not feel like thinking, but preferred the voluptuousness of an empty mind, which was where thinking led anyway. He took up his daydreaming where he had left off when Carlos arrived…. Where was he? He was trying to decide between fish and game … and there had been no need to decide: he had eaten anyway. He meditated at length without a single thought entering his mind, and this was a happy moment in his life, even though it left no trace. It did however allow him to make a slight adjustment: until that moment he had considered thought to be the true representation of the continuum; now he realized that happiness fit the bill more precisely. Happiness was the real continuum, the one that brought satisfaction.

12: Clarke's Story

WHEN CARLOS WOKE UP (BECAUSE THERE IS ALWAYS somebody who wakes up to give fresh impetus to a story), Clarke had already decided to head back for Buenos Aires. He considered their adventure over, and he was not particularly interested in any remaining loose ends. On the contrary, he thought it appropriate that some threads remain unexplained. He had had enough, he was exhausted, and felt like a vegetable, incapable of performing any fresh actions. It may seem contradictory that someone who feels this way should be in such a hurry to depart, but basically it is natural. His mistake was of another order.

"I've been thinking," he began, "and it seems to me the moment has come to turn back. I've had my fill of Indians and nonsense, and if we set a reasonable pace we could be back in Buenos Aires in a month."

"Much sooner even."

"The fact is I'd prefer not to rush. I'd like to take my time, have a rest, perhaps carry out some observations. Even so, we'd arrive in time for the start of classes, so your parents won't be put out."

"Don't worry on that score!"

"Let me decide what I worry about. What d'you think of the idea?"

"Clarke, you know I'll do whatever you think best. The only thing I'm sorry about is that you never found your Hare."

The Englishman felt a momentary flash of irritation.

"If you weren't so utterly thoughtless, I'd say you were a complete cynic. I don't know how you can stand there and reproach me about the Hare when you—who came here to paint—never made so much as a single miserable sketch, and . . ."

"I'm taking the pampa with me imprinted on my retinas, that's what matters! What would you know about art anyway? The English have never painted anything worthwhile!"

". . . And you forgot your famous Yñuy in a hurry, didn't you?"

Even as he was saying this, Clarke regretted it, but the boy was so surprised he did not even react bitterly:

"It's true, Yñuy . . . I swear I had forgotten about her."

"You see?"

"But I did search for her, you're a witness to that. Is it my fault I couldn't find her?"

"Two weeks ago you wanted to get married, now it's neither here nor there."

"No, it's not! If I found her I'd go on loving her. . . ."

"Don't talk of love, you make me laugh."

The pair of them fell silent, in a sulk.

"Look Clarke, I have to say it: you're a bit of a bastard. You had no right to say that to me."

"Sorry."

"Yes, 'sorry,' 'sorry,' but you said it all the same."

"You deserved it." But then, seeing that this was getting them nowhere, Clarke chose a different tack:

"Don't worry. After all, she was the one who left. It wasn't you who got her pregnant, was it?"

"How could you think that! When I met her, she was at least eight months pregnant."

"As much as that?"

"She had a belly. . . ."

"Perhaps she's already had it, who knows? And maybe she's had it adopted."

"I don't think so."

"It's incredible how unconcerned the Mapuches are about their newborn. They claim to be defenders of the human race, but they give up their children without batting an eyelid."

"Far be it from me to question your wisdom, but I'd say quite the opposite. I think they're very affectionate with their children."

"That's true, but I was talking about the identity of the children when they're just born."

"Yes, but that's what the birthmarks are for."

"What?"

"The birthmarks. Don't you have one? I've got one on my . . . on my buttock. A small mark that looks like a hare in flight. When we were fighting, and I was . . . well, when I was almost naked let's say, it was visible, you can't imagine how much the Indians commented on it, they're so observant."

Clarke suspected he was having his leg pulled, but let it pass.

"I've got a birthmark as well," he said, to say something. "Here, between my eyes. You can't see it because of my thick brows."

"Let's see," Carlos said, coming closer.

"It's barely noticeable. It's a V-shape that's lighter than the rest of my skin."

"But it's perfectly visible. It looks just like a hare's ears."

The Englishman exploded:

"There you go with the hare again! Are you doing it on purpose?"

Carlos rocked with laughter. Then a moment later, his gaze lost in the distance, he murmured:

"Yñuy is a very sweet girl."

"Is she pretty?"

"Beautiful. You'd have really liked her."

"We might still find her."

"I asked everywhere...."

A silence.

"Shall we head back then?" said Clarke.

"OK ... let's. The fact is, I've no idea what we're doing here. Are you sure you don't want to go to Salinas Grandes?"

"Not on your life. Besides, we're a long way away."

"Clarke!"

"What's the matter? Don't shout like that, you'll give me a heart attack!"

"We're forgetting Gauna!"

"Good. He's someone who's better to lose than to find."

They mounted. While they were ambling along, Carlos kept on about the tracker, so Clarke told him the story of the Gauna Alvear family, and the gaucho's views on it.

"You can't deny it's an ingenious tale," the boy said when his friend had finished.

"That's the worst thing about it."

Night was drawing in. They met up with some Indians. Those Indians met others ... to cut a long story short: by the next day, Gauna was back with them, and they had completely changed direction. Now they were headed south-west once more, as their guide wished. Such a rapid turn around demanded an explanation.

"Why did you listen to him?" Carlos asked Clarke (they had resumed the order they rode in before the war, with the two of them in the rear, and Gauna fifty yards ahead so he did not have to listen to them).

Clarke did not reply.

"Don't you see you're completely underhanded? You tell me, your friend, one thing, then he comes along and ..."

"I say the same to everyone: yes. What are we losing by going with him? In three or four days he'll be satisfied, we'll have had an another outing, and got to know ... then the three of us can go back to Buenos Aires, as right as rain."

"No, Clarke. You're hiding something from me."

"All right, if you want me to be frank with you, there are two things: first, I'd like to see that famous Cerro de la Ventana; and second, perhaps the Widow really does have something to do with Gauna's story, in which case we'll be able to get to know her."

"But who wants to?"

"I do, for one. Just think if she really is his half-sister."

"Come off it."

"Everything is possible, Carlos."

"Why does that make her so special anyway? What if they are similar? What if she's got the same rotten nature as him, and has us all slaughtered?"

Clarke shrugged. Then he counterattacked:

"All Gauna told me was that he had learned that the Widow had finally found a girl she could pass off as her daughter, and that she was on a forced march to get to the Ventana to celebrate the birthday. There, from the hands of the unknown Mapuche who has been keeping it all these years, she is supposed to receive a jewel that will release the inheritance that is going to make Gauna a Rothschild, if only he can get there in time. OK, so it's the most unlikely fantasy in the whole wide world. But he is going to go anyway, with me (which he says would help him, because of Repetido, our four-legged safe-conduct) or without me. Now tell me, with your hand on your heart, if you had been told a story like that, however far-fetched, and it was all the same to you whether you went or not, wouldn't you at least have been curious? Tell the truth."

Carlos laughed his fresh, childlike laugh:

"You're a genius, Clarke. You always manage to convince me."

"Oh, Good God, it can't be ..."

"What?"

"Do you see what I see?"

"You're right, it's your friend the Wanderer. Is he coming or going?"

Clarke, raised his voice: "Can you see him, Gauna?"

"Yes."

The rider seemed not to move on the horizon, to be a fixed point. The Englishman told himself he would not take his eyes off him, because he wanted to know how he always succeeded in vanishing. He regretted it was not dark enough yet for him to carry out a triangulation by the stars. There was no point doing it with the sun, because that moved. Over the previous days, the warriors he had commanded in battle were always telling him they had seen the strange horseman, but for one reason or other had never seen him anywhere but on the horizon. Clarke continued to stare at him until all at once he disappeared. It was only a moment, and suddenly he was gone. But in that instant, whether due to a visual trick or a mental fantasy, Clarke could have sworn he had seen the most subtle overlapping; it was not as though the horizon were coming nearer, which would have been the normal thing, but instead as though the whole vast expanse of the plain had been exchanged for another, which was absurd. Clarke became lost in thought.

Gauna had brought another ten horses with him, so the troop they were leading was huge. They also had enough provisions for weeks, so they would not have to go to the trouble of hunting. In their first day of riding they did not meet up with anyone, but on the second they ate at midday with a noisy bunch of Indians out hunting, and they almost found themselves obliged to dine with others. They got out of it by arguing great haste, and camped for the night in what seemed to Clarke to be one of the most enchanting spots he had ever seen: a creek, usually quite narrow but swollen now after all the rain, framed by an exquisite variety of scenic views. By the dying evening light and the first light of the next morning, they collected agate and jasper pebbles, admired thousands of yellow lilies, listened to the birdsong, took long walks along the riverbanks, and bathed not once but twice, before dinner and before breakfast. Frogs lulled them to a restoring sleep.

The next day the weather was clear and fine. Gauna rode on

ahead as usual. They had scarcely traveled half an hour when Carlos looked up and said:

"What are those ... accumulations of earth?"

He did not dare say "mountains," because the very idea seemed so out of place in these surroundings.

"They're mountains," Clarke replied; "and I think ..." He raised his voice: "Gauna, are they the Sierra de la Ventana?"

"Yes," said the gaucho without even turning round.

"They are."

"So we've arrived."

"Not quite. They're still a long way off."

They were barely visible on the horizon, an unbroken line of the brightest blue. The three carried on riding for a while in silence, their eyes sometimes fixed on the mountains, sometimes staring out emptily.

"While I remember, Clarke," Carlos said, "you have to finish the story you started the other day."

"What story?"

"Well, 'story' is just a way of putting it. You were telling me about your great love."

"...?"

"Don't you remember? About Rossanna ..."

"I told you about that?" Clarke asked, genuinely startled.

"Of course you did. It was before the war."

"I don't recall."

"And you left off in the middle."

"I must have had some reason for doing so."

"It wasn't my fault, I assure you. There was some interruption,

I can't remember what. You can't say there haven't been interruptions over the past few days."

"You're right, more than enough. But are you sure ... ? It's completely slipped my mind. But when you say her name ... it's not that I always think you're making things up, but I thought that fragment from my past was one of my best-kept secrets. Sometimes it seems to me it's the key to my entire life. In a way I'm glad I confided in you, even though I don't remember doing so."

"Sometimes I just don't understand you, Clarke."

Clarke had submerged himself in a deep well of memories, a darkly veiled expression on his face. Carlos did not insist, but after riding on for a while in silence, he asked again:

"So, are you going to tell me or not?"

"Eh, what?"

"Your story about Rossanna ..."

"Rossanna died."

"I'm very sorry. But I must say I was expecting it, from the way you began your story."

"You'll end up convincing me I really did tell you. Perhaps I was talking in my sleep?"

"Look, if you don't want to, you don't have to tell me anything."

"No, I'm sorry. Where had I got to?"

"After all this build-up, you'll think it's ridiculous if I say I can't remember, but so much has happened I reckon I do have some excuse. I can recall there was a black man: what was his name? Mandango?"

"Callango. Did I tell you about him too?"

"Stop it, for heaven's sake! You told me everything, in the classic style. Let me think." He stroked his smooth, youthful chin. "You'd been attacked by the Indians, Rossanna had disappeared, you and her father, Professor ..."

"Haussmann."

"Exactly. You were looking for her. That was as far as we had got, I think: you were heading for the glacier."

"I told you about the glacier?"

"There you go again! I'm going to ride with Gauna."

He spurred on his horse, and would have ridden ahead if Clarke hadn't quickly pushed in front of him with Repetido, who was a genius at this kind of maneuver.

"I'm sorry, I'm sorry. I promise not to say it again. From now on I'll behave as though I told you everything, which is probably what I did. When the Professor and I returned to where our camp had been before the Indian attack, who looked fierce and had even fiercer intentions, we could find no trace of either Rossanna or Callango. At first I made no connection between the two of them, and if I had done so it would have been to kindle a glimmer of hope because he, when all was said and done, was a member of our expedition. Even the despicable idea that he loved her might have given me hope. We had spent long hours fleeing in a state of despair, and now we were faced with the stormiest, most leaden and sinister nightfall you can imagine. Exhausted, desperate, both of us had the idea of returning to the place that was dearest to us. I wanted to go back to the myrtle wood, and dragged the Professor there with me; and then he, after making sure his daughter was not hidden among the trees, took me off to his glacier. I followed him like an automaton."

Here Clarke paused for a moment. Somewhere in his unconscious mind he must have realized that this was the exact point where he had broken off his story before. He began again in a different tone, with a low, troubled voice that lent an air of truth to his strange and horrible account of how the episode had ended:

"To the uninformed, the glacier looked like a massive, threatening mountain of black ice. The fact that it moved added a supernatural touch. It was something to gaze on from afar, then get away from, to talk about at a safe distance. The Professor on the other hand had spent weeks 'inside' this wonder of nature. Not that he had gone into the ice, of course, but he had got inside the system of its formation, its movement; he had weighed it up, listened to its heartbeat, had 'ridden' it at length. Together with his Indians, now dead, and with the deplorable Callango, still unfortunately alive, he had clambered up to its highest point to hang his plumblines and set up his metronomes. Wearing thick felt overshoes they had spent hours up on the crest of the glacier, measuring the speed at which the wall of ice moved forward. The Professor had grown used to considering this dreadful object as a living being, and that was what motivated him that evening. He needed to calm his anxiety with a scientific image, even though he was the one who had supplied all the science. There was a slight mishap: I would not remember it, had not everything that happened that day been branded in my memory. The Professor lost his way. As it turned out, this was unimportant, because the tragedy had already happened without our being aware of it. For a few minutes we walked along aimlessly, with the Professor wondering what had become of the glacier, and me behind him,

my mind a complete blank. Then I reacted and started to guide
him. We could hardly see a thing, not because it was so late, but
because a dense black cloud was descending upon us, with the
noise of an approaching storm. A hurricane began to blow, pro-
ducing a terrible howling as it whistled off the peaks. It was going
to pour with rain at any moment, but that was the least of our
worries. Finally we came out from the trees into the clearing
made by the thrust of the glacier's ice and rocks. Its dark mass
rose in front of us. We did not look up at it, but were only too
aware of the way darkness emanated from the glacier, and its
monumental indifference; we could hear new terrifying sounds
that the wind was drawing from its jagged needles, and a deep
resonance from sonorous depths. At that moment something
happened which you may very occasionally have seen during a
stormy nightfall. The sun, which seemed to have set at least an
hour earlier, was in fact still sinking toward the horizon. And in
the lowest part of the sky there was a border more or less free of
clouds. So that although the leaden ocean hanging over our
heads neither moved nor lifted in any way, all of a sudden a shaft
of light appeared, dazzling and theatrical, both bright and gentle
at the same time, and a ray of sun found its way through the lab-
yrinths of the mountains and shrieking winds and struck the glacier, illuminating it like a diamond against a background almost
uniformly black. . . . It was then we saw her. We saw her the entire
time, no more than a minute, that this fantastic sunbeam lasted,
and I have continued to see her every day since then, like an epiphenomenon of light, any light. Rossanna's white, naked body
was encrusted in the glacier about two yards below the top, that's

to say about a hundred feet above the ground. To our confused, exhausted minds it seemed simply like some kind of ghastly miracle that defied explanation. Nevertheless, I thought I understood what had happened. The deranged Callango had thought up this macabre proof of his love. Demonstrating a skill that could seem remarkable, and indeed was, in the way that feats of madness are remarkable, he had lowered himself on ropes from the top of the glacier, had dug a hole in the ice, had put Rossanna's body in it, and then had filled it with water which, at those temperatures, had frozen in minutes. For years now I've thought about it. I suppose he must have reasoned: if she is not to be mine, she won't be anybody else's, she will be part of this huge diamond, frozen, intact for all eternity.... He had often carried out similar tasks, with ropes, pickaxes, and buckets of water, for the Professor, so we could hardly be surprised that he knew how to do it. The light began to fade, the sun was going down, this time finally (and this adverb, in a broad sense, also applied to the feelings of my heart); grasping fingers of darkness stole the apparition from our sight. The Professor cried out and pointed: from the summit of the glacier, a confused outline of gray on black, Callango was sliding down, a bundle of ropes under his arm. He had spotted us, and was trying to escape. I raised my rifle, which I had been clutching for hours forgotten in my hand, and fired off a shot, almost without taking aim. I have to tell you that I did it as an automatic gesture, with no hope of succeeding, because not only were we four hundred yards from the target, but I was a dreadful shot, so bad in fact (I had never once hit what I was aiming for) that I had more than once wondered whether

I did not suffer from some psychic resistance to shooting. But it
so happened that hardly had the shot rung out before the ape-
like silhouette of the black man came to a halt, hesitated for a
moment, then plunged over the edge of the wall of ice. I thought
I heard, with a certain melancholy satisfaction, the thump of the
body as it crashed to the ground. In parenthesis, I should say that
ever since then I've been a crack shot. I don't think I've wasted a
bullet in fifteen years. Well, such are the mysteries of the human
soul. Night had fallen, and the delayed storm finally broke. A
hard rain began to fall, lashing down in squalls of wind, while the
sky was crisscrossed with lightning. One of the flashes lit the Professor's face. I had not been thinking of him for a few minutes,
but now I saw the mask of a man plunging into the abyss. I took
him by the shoulders and dragged him toward the wood, where
I hoped to find shelter. This was not to be; rather, the danger was
still more deadly there. The branches of the myrtles were being
whipped around, and the whole wood seemed to be on the point
of being uprooted, to topple and bury us. As we ran out again, we
saw lofty pine trees being torn from the earth, great clumps of
snow being hurled from mountain to mountain, and the waters
of the lake surging up in roaring black waves, one of which en-
gulfed us and knocked us flat.... We ran on again, crazy, desperate; vague ideas flitted through my mind, offering me a remote
hope: we could wait till morning, go and fetch Rossanna's body,
give her a proper burial, weep over her, anything. But even these
plans were swept away in an apotheosis of horror: a fresh catas-
trophe befell us, in which the elements themselves seemed to be
conspiring. First there was a peal of thunder, unbelievably louder

than all the ones which had preceded it; then a lightning bolt fell to earth with a loud boom. We looked toward the spot. Our blind flight had taken us to a place from where we could see everything: the lightning struck the heart of the glacier, which shattered with a cosmic crash of breaking glass. Thousands of tons of ice collapsed on top of each other. I could think only of Rossanna. The Professor was a rag doll beside me, unable to take more than a few feeble steps. I don't remember much more about that terrible night. I know we ran on again, unable to find shelter, that we somehow survived the following day of rain and winds, and that we ended up in the leather tents of some Indians who had picked us up just as we were about to succumb to the cold and exhaustion. We recovered, in our bodies at least, and started on a long, hazardous journey that eventually took us to Buenos Aires, and from there in a schooner to Southampton. The Professor had not regained the use of his speech, or all his mental faculties, and he died in my arms a few months later in his house in Surrey. As for my life ... well, it could be said it went on. I studied, I became a naturalist...."

The effort of telling the story had left Clarke drained, quivering. On this occasion, his exhaustion was an aesthetic reflex, bearing in mind that this was the state in which his protagonist—that is, he himself—constantly found himself in the narration. Sweat was pouring down his face and neck, making him shudder in the hot morning. Carlos was taken aback: proof of which was that he was speechless. As Clarke gradually recovered, he understood his companion's silence: there was no need to say a single word more about love, madness, or death. All that remained was destiny, but that was too vast, was akin in a way to the continuum. He also understood a persistent feeling that had been with him all through his tale, a slight unease he had been unable to place. Before he had begun the story, or what had been left of it to tell, he had been talking about interruptions. That was not right, it was incorrect. Interruptions did not exist. He would have explained this to Carlos, but he had no wish to interrupt his thoughts, which must have been edifying.

At midday they crossed a charming stream. Gauna surprised them by telling them it was the same one they had spent the night beside, which bent round like a bow. It might have been true, or not. They halted for lunch in the shade of its trees.

"Tell me something, Gauna," Clarke said once they had finished eating, "how can you be sure we'll meet up with the Widow? It's obvious that she's ahead of us, by however little. Isn't it possible that she's already finished what she had to do in the Sierra, and has left? All we would find then are cold ashes."

"It so happens that tomorrow, the ninth of March, is an important date in our family. It's my grandfather's birthday (he would be a hundred, if he were still alive); it's my mother's birthday, and it's mine too."

"What an incredible coincidence."

Carlos had become excited. "So tomorrow is your birthday, Gauna! You should have told us sooner. I don't think there's time for us to get you a present now."

There was no reply.

It was late afternoon by the time they reached the hills, which of course when seen close up were neither blue nor a wavy line on the horizon. They were broken terrain which the horses found hard going. The three men entered them almost at random. Clarke had vaguely hoped the famous pierced crag of the Ventana would present itself to his eyes straight away, but it was obviously not going to be that easy. The hills covered a wide area, with hundreds of peaks forming a real labyrinth. A creek—or rather, a river, because it must have been about a hundred yards wide—forced them to change direction; there was no point going to the trouble of swimming across it if they were not sure that their goal lay on the far side. They had been climbing the whole time, and were now breathing a different air, which affected their nervous systems and made them light-headed. There was not a single tree in sight. The silence was complete. A few birds flew out from the mountains and glided for a while without a sound. Standing out against the sky on high slopes beyond a range of low hills, they saw an endless herd of deer, rendered mute by distance. The landscape was reminiscent of a cardboard cutout, but on a huge scale, which gave the impression they were the ones who had become miniatures. The sun had been hidden as soon as they entered the hills, and must by now be falling below the horizon line, because the light took on first a bluish and then a gray tinge, while the odd wisp of lilac-colored cloud floated peacefully across the heavens. Gauna was looking round with as much curiosity as the other two: for him, as for them, this was the first time he had visited the hills. All three of them were equally lost. Clarke was thinking it would be only too absurd for the appointed day to come and go, without them being able to find the famous Ventana peak. Carlos must have been thinking the same, but made no comment, because in this more difficult terrain the three were riding alongside each other, and Gauna hardly seemed in a good mood. It was odd he had not insisted on more precise information. Had he imagined that the pierced peak would be visible from all sides? Clarke told himself that perhaps it was even hidden from the foot of the mountain itself; it could be any one of the crags around them. Then again, it might be none of them; the hills seemed to stretch on for ever. For the time being, it was already night, and since it was not a good idea to continue on this treacherous terrain if they could not see properly, they made camp in a hollow surrounded on almost every side by steep, conical peaks. The day had been a tiring one; this last stage had prolonged it even more than usual, until it was completely dark, and since they would have to be up at dawn if they were to have any chance of finding what they were looking for, they ate a perfunctory supper, saying little more than was necessary to show they were not ill-disposed to each other; then they slept.

13: Happy Families

CLARKE WAS AWAKENED BY GAUNA'S HAND TUGGING AT his shoulder. It was some unearthly hour in the middle of the night. His body clock told him he had slept several hours. He needed several more, no doubt, but even so he was sufficiently lucid to think that Gauna must have had a good reason for waking him. He sat up and looked around. Although it was nighttime, it was very bright: there was a full moon. The gaucho did not seem to want to speak. Everything was still and quiet, and the moonlight produced a strange effect on the contours of this mountain landscape ... one that was perhaps too strange, he realized a few seconds later. He wondered what could be causing it. The light was not uniform: some areas were very bright, others were in darkness, then further on there were bright patches again. As he transferred his gaze from the distant peaks to the spot were they were camped, he noted that they were in the center of an irregular circle of whiteness. This was the "reflection effect" that a heavenly body like the moon was not supposed to produce. Clarke looked again at the light, and what he saw was so inexplicable that he sat for over half a minute in complete stupefaction. The moon was shining through the far side of a tall conical mountain less than half a mile away. But that was impossible. He glanced at Gauna, who was standing beside him (he was still sitting on his bedroll, twisting round) and staring at the same spot. An association of ideas helped Clarke clear his mind. When he looked up again at the yellow face of the moon, he had already understood what was happening: by a great stroke of luck, they were seeing it through the Ventana peak. Even while he was staring thus at the moon in astonishment, it moved on, and the circle of light on the ground moved with it, leaving them at its dark rim. The Ventana, had found them, rather than them finding it.

"I'm going up there now," Gauna said, still staring at the mountain.

"You mean you're going to climb it?"

"I want to be at the top at dawn."

"Won't it be dangerous in the dark?"

"That face over there," Gauna said, pointing to the left, "looks possible, and in a few minutes the moon should be shining directly onto it."

"All right," said Clarke, making up his mind. "Let's wake Carlos."

"You mean you're coming too?"

Clarke had considered this understood from the beginning. "If we've come this far ..." was all he said. He put his boots on and went to wake Carlos. He explained the discovery they had made. The moon was no longer shining through the pierced mountain but to one side of it, so the youngster could not verify for himself what he was being told. He expressed his doubts. Couldn't it have been a hallucination, what the English called "wishful thinking"? They assured him it wasn't.

They set off at once, pausing only for Clarke to grab his shotgun and Gauna to pick up a folded piece of paper that was proof of his identity. There was something frankly pathetic in his gesture. To climb a mountain in the middle of the night just to claim a fortune was taking greed a little too far. They left the horses where they were: they had no reason to stray, unless attacked by a puma, and there was nothing they could do about that. Their excitement, the time of night, and the lack of baggage lent wings to their feet. Before they were aware of it they were climbing the mountain, something their lungs soon became aware of. The animal life on the slopes was incredible: tiny owls, gophers, foxes, bats, armadillos started up in front of them at nearly every step. It was a paradise for small game; Clarke's shotgun was scorching his hands, because he had decided to respect Gauna's suggestion that they make as little noise as possible, not so much because he shared the gaucho's belief that the Widow's men were nearby, but more to humor him. The obliging moon lit up every clump of grass. When they glanced up, the mountainside looked daunting. It seemed it would take them a lifetime or more to reach the top. But when they looked down, they were surprised at how far they had already climbed. They could feel the mountain beneath their feet, the incomparable sensation of bulk that contrasted so sharply with their abstract progress across the flat plains. They said nothing, because breathing itself was difficult enough.

The moon moved further off and appeared to climb in the sky. It picked them out. They saw themselves as almost infinitely tiny, but at the same time gigantic as they scaled the hidden microlandscapes of the mountain. The moonlight bounced off the solid objects, which remained in darkness. Everything was duality. Even the high and low. Then all of a sudden they were very high up. They had been climbing without respite for three or four hours. The moon was still in the sky, a little smaller perhaps, and with a different shape, as though they were seeing it from the side; the same was true of the Milky Way. As for the shape of the mountain itself, by now it was all the same to them whatever it was. Clarke remembered that from down below it had seemed to him to be almost perfectly conical, with a broad base—like an Egyptian pyramid. From the heights, it was nothing more than a monstrously uneven piece of ground. Possibly when they reached the summit they would be able to appreciate its geometrical perspective more, though he doubted it. And anyway, night transformed everything. Being younger and lighter, Carlos was slightly ahead of the other two, whose legs were already heavy as lead. Gauna brought up the rear, panting as he climbed. All at once, they were surprised by a change in the surrounding darkness. This was because the moon had disappeared behind a mountain in the middle distance; which was further proof of how distorted their appreciation of everything was, as only a moment before it had seemed to be overhead, and probably had been. Now its light shone round the sides of the mountain, which gave off a bright clarity like a candle. Still, they found it harder to see where they were treading.

They were not able to worry about this for long, because several human shadows suddenly leapt out at them and in a flash had pinioned them to the ground. Gauna maintained his proud silence, but the other two let out shouts of rage. All three tried to resist, but in vain. The Indians tied their hands behind their backs, with sturdy leather thongs, bound their feet, then sheathed the daggers they had been waving menacingly at their throats. When their assailants had finished tying the three men up, they sat down to get their breath back, passed round a bottle of some kind of firewater whose smell filled the air, and began to talk. Their victims listened closely.

"Now," one of them said, "we're going to have to carry them."

"Why's that?" another one asked, as if it was not obvious.

"Because we tied their feet, that's why."

"You're right," a third or fourth person said, apparently suddenly catching onto something he could never have worked out for himself.

Another Indian, most probably the one whose idea it had been in the first place, came to the defense of tying their feet up: "First, it stops them running off. We wouldn't be sitting here so relaxed now, passing round the bottle, if their feet were free and we had to keep an eye on them all the time. Second, they could kick you...."

"Once, a fellow I'd tied the feet of kneed me, so it's no great guarantee."

"That's really weird, it could only happen to you...."

"No, hang on a minute...."

The argument became more personal. But it did not offer any clues as to who these Indians might be. They spoke a mishmash of the region's languages; Clarke had taken it for granted they were the Widow's men. Until the moon emerged from the side of the mountain in the distance, they were nothing more than confused silhouettes. They were ordinary-looking savages, wearing a thick

coating of grease. As soon as the moonlight returned, the Indians stood up, removed the thongs from their captives' feet (so in
fact they had simply hobbled them like troublesome horses while
they had a rest) and motioned them to climb in front of them.
There were only four Indians, which would have been a cause
for shame, had the three white men not had the excuse of being
caught unaware. Their fears had proved correct: they had been
ambushed. But there was one good thing about this mishap: their
assailants would take them where they wanted to go, to see the
Widow, and she might even be kind enough to have their hands
untied, in which case the whole experience would have cost them
nothing. They continued to climb for some time, following a di-
agonal path they would never have discovered for themselves, at
least at night. They said nothing to each other, although they had
the opportunity. The situation did not seem particularly threatening. Their captors seemed quite fierce, but they could hardly be
otherwise; their role demanded it. At one especially steep point,
the Indians came to a halt. Two of them stayed to look after the
prisoners, while the other two loped off, triumphantly returning a
few minutes later with a third individual. He peered at the faces of
the three new arrivals, particularly Clarke's, and eventually said:

"The lady will come to see you in a few minutes, if she can."

Raising a doubt in this way was typical of the Indians. Before he withdrew, the messenger asked the others to untie their
prisoners:

"They were being overcautious. All they were asked to do was
bring you here."

"We come in peace," Clarke said.

"I would never have doubted it," the Indian said as he left.

The three white men were untied. The four Indians who had brought them did not comment on the situation beyond giving a few nervous laughs, then offering them a drink. Clarke refused, but when Gauna took one, he changed his mind. He felt relaxed, and even slightly amused at how nervous the gaucho was. He wondered what it would be like to meet a half-sister for the first time, and decided it must be even odder than meeting a full sister. In the latter case, the encounter would completely fill the gap, whereas if it were only half a relationship, the missing half would continue to cast its shadow ... Clarke's mind drifted off into these somewhat irrelevant speculations. The three of them were seated comfortably with their backs against a rock; Clarke in the middle, Gauna sweaty and agitated on his right, Carlos on his left. Clarke realized Carlos was nodding off.

"If you're sleepy," he said, "go ahead and sleep."

"Not on your life. I wouldn't miss Gauna's meeting with his sister for anything in the world."

Clarke felt himself obliged to turn to his companion on the right and say: "If you prefer to see her on your own ..."

"No."

The Indians had moved some distance away and were talking in whispers. The moon had passed through various changes, and was now high above the mountain, not because it had risen in the sky but because in the last stretch of their walk, when they had been tied up, they had traveled along the rim of an imaginary conical section, so they had almost gone right round the mountain. A vast landscape lay before them: a huge chamber of dark

air, whose sides were mountain slopes gleaming brightly like silver, while above and below all was pitch black. But what was
down below was in a kind of corridor which led the gaze back to
the foreground, with moonlit slopes on both sides—none other
than those they had seen in the first place. This nocturnal alter-
nation of planes produced a pleasant sense of confusion.

The individual who had spoken to them earlier returned, together with a female figure; they realized it was not the Widow,
although the half-light did not allow them to see her clearly. She
was too tall, too formidable. The three men stood up respect-
fully. After exchanging a few words with the woman, the Indian
hung back, and she came on toward them. When she was close to
him, with the moon illuminating her fine, proud features, Clarke
recognized her with the same leap of emotion as he had felt the
first time he had caught sight of her. It was Juana Pitiley, Cafulcurá's legendary wife. Their adventure was taking yet another
unexpected turn. The three men thought she was going to come
to a halt, but she kept advancing until she was only a few inches
from Clarke, whom she was staring at intently. The Englishman
was nervous, unable to move. He wondered if the woman was
shortsighted. He thought that all her life she had been a queen,
and so he should not be surprised that she behaved like one; he
was an unusual object, and she saw no reason not to examine
him closely. She was so near, he could not avoid studying her as
well. There was something strangely familiar about her; she was
too intense and beautiful, and he was compelled to lower his
gaze. She gave a faint smile, and stepped back. Then she asked
them to sit down again, and did the same herself. She sat op-

posite Clarke, whom she had not taken her eyes off. When she spoke, her voice was deep and soft:

"Mister Clarke, I believe?" Clarke nodded. "The son of Nehemias Clarke?" This was quite incredible, and presaged some fresh revelation. "I knew your father," the woman said, "many years ago, in a place west of here. Is he still alive?"

"He died almost twenty years ago," said Clarke.

"I'm sorry to hear it. We knew each other only for a few days, and in very special circumstances. But we were united by a gift I made him, and which I sincerely thought I would never regain. I suppose he never mentioned it."

"No, he didn't."

"That was what he promised."

His father had told him a lot about his adventures in the Americas, but Clarke had always had the impression that there was a blind spot in them, and this was what was being revealed now. Juana Pitiley sat in silence for a while, recalling those distant events. Then she raised her eyes and stared up at a point near the mountain summit. The Englishman kept his lips sealed; he knew it was not the moment to ask questions.

"It was many years ago, and right here." She lowered her gaze, and stared once again at Clarke. "There's even a legend, the legend of the Legibrerian Hare, which arose from what happened here thirty-five years ago. A month ago when I heard in Salinas Grandes that someone had come in search of the Hare, an Englishman who bore a supernatural resemblance to my eldest son, I could see it all, as if I had always been expecting it. The paths of fable are usually the most real ones."

"And you," Clarke said, with tremulous voice, "you conceived a child on the summit of this mountain...."

"Ah, I see you've heard the old story. Yes, this is where my wedding night took place. It was here I rescued my husband from his captors, it was these mountain sides we scoured in search of a place of refuge, which we found in the gap pierced at the top. When we came down the next day I was already bearing my offspring in my womb. You will also have heard of the lengthy flight that followed, and of the gap that there is in the story, when I became separated from my husband before I gave birth. He arrived alone at Salinas Grandes, thinking me dead, and I appeared a couple of months later with a child in my arms: Namuncurá. And I suppose they couldn't resist insinuating what has by now become a common belief: that Namuncurá is not in fact my child, and so on. Since I had no more children, the logical thing has been to assume that I was sterile, but that since I needed to be the mother of a legal heir to strengthen my political position, I dreamt up this hare-brained scheme so as to pass a foundling off as my own son. I preferred to let this inept lie circulate rather than have anyone suspect the truth, which nobody has guessed at ... not even now."

She fell silent for a long time. So long in fact, that it seemed as if her tale was over. Clarke did not dare move, speak, think, hardly even breathe. He held his breath for so long he almost passed out. A remote part of his brain, the most English part, was aware of the effect that Juana Pitiley's words were having on the other two. Gauna seemed thunderstruck; Carlos Alzaga Prior was beside himself with excitement, and in anticipation of the great revelation was glancing first at Juana and then at Clarke, eyes shining.

"It was during that interval," she said, "that I met the person who from that moment on became your father, Nehemias Clarke. I had just given birth, not entirely on my own as legend has it, but in quite primitive conditions. When I met him, I had already decided to give up one of the twins, and the possibility that he would be going somewhere far from me and all the Mapuches finally convinced me to give him the boy. He was a silent, modest, crazily romantic man. There was never anything between us of course (the fact that I was so recently a mother prevented all thought of that) but I could tell he had fallen in love with me, and without the slightest cynicism on my part (or at least so I believe), I understood that this love was a guarantee for my plans. I made him promise he would never tell the boy of his true identity, that he would bring him up in England, where his childless wife was waiting for him, and that he would never return to America. He left at once, and I can see he was as good as his word."

The moonlight took on a fresh meaning for Clarke. He knew deep down that it was no longer a question of seeming ridiculous or not. He felt calm and collected again, in a way that left all confusion behind.

"So then," he said, " you are ... my mother."

"That's right," Juana Pitiley replied, "are you surprised?"

"Well, I had my suspicions," Clarke lied.

"Son of a gun!" said Carlos, who had begun to weep for no reason except generosity of spirit.

"Son of the Piedra," Gauna corrected him, also clearly affected by the scene. He was referring to Cafulcurá, the father, whom nobody had mentioned until now.

Clarke was trying to order his racing thoughts.

"So Namuncurá is my twin brother. He was the lookalike I met a few days ago."

"You did?" Juana asked. "The poor man has been pursuing Rondeau's Widow for years, but I think he's finally accepted it's hopeless."

"Just a minute," Clarke said. "In Salinas Grandes, when Cafulcurá, and Mallén, and all of them saw me ... and Namuncurá's wives, whose tent I stayed in ... they must all have seen the likeness."

"Of course!" said Juana.

"So why did they say nothing?"

"They were waiting for Cafulcurá to speak first. There are certain codes of honor which determine how things are done in these matters...."

"Why didn't he say anything then?"

"He had his reasons. He preferred to disappear."

"You mean he decided to disappear? He wasn't kidnapped?"

"Of course not."

Clarke was beginning to glimpse the thread linking the complicated events his arrival had set in motion. But he understood that nothing could be explained without returning to the start of it all, to his life and its secret.

"What I don't understand is why ... why hide me, why send me to England?"

His mother paused for thought, and before she could reply, a man emerged from the shadows and whispered into her ear. She listened, nodded, and told them:

"You'll have to forgive me, but little Yñuy's time seems to have arrived…."

"Yñuy!" exclaimed Carlos.

"Do you know her?"

"My friend here," Clarke said, " has been searching for her ever since we left Salinas Grandes."

"Well, he's found her, although perhaps at a rather inopportune moment for any great show of affection. I'm acting as her midwife, and the time has come to offer her my services. Excuse me, please …"

She left, leaving them so shocked they did not even think to stand up.

"We've found Yñuy!" Carlos purred. "I can't believe it. But Clarke, your story is even harder to believe. You're Cafulcurá's first-born! You've found your mother and your father! I can imagine how you must be feeling."

"I can't think clearly about it yet. This kind of thing only happens in novels … but then, novels only happen in reality."

"What do you make of it, Gauna?"

"I'm astounded. I congratulate you both."

"And there we were thinking you were the one who'd be having a remarkable encounter!"

"I think he will," Clarke said. "It's very likely that the Widow is here as well. Do you remember we heard she was looking for a young girl, and that she had finally found one?"

"That's true. Do you mean Yñuy?"

"That would explain her presence here."

"Why don't we go and find those Indians and ask them?" the boy proposed.

"Where can they have got to?" Gauna asked, peering into the shadows.

"Just a moment. Someone's coming."

It was Juana Pitiley. She sat down in the same spot as before.

"It was a false alarm," she said, "she's still got at least half an hour to go. She's a very brave girl," she added, then, glancing at Carlos, "I told her you were here, and she was overjoyed. Would you like to see her?"

"Can I?"

"I think it might be a good way to take her mind off things." Don't talk too much.

She signaled to one of the invisible men in the shadows. He got up and led Carlos away.

"One other small thing," Clarke said. "My friend Gauna Alvear here is brother on his mother's side of the woman known as Rondeau's Widow, whom you spoke of earlier. In fact, it was her we came to the Sierra de la Ventana in search of, and just a moment ago we were wondering whether she might not be here as well."

"She is indeed," Juana Pitiley said, looking across at Gauna. "This is like a family reunion. Would you like to see her?"

"Yes, I would," said Gauna.

Another gesture, another Indian stood up, and Gauna followed after him, stiff and ill at ease. Mother and son were left alone together.

"There was something I still had to explain to you," she said. "We have a little while before those babies decide to come out into the world, so I'll try to satisfy your curiosity. But don't expect to understand."

"A few difficult arguments have managed to penetrate my thick skull."

"None of them as difficult as this one, I can assure you. In fact, it's not that it's so difficult, more that it is such a broad issue. It's one of those things that the whole of life, with its infinite variety, is insufficient to contain, precisely because that is what it is all about: the variety of life in its entirety." She fell silent, then after a while began again on what seemed to be a completely different subject: "The Widow is a good friend of mine; and if she is here it's because I asked her to come. It so happens that this girl Yñuy had a brief romance with one of my husband's sons, Alvarito Reymacurá, and she became pregnant. After a few months I began to suspect she might be having twins. Although I said nothing, and advised her to do the same, Alvarito must have got wind of something, and he put her under the strictest surveillance. So we planned her escape, just at the moment when you were arriving at Salinas Grandes. Alerted by me, the Widow set out to look for Yñuy, and after a string of adventures finally caught up with her. Alvarito had also set off after her, and we learned you three were on her trail, for reasons we could not possibly imagine...."

"It was simply because Carlos thought he was in love with her. But what were your motives?"

"The Piedra royal line is said to be based on twins, twins nobody has ever seen, although my husband encourages the belief that he is the twin of a dead brother. This could be seen as simply another of those harmless fantasies our menfolk are so addicted to, if it were not for the fact that it seriously affects us women. If we really did show them the twins, we would be finished."

"Why's that?" asked Clarke. Juana had pronounced her last sentence with such finality he was afraid she would not give any further explanation.

"We can put up with polygyny, war, word games, hallucinogens, shamans ... no one can say we aren't broad-minded. But there comes a point where we have to draw the line, otherwise we would no longer be women, which would mean the disappearance of a function that is all-important for the Mapuche: the continuation of the species. And that line is the one that separates fiction from reality. On this point, and only this one, we are completely inflexible, and we are not afraid of taking things to their ultimate conclusions, as recent events will have shown you. For the real world to continue to exist, the multiplication of the identical, of repeated images, must remain part of the imaginary world."

"I don't understand."

"I didn't expect you to. You yourself are part of the system of separation. And yet our mechanism, which keeps this real world turning, must have had its effect on you too. Because the dividing line is the sum of all our lives, it offers the possibility of love, adventure, knowledge. It is reproduction. One day you will understand."

She had pronounced these last words, so typical of a mother, in great haste when she saw another Indian approaching. He bent down and whispered something to her. She looked up at the position of the moon, and stood up.

"This time I'll wager it's for real," she said. "I'm going to Yñuy."

She went off, and Carlos appeared almost immediately afterward.

"She's about to give birth," he said, both excitement and fear in his voice. "She's having contractions all the time. Poor thing! She's more beautiful than ever. Do you know she's going to have twins?"

"Yes, my mother told me."

"Your mother! Isn't that incredible? Aren't you all shaken up? Do something, say something, Clarke, forget your English stiffness for once in your life. You know it could do you harm, it could cause heart failure. If I were you ..."

"What?"

"I don't know ... I would have thrown myself in her arms, I would have called her 'mother! mother!'" Carlos's face was streaming with tears again. He jumped about like a man possessed.

"Don't be crazy. Let me be as I am."

"All right. Don't get me wrong. Of course you're fine as you are. It's not for nothing that you're my best friend, Clarke." He embraced him, fighting back another flood of tears. "It's just that so many things have happened...."

"Did Yñuy recognize you?"

Carlos stared at him, surprised and somewhat offended.

"Of course she recognized me! She told me she had spent the whole time thinking of me. She's entranced by me."

Clarke thought better of reminding the boy that it was he who had not seemed so faithful. At that point, Gauna arrived.

"Well, was it her?"

"Yes. She is my sister. She told me she had brought the girl here because your mother, Clarke, had asked her to, in order to conceal the twins she was about to give birth to ..."

"Yes, we've already heard that," Clarke butted in, not wanting to go into detail in front of Carlos. "What about the diamond?"

"She told me it didn't exist."

"And you believed her?"

"I'm afraid I had no choice."

This sounded odd to the Englishman, coming as it did from someone normally so suspicious as Gauna. But he could see something had made a great impression on the gaucho, which was probably the reason for his strange meekness. Carlos must have dimly felt the same, to judge by the question he asked:

"Is she pretty?"

Gauna took time before he replied, in the hushed voice of a threatened conspirator:

"I think she is the most beautiful woman I have ever seen in my life."

"So what does it matter that the stone doesn't exist!" Carlos exclaimed. "Look at all we've discovered anyway! Clarke's found his mother, which is the most important thing; I've found Yñuy; you, your sister. It's more than we could ever have hoped for, always supposing we were hoping for something."

"That's true."

"But we have to meet this great beauty," the boy gushed. "You'll introduce us to her, won't you, Gauna?"

"Oh, I was forgetting," the gaucho said, giving himself the classic slap on the forehead. "She asked to meet you. Come on."

As they got up, they were surprised to find that the darkness was lifting. The faintest of glimmers had spread through the night, and at this first instant of what soon afterward became nothing more than the sad gray of dawn, all the shadows had taken on a transparent quality. It was still night, but it was also day, and at the same time was neither one nor the other.

"Here she comes," Gauna remarked before they had gone more than a few steps. They looked up. The path rose in a steep track that must have been made by deer. A lone woman was coming down toward them. They waited for her. In this half-light that did not dispel the darkness but still allowed them to see, the Widow seemed to them almost painfully beautiful. They stood there with their mouths wide open. She looked up and also stopped, searching out Clarke's face. There was a moment of mystery, and then one of those "serious smiles," such as a man sees only a few times in his life spread across her face. Her gaze showed a confidence, an acceptance that were totally absent from Clarke's features, which were a picture of horror and misery. His heart had finally failed him. He felt that the whole of his past life was rushing uncontrollably to this moment, to this instant which because it was too close and too enormous, risked escaping, risked crushing him.

"Rossanna ..."

"Tom ..."

"Am I dreaming?"

"No."

"But ... weren't you dead? In the glacier?"

"No. I escaped. There was a flash of lightning—I don't know if you saw it—the ice I was imprisoned in shattered and melted

... the next day, some Indians rescued me ..."

"I can't believe it! It's not possible!"

"Tom ... it's me."

"Rossanna ... How? ... How are you?" A stupid question, but he found it hard to think.

"You're exactly the same."

"So are you. You're more, much more ..."

"More the same?"

"More beautiful."

"I'm not young anymore."

"Yes you are!" Clarke said, raising his voice from the level of a stuttering mumble for the first time. But then at once he returned to a whisper: "Did you ... did you remember me?"

"What about you?"

"The whole time."

"Still?"

"Yes, yes, always!"

He was sincere, there could be no doubting that. They came toward each other and linked hands, still staring into each other's eyes. They were in their own little bubble; the world had ceased to exist for them. Carlos, who had been watching the scene with the most passionate attention, exchanged radiant glances with Gauna, and was beside himself with the desire to join in.

"Clarke, Clarke ..." he hissed. "Señora ..."

She turned to him with a gentle smile:

"You're the one who's in love with the girl, aren't you?"

"I can vouch for the fact that Clarke, who's my best friend, is still in love with you.... There's no other woman for him...."

Clarke did not bother to shut him up because he did not even hear him. Rossanna turned to look at him again:

"When you looked at me just now I saw in your eyes exactly the same gaze as on that fateful day when I was trapped in the glacier...."

"You mean you saw me then?"

"Of course I did."

"You saw me?"

The horror came flooding back. Clarke had survived all these years absolutely convinced that he had seen her dead, and now it turned out that not only was this untrue, but that she had seen him looking at her. It seemed to him that the whole of his life (and this was the real revelation) had been impregnated with a diffuse, usually repressed terror. It was then, and only then, that love—an overpowering, immense love—was rekindled in him; love for this woman who was more beautiful than anything, the love of his life. Clarke thought that this was the first time he had ever truly loved; what had come before was fantasy, youth, nostalgia; what he felt now was genuine and lasting. Relieved, he turned toward Carlos, who was gazing transfixed at the transformation of his friend's features. He was about to say something, anything, to him when they heard the sound of laughter.

It was Juana Pitiley, surrounded by several people who were staring at something with great curiosity. She came over to them, and they could see she was carrying two babies, one in each arm.

"Two girls," she said.

The babies, wrapped in clean white cloths, were tiny and perfectly formed, like two little dolls. They all stared at them enchanted for a few moments.

"What a remarkable proliferation of twins," said Clarke.

"I'm delighted they're girls," Juana Pitiley said. "It's as though a curse were finally being lifted."

Rossanna, her arm linked through Clarke's, said to him:

"There's something you should know, Tom, and now seems to be the right moment. When we two were separated fifteen years ago, I was pregnant. At the time I hadn't told you because I was waiting for the right opportunity, which never came. And I also had twins, a boy and a girl."

"No!"

"It's as though we all belonged to the same family."

"But we do! This lady has just told me I'm her son."

Perplexed, Rossanna looked toward Juana Pitiley, and saw the confirmation of Clarke's words on her face. She murmured:

"That explains how similar you look to Namuncurá, my constant suitor."

"Yes, we're twins too. But why did you never say yes to him?"

A "serious smile" was her only reply.

"And those children?" Clarke was anxious to know. "Our children? What became of them?"

"You may find it hard to forgive me, but I gave them up for adoption almost as soon as they were born. I gave the girl to some Mapuches from Saliqueló, and the boy to a cousin of mine in Buenos Aires, Susana Prior."

At first, Clarke did not make the connection, but the shout of joy from Carlos soon forced him to do so:

"Susana Prior is my adoptive mother! It's me! It had to be me, Clarke!"

Rossanna, whose aristocratic reserve stood in such stark contrast to the hysterical enthusiasm of this alleged son of hers, asked him:

"Are you sure? I know Susana adopted other children...."

"No, it's me! My heart tells me so!"

He was laughing and crying at the same time. Clarke felt a wave of laughter welling up inside his own chest.

"Well, anyway," Rossanna said, "it would be easy enough to prove it, because my twins had a birthmark, in the shape of a tiny hare, on their butt ..."

"Here it is! Here it is! What did I tell you, Clarke, I mean father!"

Without the slightest regard for convention, Carlos turned round and pulled his trousers down. He was so nervous and fumbled so much he snapped his belt. But it was true, in the center of his right buttock he had a long birthmark that looked like a hare in flight. When he turned round to them again, his face was red and wet from tears. He could not speak. Clarke took him into his arms to console him.

"I saw a birthmark just like that," said Juana Pitiley, "on Yñuy when she was giving birth."

"Yñuy?" everyone said. Carlos raised his head from his father's shoulder.

"Where did you say you had your baby girl adopted?" Juana Pitiley asked Rossanna.

"In Saliqueló."

"Well, Yñuy and her family arrived in Salinas Grandes from Saliqueló a few years ago!"

"So there's no doubt it's her."

"So then ... Yñuy is my sister!"

"Yes, your sister ..." Clarke said. "Tell me, you didn't ... did you?"

"No, don't worry," Carlos replied, smiling through his tears. "You're always the same, aren't you? You can relax, there was no incest."

Rossanna was smiling at him.

"I'm going to tell her!" Carlos exclaimed.

"Not now," Juana Pitiley said, holding him back. "She's asleep. We'll tell her when she wakes up."

"These little girls are our grandchildren," Clarke said to Rossanna.

"I told you I wasn't so young."

"And they're my great-grandchildren," said Juana Pitiley.

"Clarke, father, I think I'll die, I'm so happy!" Carlos roared. "I knew it all the time: you had to be my father ..."

"Don't forget that this is your mother."

"It's true! So I was in the glacier as well!"

"That wasn't what I meant. Didn't you say that if you ever met your mother, you'd throw yourself in her arms, and all that kind of thing?"

Carlos shyly evaded Rossanna's smiling face.

"Now that I know I'm your son, a certain British reserve ..."

"In fact, you're more English than I am, thanks to the blood of poor Professor Haussmann." Clarke saw the moment had arrived to say something which would not only delight the boy, but was also true: "I have to admit that if I had been asked how I would like my son to be, I would have said like you."

"That goes without saying," Carlos responded at once, sincerely convinced of it.

They were all sitting round in a circle. The light had grown stronger. Suddenly Carlos thought of something:

"So that means Gauna is my uncle! Come and give me a hug, uncle. Gauna, you're going to have to be nice to me from now on."

"Whatever will he think of next?" said his father.

"How about having some breakfast?" Rossanna asked.

"Wait a moment," Juana Pitiley said. "I think the sun is about to rise, and perhaps my son, my delightful grandson and Mister Gauna would like to see it through the Ventana, just as I did when all this began."

They agreed and everyone set off, leaving the babies in the care of an old Indian woman. They were already only a short distance from the summit. It took them no time at all to reach the Ventana itself, which was a fairly large window-like hole in the topmost rock. They climbed up, picking their way through huge boulders. There was no wind, which could have made the spot unpleasant. As Clarke reached the top, a huge orange sun was rising, exactly opposite him on the eastern horizon, which seemed not nearly so far away as when they were out on the plain. Gauna pointed downward: among the shadows on the prairie at the foot of the mountain, their horses had scattered far and wide. Clarke looked for Repetido. When he found him, the horse was standing with its head lifted nervously. Then he saw it dart off in an unlikely gallop toward the rising sun.

"Where's he going?" Clarke asked in alarm. The others also gazed after the horse, half-closing their eyes against the bright glow the animal was running toward. And they were all equally shocked when they saw the silhouette of a rider appear on the horizon line.

"The Wanderer! Repetido's got tired of only seeing him in the distance as well!"

But it was not mere curiosity on the horse's part. The Wanderer's horse was another Repetido, and suddenly the two of them reared on to their hind legs with exactly the same movement, standing poised for an instant like two chess knights. And then it was as if the page of the world were finally turned, and the Wanderer was on this side, and they saw him coming to meet them. They all recognized him at the same instant: it was Cafulcurá.

Juana Pitiley roared with laughter.

PRINGLES, 6 SEPTEMBER 1996